Out of Sorrow

CARY MORGAN

Tipsy SAILOR PRODUCTIONS

OUT OF SORROW

Copyright © 2021 by Cary Morgan

Published by Tipsy Sailor Productions

Digital ISBN 978-0-9861938-0-4

Print ISBN 987-0-9861938-1-1

Cover design & formatting by Clarity Book Cover Designs

https://www.claritybookcoverdesigns.com

OTHER BOOKS BY CARY MORGAN

By Cary Morgan

Contemporary Romance Short Stories

Red Soles at Night, Christmas Delight 2013

Red Soles in the Morning, Valentines Soaring 2014

By Morgan O'Neill (Books Co-written with Deborah O'Neill Cordes)

Time Travel Romance/Historical Fiction

Italian Duo 2nd edition

The Other Side of Heaven 2014

Time Enough for Love 2014

Roman Trilogy 2nd edition

Love, Eternally 2015

After the Fall 2015

Return to Me 2015

Elizabethan Trilogy 2nd edition

The Thornless Rose 2017 / Audiobook Publication 2018

Begun by Time 2017 / 2018

Ever Crave the Rose 2017 / 2018

Upcoming Works

I, Guinevere - Spring 2021 Historical Fiction

Dead Reckoning - Summer 2021 Contemporary Fiction

Anthology of Short Stories - Fall 2021 Mixed/Fiction

Elizabetha Regina – 2022 Historical Fiction

Yellowman – 2022 Contemporary Fiction

You can visit our websites at carymorgan.com and morganoneill.com

To Claire, who offered the first spark of inspiration.
To Effie, who kept 'em gettin' up.
To my mom, whose trove of memories helped lend realism.
To Abbeville, S.C., my ancestral hometown.
And to those on the Thin Blue Line.

CHAPTER ONE

ALL TOO SOON, HER PRECIOUS ALTAMONT WOULD BE NO MORE. Or at least, no longer hers.

Vivian pushed a strand of wispy, gray hair off her brow, then reached out and took her young friend's hand. "This has been so difficult, and would have been impossible to manage alone. I don't know how I'll ever be able to repay you for the help you've given me," she said, as she gazed at the final room they needed to tackle.

"Are you kidding?" Stephanie replied. "You are our *grande dame du benefactrice par excellence.* How could I not, for all you've done?"

Vivian chuckled. "Your French needs some work."

Stephanie grinned. "Maybe I'll get lucky and a Frenchman will appear on my doorstep with every intention of improving my language skills."

"Ha! First, may I remind you your husband would disapprove, and second, my father was French," Vivian said. "Came over before the Great War. I don't recall that my mother ever learned a single word of French."

"You're joking. Didn't you tell me you had seven siblings? Sounds like she learned French *trés bien*, to me."

Vivian laughed. "*Vous êtes terrible.*"

As their laughter died out, she looked around the smallest guest room. Once it had been busy. Once all three of her guest rooms had been busy. She and her husband welcomed visitors from around the world, well into their seventies. Seemed hardly a week went by they didn't have one or two guests, plus dinner parties in their honor. The only time her home wasn't full of bustle was when she and Thomas travelled to visit those same, far-flung friends.

But life had slowed considerably in the last five years. She didn't have the strength for it anymore. Plus, since her husband, and so many of those dear friends, had passed, there was almost no one left to visit.

Her mind was still plenty sharp. She loved her history, and could bring eras to life in minute detail, when asked. However, recently she'd become more interested in her own life, remembering the love, the heartache, the loss, and so much joy. In the last few years, this room had become her 'life' room, as she thought of it. Once it had belonged to her daughter, which seemed only yesterday, and yet...

The room contained her precious, albeit unused, past. Those trinkets she treasured; photo albums of people long dead, hand-written letters from the same group, her high school prom corsage, and a white rose, now brown, clipped and carefully dried from her first wedding bouquet. There was her son's swaddling blanket. Her daughter's baby shoes.

Vivian came back to the moment when Stephanie put an arm around her shoulder and gave her a squeeze.

"Can we go downstairs and sit a minute? Maybe have a cup of tea? I need to, um, go over a couple of things with you – tell you what the historical society has been planning. They want to surprise you, but I feel like you need to sign off on it.

Before the surprise. If you approve, then you can look surprised later on. Only we two will be the wiser."

Vivian looked at her. "I'm certainly intrigued. Should I be worried?"

"Not at all. If you don't like the idea, then I'll nix it before it ever gets off the ground."

Vivian set about making tea, and soon they were seated across from one another at her kitchen table.

Before they spoke, she looked down the hallway toward the foyer, and sighed. Most of her things had already been taken away, but a lot still remained. There were three pile groups. The first would go with her to the senior living condo, and it was much the smallest. The second, much the largest, was designated for St. Vincent de Paul. And yet, there was still a sizeable amount earmarked for the Historical Society, and this was by far the most valuable.

She might have passed it on to family, but she had none. Harold. Robert David. Opal.

And Thomas. Dear, dear Thomas. How had she been so lucky as to have two great loves in her life? Vivian smiled at the warm memories. She and Thomas had purchased this grand old house early on in their marriage, and it was so much a part of them, of him.

"Viv?"

Startled out of her reveries, she smiled. Stephanie, with her dark hair and clear, blue eyes, brought her thoughts back to her daughter. What would she look like today? Had she ever had any children? Known real love? Was she still living? And did she still detest her mother?

"Viv?"

"I'm so sorry, dear," Vivian said, waving her hand. "I was back in time. All this, well, I'm afraid it's forced me to trod some very old paths, ones filled with all sorts of memories. What was it you wanted to discuss?"

Vivian noticed Stephanie's knuckles turn white as she gripped the table's edge. The poor dear took a deep breath with a look of terrified excitement on her face, and finally plunged in.

"So, okay, we are going to name a hall for you."

She quickly held out a hand when Vivian started to protest, aghast at such an extravagance.

"No, sorry, that much is set in cement and not open for discussion. What I want to talk about is another idea some have floated. There has been talk about setting aside a small, well, medium sized room with your most personal effects, those that tell your personal story. Harold. The war. Thomas. Your daughter and her disappearance. The triumphs, the tragedies, in short, everything that made you the exceptional person you are. We don't want anyone to think we named the hall for you simply because you gave us a lot of money. Nope. We want them to know you. The real you. The whole you."

Speechless, Vivian sat, thunderstruck. Her instincts told her to protest, but the historian in her would have loved to know the day to day, intimate details of the lives of those she studied. Not only their titles, but their wants and needs, their hurts, and their most cherished moments.

"What do you think?" Stephanie held her breath, her hands clasped under her chin, as though in ardent prayer.

"I loathe the idea."

"But...?" Stephanie looked crestfallen.

Vivian patted her arm. "I loathe the idea because it's all about me, me, me. On the other hand, I'm plenty vain enough to think my personal story might be of interest, might go forward, even when I'm no longer around to bore anyone with it." She shook her head. "As a historian, though, and looking forward a couple of hundred years, I'd give my eye teeth to have information like this on someone I was studying. It would tell my story, but it would also be a window in time."

Stephanie leaned forward with a broad grin. "So, is that a yes?"

Vivian smiled back. "Yes. It's a yes."

"Woo-hoooo!" Stephanie leapt out of her chair and began a very bizarre victory dance. Once she'd spun and hugged Vivian two or three times, she calmed, and started planning out loud as she paced the kitchen. "We'll need to re-separate what you've given us, with a group of the most personal items set apart for your private room. We have pictures of Harold and Opal, right? I know we have loads with Thomas. And I have to confess, we've kept some of your donated clothing, period specific things, or specific to a certain event. Dresses, hats, gloves, purses, you know, to set mood and the period."

"And all this time I thought the lot of you were perfect, the epitome of genteel Southern Ladies. Now, I see you are all a devious lot of scallywags. Have any of my donations designated for St. Vincent de Paul actually gotten there?"

Stephanie smiled impishly. "Some." She abruptly stopped her pacing and knelt beside Vivian, clasping both of her hands. "I need to ask you for something more. Ask you to *do* something. Nobody else is talking about this. I, it's something I've been thinking about. A lot."

Vivian smiled. "What else can there possibly be?"

At first, Stephanie wouldn't meet her eye. "I, um, I was wondering if you'd like to submit a DNA sample. I mean, it'll show your ancestry. It'll even show historical kinship to others from the area. Or, it might show…descendants. What do you think?"

DNA, Vivian thought. Her mind reeled. She'd read a lot about it. Had Opal ever considered submitting hers? Would the DNA people be able to link her to her daughter? Could they possibly be...reunited? After all these years?

"Viv?" Stephanie said quietly. "If it's too personal, then no. But, well, you've spoken about Opal, and I thought, she'd be what, in her seventies? I mean, she obviously has longevity in her genes, so she might...she might... but it's not like, if they do find a connection, we'd be forced to make contact if you weren't comfortable with it."

Vivian shook all over. She tried to quell the onslaught of emotion, but was unable. Opal? Alive? A reunion? She could feel hot tears pricking her eyes, demanding release. When had she last cried? When had she last cried in front of someone? Never. At least not since news of Harold's death in Italy.

In private? Oh, she'd cried many times, but only over her split with Opal, who'd cursed her upbringing, abandoning her family for the life of a drugged, n'er-do-well hippie on the streets of far off San Francisco.

Had her daughter lived long enough to become a real adult? Vivian always supposed her daughter had died, like Joplin and the others, because of the drugs they'd chosen to take. Otherwise, wouldn't she have gotten in touch, after so many years? Wouldn't her daughter have tried to bridge the rift? She had never known where her daughter lived, beyond somewhere in San Francisco, and her name was too common for any realistic search.

On the other hand, Opal knew where *she* lived. She'd spent several years in this house, and Vivian hadn't wanted to part with the old place, partly in hopes her daughter would, one day, find her way back.

She, Vivian, was findable. But there had never been an attempt to contact, to reunite. Never.

"Viv? Is this too much?" Stephanie looked dismayed. "I'm so sorry if I've upset you. I shouldn't have mentioned the situation with your daughter. I've overstepped."

6

Once again, Vivian forced herself out of her reveries and into the present. She smiled. "You've nothing to be sorry for, my dear. On the contrary, you've given me hope. I've heard of this DNA stuff, but I never thought about it for me. Yes, let's give it a go. After all, hope, however tenuous, never, ever dies."

Stephanie grinned, rummaged in her purse, and drew out a box. "Southern ladies never spit, I know, but, this once, you're going to have to make an exception."

CHAPTER TWO

Tia took her cuffs from the corrections officer, wiped them with an antiseptic cloth from a tub on the receiving desk counter, and put them back in their holder on her duty belt. She watched as they frisked her guy, then sent him into the changing room to put on his jail uniform.

Sweating and sick from coming off his most recent injection, the guy was a frequent flyer. She'd brought him to jail countless times. He was always pleasant, even friendly, when he wasn't stratospherically high, but he refused to entertain the idea of getting clean. One day, she was sure, somebody would find him dead from an overdose, disease, or infection. She wondered, when the moment inevitably arrived, if anybody would be left in his life who would care.

He'd told her he considered heroin a party drug in high school, one he'd only use on weekends. And of course he'd been confident he'd be able to handle it.

Tia didn't know who fed him such a load of crap, but, in an effort to find a common thread, she always asked users why they'd ever entertained that very first thought, that trying heroin was a good idea. She'd heard similar stories to his nearly every time. She shook her head. She found it unfathomable. Unfathomably stupid.

You can't fix stupid, she thought cynically. And he was stupid for believing he could control poison.

"Numbers?" the desk officer asked.

"Forty-two eighty." Tia replied. Her badge number.

Her druggie came out in his new outfit, handed over his old clothes, got patted down again, and was directed to take a blanket before being sent to a holding cell to await the rest of the booking process.

"You're good to go." The officer barely glanced at her. She had three more cops inside, waiting with their perps, and a long line of police vehicles outside. It was a busy night for stupid.

"See ya soon." Tia replied, and headed toward the door. "Hopefully not tonight, though. I was off shift before I even headed here."

A short laugh. "Gotta love overtime. I'll keep my fingers crossed for you."

The exterior door was buzzed open and Tia stepped into the brisk, clean air. The jail never smelled bad. They had to have an excellent air filtration system, since inmates weren't known for their stellar hygiene practices, but she was always happy to get out of the recycled atmosphere.

She climbed into the transport van, which she liked to call 'the paddy wagon,' and radioed she was enroute to the station.

It was late, dark, and traffic was light. She did the return drive on auto-pilot, and let her mind wander. *Need new tires on my truck. Need to find a cheap plumber for the bathroom remodel. Need a vacation.* She wanted palm trees and sun, an eye-candy pool boy who brought endless margaritas, but who didn't bother her otherwise. And quiet. She needed some quiet.

And when was the DNA test she got her mom for Christmas ever going to arrive? It was what, six weeks since they'd sent it in? Her mother had no information about her maternal origins, and they'd both been intrigued by what might be revealed. Actually, Tia had to admit she was well beyond intrigued. She was restless, uncomfortable, even nervous about what the results might show, although *why* she was made her wonder.

Her maternal grandfather, Michael Williams, dead nearly six years, was of Welsh extraction – an extraction countable in centuries, so plenty diluted and providing no close cousins to visit, or who wanted to visit them.

She still missed him. He was funny and lighthearted, but at seventy-three, as a life-long smoker, he'd died from lung cancer. She'd readily promised him she'd never take up the evil weed. When he was sick, she pestered him for information about her grandmother, who'd died when Tia was only three. He told her everything he knew about her grandmother's life before they'd married, which wasn't much, and nothing more than what her mother had already imparted.

Her maiden name was Henderson, she knew. Barbara Henderson Williams

Grandma Barbie and Grandpa Mike met in San Francisco. Grandpa said she was lovely, with curly, dark hair and piercing blue eyes. Tia was a mirror image, or so he said, except her eyes were green – like her mom's. They had been ardent hippies back in the day, he ruefully admitted, and although Barbie had done a lot of experimenting, he swore he never did anything worse than pot. She got clean soon after they met, and they abandoned their hippy days once she knew she was pregnant.

That was all anyone knew about Grandma Barbie's past, which was practically nothing, and impossible to trace. There were a lot of Barbara Hendersons born in 1942.

When Tia thought of hippies, she saw muddy, commune-dwelling, drugged-up idiots flashing the peace sign. She couldn't square this image with her grandfather at all. They had, however, named their only child Cherish, which did fit the profile.

Tia's mom said she hardly knew her mother. And there had never been any mention of a grandmother. Ever. Tia's mom said she thought not having a grandmother was normal, didn't think about it at all, actually, until she realized all of her girlfriends had grandmothers. But when Cherish, or Cherry, as everyone called her, tried to find out the truth, she said Grandma Barbie would ignore her. No information was ever forthcoming.

As an adult, Cherry moved away from California to study Interior Design and Architecture at the University of Washington, and stayed in the area after graduation.

Cherry hadn't been close with either of her parents until much later in life. In her childhood, so she claimed, the family atmosphere was friendly, functional, but not warm. The one-eighty on warmth and closeness happened after Grandma Barbie's death.

Devastated, Grandpa Mike moved to Washington to be near his daughter, and only then discovered the wonders of fatherhood, grandfather-hood, warmth, and a loving family.

Alls well as ends well, right? Let sleeping dogs lie? Tia shook her head. *Only if you didn't care about answers, or facts.*

Tia liked facts. She wanted a straight line. Who were her great-grandparents? Her grandfather's side was known, but not Barbara's. Where was she from? California was the likely answer, since people weren't as mobile in those days, but she didn't have any information as to Grandma Barbie's, origins. California was only a supposition. She didn't have any hard facts to add, beyond her grandmother's maiden name and birth year, and nothing popped in California that fit the parameters before her grandparents married and bought their first home in Santa Rosa. Before her marriage, Barbara Henderson Williams was a ghost.

Tia sighed, put on her blinker, turned into the police station driveway, and radioed her arrival.

When were they ever going to get the results of the DNA test?

She parked the van, checked her watch, and went inside. She should have clocked out two hours before, but they'd needed the transport. Overtime was good. And timing didn't matter, since no one awaited her homecoming.

She keyed her mic. "Paul Eight out of service."

"Copy, Paul Eight, out of service," came the dispatch voice. "Good night."

Changed out of her uniform, Tia turned on her personal cell as she left the station and checked texts, social media posts, then clicked on voice mail to listen to the message her mother left in the early afternoon.

"Hi, Honey," her voice said. It sounded a little wobbly, and Tia instantly focused to hear the rest.

"Um, I got the DNA results today. I think you should call. It's...it's interesting. Call me."

Tia checked her watch. 10:35pm. Her mother usually went to bed around nine. Call or wait? Call or wait?

Tia got into her F-150 and made sure her phone was connected to Bluetooth. Call or wait? Nah. It took her twenty minutes to drive home to Snohomish, and she wouldn't mind the conversation. Besides, the sound in her mother's voice made the decision for her, so she dialed, and got nothing but endless ringing.

Damn. Tia reached out to disconnect.

"Tia?"

"Hi Mom. Sorry for calling so late, but I just got off. Hope I didn't wake you, but you sounded like it was urgent."

Tia sat back and shook out her 'cop do' – a French braid with the tail tucked inside so there was nothing for bad guys to grab hold of. Some said the hairdo was elegant, but she styled it that way because it was easy and practical.

"Oh, Tia, I'm so glad you called. I couldn't have slept a wink without talking to you."

"What's going on? Is this about the DNA test?"

"Yes! It, it seems I have a grandmother," Cherry blurted. "Well, I mean, of course I do, but the email said she's living, and she's a maternal match! How…? I mean, I'm blown away. I don't know what to think, or say, or anything. I've never used 'flabbergasted' in my life, but I think it fits. I'm floored. I'm more than that. I am actually flabbergasted."

Tia laughed. "Do you want me to come over?"

"No, no, not really. This is your Friday, right?"

"Yes. I'm headed home, but I can come by if you want."

"No, no need," her mother said. "I had to blurt, to tell you. The rest can wait for the morning. I think I'll be able to sleep now. Oh my God! Can you be here by nine?"

"Sure. I'll see you then."

After the call, Tia couldn't suppress a grin. She had a living great-grandmother. Wow. What would she be like? Where did she live? What in the world was the story between mother and daughter? Adoption? Abandonment? Feud? Maybe they were all a part of the Hatfield and McCoy saga?

Tia laughed at her silly musings. She loved a mystery, and could hardly wait to peel back the facts of this case, this very personal case. She put her truck in drive and headed home.

NEXT MORNING, Tia did her workout at the gym, then headed for the diner in town. She greeted the crowd of all-male retirees who were there every morning. She'd gotten to know most of them over eggs, bacon, lots of coffee, and plenty of lighthearted BS since moving to town, and was pretty sure they thought of her as their adopted daughter. Or maybe a puppy. In any case, they made her grin.

Laurie poured her coffee and asked if she wanted her usual.

Tia nodded, but before Laurie could turn in the order, the cook, with his Sam Elliott mustache, was beside her.

"Man, you should have been there last night. I made the best grilled Elk sirloin with …"

She smiled, leaned back, and listened to his description.

He was always promising to invite her to his epic dinners, but to date, she'd only heard about the events, on social media, which dereliction she reminded him of repeatedly.

It didn't take her long to finish her breakfast. After reading the local news on her phone, Tia glanced at her watch. 7:30am. She had plenty of time to kill before heading to see her mom, so she accepted another cup of coffee, chatted with Laurie, bantered with the guys, and gave the cook some grief, before giving a fond farewell to all and heading home for a shower.

TIA ARRIVED RIGHT ON TIME, and sat at her mother's kitchen table in Kirkland, her hands wrapped gratefully around a steaming, aromatic, better cup of coffee.

Her mother was as nervous as a cat on a barbed-wire fence. Cherry bustled silently, making scrambled eggs, bacon, and toast, then flitting about while Tia ate. Again. It didn't matter when she said she'd already had breakfast. Her mother always made sure she was eating properly, which meant eating what she prepared. So she ate. Tia knew her mother wouldn't mention her own issues until her daughter was done.

"Mom, I'm full," Tia said as she pushed her partially eaten

plate away. "Please, tell me what they said. I can't stand the anticipation anymore."

"Okay." Cherry opened her laptop, got into her email, then spun it around so Tia could read the pertinent message for herself.

Tia read: 'Vivian G. 100% maternal lineage match. Living. Grandmother. Aged ninety-five years."

There was a button to click if they wanted to make contact. A blind contact. Smart.

She looked at her mom.

"Well? What should I do?" Cherry asked.

Tia shrugged. "Email her. She won't get your info, and you won't have hers, unless you both decide to share. It looks safe to me. The site is solid. What have you got to lose?"

"But, I feel like I'm betraying my mom."

"Why? Did she ever say anything negative about her mother?" Tia asked.

"No. She wouldn't talk about her family, or her past, at all. She'd shut down."

"But there's nothing bad, right? I mean, she didn't go off on how horrible the woman was, or abusive, or anything like that?"

"No, never anything negative. Just…" Cherry lifted her shoulders. "Just nothing."

"Do you want me to write the email?" Tia enquired of her mother.

"Oh, thank God, yes. I thought you'd never ask."

Tia took a deep breath, scratched her head, blew out with a huff, and tucked a strand of hair behind her ear. Once she felt ready, she began typing.

After she finished, Tia slid the laptop back to her mother. "Look good?"

Cherry read the text, smiled, then nodded. "That's a lot of parentheses and question marks, but yes, it's perfect."

Tia clicked the 'send' button before either of them could reconsider, then grinned and wiggled her brows at her mom. "Let the circus begin."

Her mother heaved an unsteady sigh. "Alea iacta est." The die is cast.

CHAPTER THREE

VIVIAN FELT QUEASY. SWEAT BEADED ON HER FOREHEAD AND her hands shook. She dialed Stephanie.

"Hi, Viv. How are you?"

"Can you come by, please?"

There was a pause, then Stephanie's voice changed, lowered. It was edged with worry. "Is everything okay? Are you sick?"

"I'm quite well, dear," she replied, her tone flat. "At least, I believe so. I received a letter on my computer. Actually, two of them. From the DNA people. I don't want to open them without someone here with me."

"On my way."

"Stephanie?"

"Yes?"

"I'm absolutely terrified."

The air seemed thicker than usual, like a heavy blanket enveloped her. Sound seemed muffled, and time itself had grown heavy. Too heavy to breathe...

Suddenly Stephanie was beside her, gently taking the phone from her hand.

"Hi, Viv. I'm here. So, you got an email about the DNA results, right? When did you get it?"

Forcing herself to focus, Vivian looked at her young friend. "Oh, I'm so glad you're here. I have no idea when they arrived. Beyond dusting it, you know, I don't pay much attention to my computer. I don't check it very often, I'm afraid, so I forget how to use it. Besides, who's going to write me? The blinking was annoying me, though, so I did check. There are at least two letters that mention DNA. Perhaps more. I didn't want to look without you."

Stephanie sat beside her. "Why not?"

"All of my choices seem so…life altering," Vivian said. "I hadn't considered it before, but, what if they say there are no connections? I would be devastated. It would mean no one is out there in my line, or that they are not trying to find out for themselves, or, or what if there is someone? What if she's dead, or what if she's…looking for me?"

Stephanie smiled and hugged her. "Then we will have answers we didn't have before. Would you like me to read them silently first?"

"Yes, please, dear."

Stephanie pulled the laptop toward her and opened it. The screen brightened as soon as she touched the pad. "Uh, you should have a password protect on this, Viv. Anyone could get it and see everything you've got on here."

"I haven't got anything on there," Viv smiled wanly. "Sometimes I read the paper on my computer. Periodicals. Studies. Research findings from the Historical Society, and others. But that's all. I prefer having something in my hands to read, so I don't truly see the use of even having one, but there you go."

"You don't do social media? No online banking or purchases?"

"I like to see my banker in person," Vivian said. "I go to

stores for my needs, and I have no family with which to be social. The historical society set up my email for me, and except for the DNA people, they are the only ones who have it. I don't need a password I'd be sure to forget."

Stephanie chuckled. "Okay, point taken." She opened Vivian's email and scrolled through. "The first one says you have several matches, some third and fourth generation, and...and two, oh boy, three close-match, matrilineal *descendants*. Two Living."

Vivian could make out Stephanie's tentative smile through her tear-filled eyes.

"Does it give their ages?" she asked.

"No, but there's a way to connect with them anonymously, if you'd like," Stephanie responded. "You can write them an email, and decide whether or not to give more personal information as your interactions go on."

Vivian took a deep breath and blew out hard. "My daughter, then. And a child of hers, I'd guess. Heavens, I have a granddaughter." She felt shaky and vulnerable.

Stephanie nodded. "Oh! They're reaching out. The second email is from one of them."

"Read it, please." Vivian said, her voice almost a whisper. She ran her hands over the wooden arms on her favorite, wing-back chair, then gripped the rounded ends and held on. "Please. Yes. I'm ready. Go ahead."

Dear Vivian G.,

Greetings. It seems we are a DNA match, and I and my mother (your granddaughter?) are eager to find out more about our possible (probable?) connection. No familial information was ever passed on, so, as you might imagine, we are curious to find out as much as we can. Please let us know if you are willing to continue this communication, or to meet at some future point. We very much look forward to hearing back from you.

    Best,

    Your progeny (?), Cherish (granddaughter?) and Cynthia (great-granddaughter?)

Stephanie finished and smiled at her. "They sound nice. Right?"

Vivian turned her head and looked out the window at the bleak, rainy day outside, at the leafless trees, at the dismal gray.

"She is gone," Vivian mumbled, and put a hand over her mouth. She tried to hold back her emotions, but the news was too much to bear. "Opal is gone. They said 'no information *was* passed on,' which means my daughter has died. And, it seems, she died without ever mentioning me, or her past."

Vivian let the tears fall, and didn't care. She could hardly catch her breath for the sobs wracking her body. The rift would never be healed. They would never hug, never talk again, never forgive.

"Oh, Viv, I'm so sorry." Stephanie knelt beside her and held her tight.

Vivian let her emotions pour out on the welcome shoulder.

After a few minutes, Vivian gathered herself, straightened, and mopped her face. "I'm so sorry. Where are my manners? May I get you a cup of tea?" She needed to be busy. She needed time to think.

Minutes later, with a steaming cup in front of them both, Vivian faced Stephanie over the kitchen table. She ran a finger along a crack in its red-flecked Formica top, and smiled. "I intended to get rid of this years ago. It belonged to my first mother-in-law, and was given to us when we wed, in anticipation of the first little apartment we'd get after the war. It was old even then. Now, instead of simply being old, it's antique, just like me." She paused and sighed. "What do we do, now, Stephanie?"

"I'm so very sorry about your daughter, Viv. I'm sorry to have suggested this path, and opened, or caused, such hurtful wounds." Stephanie looked, and sounded, devastated, as she took a nervous sip of tea. "That being said, unless you want to pretend it never happened, I think the only way forward is to answer them. Get the truth, and maybe get to know the family, because they are your family. They are a very real continuation of the family you've been missing all these years."

"Indeed." Vivian continued to trace the swirl pattern with her finger. *Family. Her family.*

"We can offer to meet at some neutral location, or arrange for a call from an untraceable phone." Stephanie suggested, then patted her hand. "I'll be with you every step of the way, so don't worry. Whatever you need."

"All this time spent," Vivian waved a hand toward her surroundings. "I worry I'm taking you away from your own family, from your husband."

"My husband is a cop with the Greenville police, you know that," Stephanie said with a chuckle. "I'm always home before he is, so no worries there. Plus, there's nothing he likes better than solving a mystery. He'll back this project one hundred percent."

Still deeply saddened, Vivian nodded. "I must come to grips with it all, of course, and forward is the only way to go. Yes, write them back, if you would. Make plans for a phone call. Can we do one of those video chats, do you suppose? I'd love to get a look at them."

"Sure, but first, what do you want to say?"

Dear Cherish and Cynthia,

I was delighted to receive your email. I would very much like to pursue our apparent familial ties. I live on the East Coast. May I ask where you are located? Do you live together? I hardly know what to ask, or say, except I am anxious to make your acquaintance. My assistant, Stephanie, can look into a video chat, if you are agreeable.

We await your response.

Sincerely,

Vivian

Vivian stopped dictating and watched Stephanie push the send button, then they locked eyes.

"How long will it take?"

Stephanie grinned. "Who knows? I mean, they have it already, but it might be the middle of the night where they are, so they wouldn't see it until their morning."

"Opal lived in San Francisco, last anyone knew," Vivian said.

"Well, then maybe they're surfing or something. Or maybe they're jumping around and trying to figure out what to say next," Stephanie pointed out. "There's no way to predict—"

A ping alerted them to an incoming email.

"Oh, dear heavens," Vivian breathed, and put a trembling hand over her mouth.

Stephanie opened the email and read the missive silently, then grinned. "They want to come for a visit as soon as possible. They say distance is no matter."

CHAPTER FOUR

TIA DRUMMED HER FINGERS NERVOUSLY ON HER KNEE. SHE'D caught a very early flight to Denver, then on to Charlotte. She had an aisle seat, and craned to see out the window. They were on final approach. She didn't have a problem with flying, but she sure had an issue with meeting their supposed long-lost family.

Solo.

Couldn't they have chosen an airport with a non-stop? She thought grumpily, then reminded herself she and her mother had not chosen to disclose their location, so how could Vivian and Stephanie have known which airport might be the best? For all they knew, Tia was flying in from Kuala lumpur, or maybe Peoria. She wondered if those places had non-stops to Charlotte, NC.

The wheels touched down and the engines reversed thrust for several seconds, slowing the plane before it turned to the left.

Tia checked her watch. She was to meet two perfect strangers at a Starbucks in the city center in less than an hour. She had a photo of the assistant, Stephanie, for recognition purposes, and she'd sent one of herself. Nobody had shared surnames, as yet. These ladies were being very careful, and she could appreciate the caution. In this day and age, it was sensible.

With only a carry-on, Tia was settled in the ride-service vehicle within minutes of landing. She checked her watch again.

"How long will it take to get there?" she asked.

"Twenty minutes, unless there's an accident," her driver said. "But the road looks clear."

Tia started drumming her fingertips again. Her mother had declined to take the trip. In a rare show of nerves, she'd backed out.

Fine. So she got to use three days of vacation time and visit some doddering old woman who may, or may not, be her long lost great-grandmother. How would she know? What proof? Well, except for the DNA profile.

"This is ridiculous."

"What? Is there a problem?" the driver asked.

"No, no, not at all. Just talking to myself and mentally going over why I'm here in the first place," Tia smiled.

"It's a beautiful city, beautiful state," he said, hopefully. "We have the Panthers. They're a very great football team."

Tia laughed. "I'm, well, I was a Seahawks fan. I'm in law enforcement, so, when the NFL started kneeling, I stopped watching. Don't support anyone, these days."

"Ah, yes, I don't like the controversy, either," he said. "You're a cop, uh, a police officer?"

"Cop is fine, and yes. In the Seattle area. North of there." Nobody outside the Northwest knew anything about Washington State outside of Seattle, so she generalized.

"Cool. Thank you for doing what you do. You're brave," the driver said.

"You're welcome. It's my privilege," she replied, and meant it.

It only took minutes before they were in the city, and Tia could make out a few tall buildings. It reminded her of Bellevue, a neighboring city to Seattle – suburban-urban, clean and trendy, instead of stark and gritty.

Tia thanked the driver and went inside.

She glanced around, and found she was the first to arrive. *Thank God.*

She got a bottled water and chose a seat near the back, facing the door. She'd given, and gotten, a general description of what they looked like – elderly lady with gray hair, and a twenty-something woman with long, dark hair and blue eyes, and of course there was the photo of the younger woman to go by.

She was hardly settled when they came in, looking equally nervous, worried, scared.

Tia immediately read honesty, vulnerability, and rose with a smile to wave them over.

They were dressed beautifully, skirts, sweaters, and pumps. She felt scruffy after her flight, but what could she do? She held out her hand. "Hi, I'm Tia. Do you want to take a minute and get something to drink?"

"No," the elderly woman responded. She didn't seem able to take her eyes off Tia, and Tia wondered how much of the old woman's mind was still functioning normally.

The younger woman shook her hand. "Hi, I'm Stephanie. I'll get us some tea. Why don't you, eh, I'll be right back."

Tia smiled. She wasn't alone. Everyone was nervous.

"Have a seat, er, Vivian." Tia waved the elderly lady to a chair opposite hers. "It seems we have a lot to talk about. Let's wait until Stephanie gets back with your drinks, okay?"

Her great-grandmother stared back with a vague smile, and nodded mutely.

Impulsively, Tia reached out and took Vivian's hand. "This is awkward, but let me set your mind at ease. I'm a deputy with the Snohomish County Sheriff's Office, which is about thirty miles north of Seattle. It'll be ten years in April. I'll show you all of my credentials, so you know I'm not trying to scam, or anything. Honestly, my mom chickened out. I couldn't believe it, but she couldn't face the uncertainty, so she sent me into the lion's den all by myself." Tia felt herself flush. She was jabbering. She closed her mouth, smiled, and forced a pause.

The old woman broke into a smile, took a breath as if to speak, held it a moment, then let it out again, without saying a word.

Better they both wait for Stephanie, who, Tia fervently hoped, would be a more adept ice-breaker than she.

This woman is ninety-five, she reminded herself, steeling herself for disappointment. *There might not be a lot there to get to know...*

Two good-looking men came in and glanced around. Tia immediately sensed they were cops. Their presence – the way they stood, the way they scanned the room – it was obvious. They probably wanted the seat she'd chosen. Yep, one of them was looking their way. She checked their belts, but didn't see a badge. Off duty, then.

She was surprised when the other one went over to Stephanie and hugged her. She pointed at their table.

Moments later, Stephanie-the-assistant slid into her spot beside Vivian, handed her a cup of tea, then introduced the two men who'd followed her over.

"Cynthia, this is my husband, Rob O'Conner, and my brother, Seth. They're both with the Greenville police department, and insisted on providing a protection detail, just in case." Stephanie rolled her eyes and laughed. "Husbands and brothers. What're ya gonna do?"

Tia mentally thanked the heavens, and shook their hands. "Nice to meet all of you, and please, call me Tia. And," she looked at the two men, "I'm a deputy with the county sheriff's office one county north of Seattle, so I can appreciate the concern."

She and the guys exchanged tidbits in a conversational tone, but she knew it to be their way of verifying her claim. They seemed to relax, and then so did Stephanie.

And then, silence. Awkward.

"Um…" Tia began, searching for something to say.

The assistant raised her hand. "Can I take a minute to explain some background to get started?"

Tia nodded, and the old woman looked relieved.

"Your great-grandmother is a wonderful woman, and highly thought of in, eh, where we live. She has decided to leave her home for something smaller, which led to her to donate a rather large portion of her worldly belongings to us, her, eh, to us. This led to my suggesting she submit to a DNA test, which she did, and which, in turn, led us all to," she spread her arms to include the whole of Starbucks, "our meeting, today."

Tia looked at one, then the other, then took a deep breath. "Great," she began with a matter-of-fact smile. "I want to put your minds at ease. I am not looking for anything other than information, and should everything pan out, maybe we can pursue a relationship, to whatever degree you should desire, nothing more."

She turned to look solely at Vivian. "The DNA results say I am you direct descendant. Your great-granddaughter."

"Yes," Vivian whispered.

"Let me tell you everything I know about my heritage," Tia stated. "I assume you want to know what I know?"

Vivian nodded.

"So. My mother is wonderful, except she totally chickened out on this meeting. My apologies. I never expected this of her. She's usually stronger, but, well, let's stick to the fundamentals, shall we?"

Vivian smiled.

"Okay," Tia resumed, after taking a deep breath. "This part is going to be difficult for you to hear, and I'm sorry if I'm too blunt, but there you go. My grandma died in 1989, when a drunk driver T-boned her on a rainy, remote section of coastal highway near Tillamook, Oregon. Both drivers were killed on impact. Both had elevated blood-alcohol levels, but she was not at fault. The other driver was going too fast for the conditions and lost control of his vehicle."

Tia watched as tears welled and spilled onto the old woman's cheeks. She sighed mentally. These things were always so damned difficult.

"She didn't suffer. Actually, neither of them did. It was very quick, and no one else was involved," Tia went on. "Okay, so those are the facts. Now for the family part, which, arguably, might be even more difficult for you."

Both women looked confused. The guys looked interested, but remained in the periphery.

How could it get worse, right? Tia gave herself a mental knock upside the head. *Geez, show some empathy!*

"Look, it hurt my mother deeply," she explained, trying to find a way to soften the blow. "I was three when it happened, so I apologize if my delivery is mechanical, but it's because these are historical factoids to me, not flesh and blood reality, at least not until now. So, what it comes to is facts. All I can tell you is what my mother and my grandpa knew, or didn't, about, eh, about your daughter."

Tia waited, uncomfortable, and cursed her mother's absence yet again, while the elderly woman dried her face, and Stephanie comforted her. Tia took a swallow of water.

She avoided looking at the men, although, as cops, she felt

like she had more common ground with them. Nevertheless, she couldn't help but notice the brother, Seth, had a rather compelling little smile on his face.

After several minutes, Vivian nodded, and Stephanie addressed Tia.

"Please continue."

"Like I said, my mother chickened out on all of this. She's wonderful, but this was all too much for her."

Stephanie smiled. "We understand. We have both felt like bolting several times."

Tia liked Stephanie. She was strong, direct, and protective of the woman in her care.

"Very well," Tia said. "My mom, Cherry Williams, hardly ever spoke of her mother, until this all happened. She told me her mother had an artist's soul, although she says her mother never did anything artistic, so I'm not sure what any of that means. Mom grew up in Santa Rosa, north of San Francisco. She and her parents were not close. Nothing bad, just a kind of a neutral nothing, and no one ever spoke of the past. When her childhood friends talked of family, and specifically grandparents, she'd asked about her own, but her father's parents were gone, and her mother refused to speak of hers, at all."

Tia looked for reaction, but for now, the two women on the opposite side of the table kept their feelings in check.

"I knew my grandfather as a very loving man, but mom says his attitude changed for the better after he'd lost his wife. Suddenly, he made every effort to learn how to grow closer to his family. He died a few year ago. Still, when asked before he died, my grandfather had no information about his wife's family. She had never divulged anything to him, either. They hadn't met until later on in her high-living days of Haight-Ashbury, which she confessed to, but she refused to talk with any detail about her life before they met, and never about family. I'm sorry."

Tia looked at one, and then the other. *Oh, crap crap crap!*

Vivian had started crying again, and Stephanie, who looked miserable, consoled her.

So much easier to deal with a smelly, druggy, frequent-flyer, than all this emotion, she thought.

She anxiously drained her water bottle, and wished it was Scotch.

"Look, I can't mend the past," Tia said, desperation making her blurt the first words that sprang to mind. "Let me tell you about us, how we are now, okay?"

Vivian nodded, and gave a watery smile. "Yes, please. Forgive me, I just…never mind. Please, go on."

"Okay. My mom, Cherish Williams Benson, was born in 1967, to Barbara Henderson Williams. My mom, Cherry, married Don Benson in 1985—"

"Wait a moment." Vivian straightened and gave Tia, then Stephanie, a confused look. "Barbara? Who is Barbara?"

Suddenly just as confused, Tia also sought clarification from Stephanie. "My grandmother was Barbara Henderson Williams. We called her Barbie. She was born September 28, 1942, although…although she never said where. I think she intimated it was somewhere in California, at least that's what my mother always believed, and that's where I tried, but failed, to find her records."

"Are we all talking about the same person? Did the DNA people have a mix-up?" Vivian asked Stephanie.

"Hold on a sec. Let's not go there just yet. Maybe I know how we can clear this up." Tia called her mom.

"Hi honey. Have you landed?"

"Yes. Where are you?"

"Home. Why?"

"You have a photo of Grandma Barbie, don't you? Can

you take a picture of it, a good one, and text it to me immediately, please? It's important."

"Oh, that's a good idea. Can't believe we didn't—"

"Mom, hurry. Please. I'll call later and explain."

"Okay, okay. Say hi to them for me when you get there."

Tia hung up and placed the phone in the middle of the table. "If we sit here and watch the phone, it's never going to happen," she said with a weak smile. "I can't believe the DNA people messed up, so let me go on with what I was saying before, while we wait. All right?"

Vivian held Stephanie's hand in a death-grip, but she managed a smile and a nod.

"Okay. I was born in 1986. My parents are still alive and well, and I have a brother and two sisters. They are all married with children. I, however, have never married, and don't have any children. Yet."

Stephanie was taking notes with her free hand, but Vivian suddenly gave Tia a quizzical look. "Are you a lesbian?"

The men looked shocked, and Stephanie, a deep shade of crimson, was about to intervene, but Tia laughed. "No, just never found the right guy. Would gay be a problem?"

"No, simply a footnote. I don't believe we have any in our family."

Tia laughed again, happy for the unintentional comic diversion. "Duly noted." She shot a glance at the men. The husband looked to be enjoying himself immensely. The brother, Seth, was watching her closely, but she couldn't gauge whether it was interest in his eyes, or analysis. She shrugged mentally.

She liked Vivian, she decided. Very much. And her mind seemed plenty sharp. Now if they could just clear all this up and move forward.

Thankfully, her phone buzzed, and she quickly found the image she'd requested. It was of the three of them, when Tia

31

was a newborn. A generational photo. Her mom was beaming. Grandma Barbie just stared at the camera.

She turned the phone around. "Do you recognize this woman? My mom can find an older one, if—"

Vivian put a hand to her mouth and nodded, as silent sobs wacked her body.

They all waited, while Stephane sought to comfort Vivian. Everyone was uneasy, and fidgeted until Vivian regained some composure.

On instinct, Tia reached out and took her great grandmother's hand. "I'm truly sorry for all of this. What was her name, if not Barbara?"

Vivian swallowed a couple of times, then whispered, "Euphemia Opal Henderson. I named her after my mother, and Opal is my middle name. We called her Opal, instead of Effie, to avoid confusion with her grandmother. I suppose that is why we could never track her down. She'd changed her name. First and last."

"And why I couldn't find her, either, in any databases. I'm pretty sure my grandfather didn't know. He told us everything he could think of, before he died, but there was never any question on the name. Do you know where 'Barbara' came from? Was there someone in the extended family with that name?"

Vivian shook her head. "No, no one I can think of."

"I'm sorry I don't have more information to fill in the gaps," Tia added. "It seems like one mystery just leads to another."

"Don't you worry about it, dear. You have given me more than you can imagine. Some of it was hard to hear, I'll admit. Very hard. And I suppose we will never know what was going on in her mind, but she left the drugs behind, it would seem, and found love, which does me so much good to hear. And then she had a child who had a child in her own time. I feel so blessed. I am delighted to know so much. Truly."

"Would you mind if I asked you some questions?" Tia ventured.

"Please, go right ahead."

"Did you raise your daughter on the East Coast?"

"Yes, in, er…" Vivian glanced at Stephanie, who was back to taking notes, then at the others, who shrugged a 'fine with me' sentiment. "Yes, in South Carolina. Greenville."

"How old was she when she left?"

"She was twenty-three." Vivian's voice took on a soft, sentimental tone, and her eyes drifted off as she gazed into the past.

"She'd recently graduated college, had a degree in Finance, and was thinking of getting her Master's. Then, one day in mid-summer, she announced she was leaving. California was where it was happening, she said. San Francisco was the big scene, and all the kids were going there to change the world and make it a better place. Something we adults had failed at miserably, apparently."

Vivian waved a mock peace sign. "Pure horsepucky, her stepdad told her, and we refused to allow it. She tried to convince us it was a good idea over a couple of weeks, saying she would continue her schooling out West, but we held firm. There would be no more financial help for schooling, or anything else, if she left. Finally, furious and defiant, she held up one finger, and left. I found out later she'd been dating a beatnik-turned-radical, something she'd never divulged to us." Vivian heaved a sorrowful sigh at the memory. "I suppose he was the one she left with. At any rate, that was the last time I saw her, and the middle finger was the last communication I ever had from her."

After a long silence, Tia spoke with sincerity. "Wow. I'm so sorry. I wish I could say we'd found a long-hidden diary, in which she poured out her remorse, her regret, and the shame of it all was why she never spoke of her past, or sought forgiveness."

Stephanie looked a little taken aback by the statement, but Vivian smiled. "I have prayed for exactly that, for years and years."

"Well," Tia replied. "It seems to me if she hated you, she wouldn't have spared anyone knowing about it. So maybe we can assume contrition, maybe even shame, through her silence, and let it go?"

Vivian reached out and took Tia's hand. "Thank you, dear. Yes, I think that would be the perfect way to think about it."

By the end of the meeting, they'd exchanged personal information, and Tia and her mother were invited to see Vivian's home, meet her work family, and tour the familial hometown of Abbeville, an hour south of Greenville.

There was so much to talk about. So much to learn.

They all shook hands, and a flicker of...something, sparked between her and Seth when he held her hand a skosh longer than necessary. He was interested.

She smiled back. Dang if she wasn't interested, too.

Tia had only flown out for the weekend, so plans were made for a visit and grand reunification in the spring. This time with her mom. For sure.

CHAPTER FIVE

A FULL TWO MONTHS FOR TIA AND HER MOTHER TO PLAN AND prepare, and she was off for a return visit to the Carolinas.

Solo.

Again.

At least her mother had a decent excuse this time; one of her off-the-charts high end clients in Medina was having an interior design meltdown. The builder did blah, blah, blah to the crown molding in the solarium, and blah, blah something about the wood inlay design at the front entry.

The woman was not usually hysterical or demanding, but a crisis was, after all, a crisis, and Cherry couldn't abandon her cash-cow for personal reasons. She'd probably make enough on this gig alone to fly them both to Greenville on a private jet – the moment she got some free time.

Even though she knew Greenville/Spartanburg airport was her best option, Tia still chose to book the same flight as the first time, taking advantage of the drive from Charlotte to Greenville in order to get a visual feel for the state.

Simply put, it was beautiful. And *warm*. And *sunny*!

The Seattle area she left behind was a gray, rainy, and forty-eight degrees, with a lot more of the same in the forecast. Months of it.

Vivian invited her to stay at her home, which was bold of her, and a nod to her faith in family, but Tia opted for staying in the closest hotel, at least for the first couple of nights. Even though she'd used a week of vacation for this, and was determined to make the best out of every minute, she wanted a little space, until she had a clearer idea what she was getting in to.

Her onboard GPS took her across the border from North Carolina to South, then within sight of Spartanburg. There were historical markers along the way, and several roadside stands offering boiled peanuts. Not a Seattle thing, for sure. She made a mental note to ask someone.

Ninety minutes into the drive, she pulled off the highway, and eventually made her way into a lovely neighborhood in Greenville.

Tia drove slowly, absorbing the colonial grandeur of some of the homes she was seeing. After a few turns, the map guide said her destination was on her left in three hundred yards.

Excited, she pulled up to a wrought iron gate, behind which lay a long, tree-lined, gravel lane, leading to a slight incline, and on out of sight.

"Well, damn, Vivian," Tia mumbled.

She pushed the call button, smiled at the security camera, and the gate opened almost immediately.

"Boy-howdy, we got a live one, Bernadette."

It was something her first training officer said all the time. He was retired, now, and he'd laughingly handed over usage to her.

The old, stately trees were coming into bud. She had no idea what they were, since her tree knowledge stopped right after conifer and maple. And Palm. But she mostly only knew palms from those Christmas beer commercials.

At the top of the rise, the gravel drive leveled off and turned into a wide, circular driveway, with spaces for guest parking along the perimeter. She parked between a mid-sized white Mercedes, and a silver XTerra.

Feeling anxious, Tia looked in the rearview mirror to check her makeup and hair, then got out and adjusted her pea coat, black jeans, and V-neck red sweater. It was way too warm for the pea coat, but she looked more professional with it on.

When she was ready, she paused to take in the view.

Everything was perfectly trimmed, mown, and raked. The place was a postcard vision. If it ever snowed here, it would be straight out of Currier and Ives. But what took Tia's breath away, was the stately, Antebellum home gracing the property. White with black shutters, a colonnaded, wrap-around porch complete with rocking chairs, and a Trumanesque, half-round, second story balcony. It was breathtaking.

"Tara. Holy…. it's freaking Tara," she mumbled. Was this Vivian's home, or a B&B?

Tia made her way onto the porch, more than half expecting Mammy to come out the front door to greet her.

Instead, Stephanie opened the door with a broad smile on her face, and gave her a hug. Oh, yes, Stephanie was a hugger. Her dark hair was in a soft, up do, and she wore a pale pink angora sweater with a scoop neck, a double strand of pearls, a drop waist, pink and black plaid skirt, and black pumps.

"You found us. Welcome to Altamont. Come in. Come in."

I'm so underdressed. Tia suddenly recalled both ladies had worn skirts and pearls for their first meeting at Starbucks, too. *Damn.*

She stepped inside and had to stop to take it all in. The

entry had a beautifully patterned marble floor – white with soft gray veins, and black inlay for accents. There was a grand, horseshoe staircase of dark wood steps with carpet runners, rising to the second floor. Intricate molding seemed to be everywhere she looked, including along the contours of the stairs. An enormous chandelier hung from the second floor ceiling, high overhead. It was breathtaking.

Tia gestured broadly with her arms. "This is incredible. Beautiful."

"Thank you, and yes, even for the South, it is," Stephanie said with a smile. She took Tia's elbow and escorted her to a side room with tall windows that let the sun pour in.

"Let me take your coat. Vivian's awake and will be with us in a moment. She wanted to rest a bit before you came. She usually takes a little nap in the early afternoon," Stephanie explained.

Tia felt awkward and oafish as she shucked out of her heavy coat.

At the sounds of brisk, heeled footsteps, both women turned around. A beautiful, stately, forty-something black woman came around the corner carrying a heavy, silver tea tray. Tall and model-thin, she wore a dark blue pencil skirt, white silk blouse, and black stilettos. And pearls.

Shaking off her earlier thoughts of expecting to see Mammy, Tia knew her stop-motion reaction was plain to see. *Double damn.*

"Hi, I'm Naomi. Hold on a moment," she said, and placed the tray on the coffee table in the sitting room. She turned to Tia with a smile, and held out her hand.

"Have we met before? You looked as though you recognized…never mind, I'm sure we couldn't have. I'm Naomi Connelly. I'm curator at the Greenville Cultural Heritage Museum," she said, shaking Tia's hand with enthusiasm. "I work with Stephanie, and Vivian has been an important part of our program for years. Long before any of us got there. Actually, long before most of us were born. Everyone in this business revers her, and will do any and everything we can to make this transition as easy as possible for her."

"Transition?"

"Sorry, I'm jumping the gun. We'll wait until she's with us before we go over everything."

"And I'm sorry I looked so stupid," Tia admitted. "I didn't recognize you. It's just, well, we don't have homes like this in Seattle, and I was going all 'Tara' when I saw this place. Then, when you came in with the tray it kind of jolted me, like I'd stepped onto a movie set, or The Twilight Zone, or something. Sorry."

"Oh, gracious, you thought I was the help?"

Tia could feel a deep blush bloom across on her pasty Seattle skin. "Well, not exactly, but like I said, it was a – 'where the hell am I?' sort of moment. My apologies."

Naomi and Stephanie gawked at her, then at each other, and both burst out laughing.

"No apology needed," Naomi assured her. "The house is actually called Altamont. Come, sit. And I am not the help, although I do help out when I can."

These women were elegantly dressed, genteel, soft spoken, courteous. Apparently they didn't even cuss.

Everything I'm not, Tia thought, and corrected her posture.

"I see you've all been introduced," Vivian said, making her way into the cozy room, looking lovely in a beige sweater set, brown wool skirt, and black flats. No pearls, but she did have a diamond broach.

On impulse, Tia hugged her. Vivian looked surprised and pleased.

"You have a beautiful home," Tia said, taking in the

matching floral chintz curtains, arm chairs, and settee, and the a white, baby grand piano in the corner. "It's incredible. I probably should have dressed up a bit more, but this is about as fancy as anyone gets in Seattle, at least for flights."

"Not at all, you look wonderful," Vivian replied, beaming. "And thank you. I'd take you on a tour, but I haven't the strength anymore. One of these lovely ladies will show you everything later. As you can see, I've loads of space, so if you choose to stay with us, there is a room available for you to use."

Tia smiled, but chose not to accept.

They all sat and Stephanie served the tea.

"Naomi, why don't you explain the business end of things," Vivian said. "Then the tour, and we'll have a little chat about her heritage, afterward, if time allows. If not today, then tomorrow."

"All right, I'll get started," Naomi said, turning to Tia. "Vivian has been a part of the Historical Society since the early fifties. She has been our curator, as well as curator at a couple of other locations around town, and has been on the board of the State Historical Society since, what, the sixties?"

Vivian gave a nod of affirmation.

"She has done endless research for herself, for us, and for many others. She's taught, collaborated on digs, written books and treatises galore. Any and everything, you name it, and she's done it. Had she bothered, she could have earned her PhD. in several subjects."

There was a slight eye-roll and a dismissive wave of her hand from Vivian.

"Recently, she decided it would be wise to move into an apartment in an independent senior living facility, and because of her life-long dedication and extreme generosity, Vivian decided to sign over the deed to this wonderful home to us."

Tia looked at Vivian with surprise. "Oh my God, you are so generous, and thoughtful, and, how did we ever get so lucky as to be a part of your family?" Tia leaned over and hugged Vivian again. "You are more awesome with every minute that goes by."

Vivian hugged her back, chuckling.

"Not to be rude," Naomi continued, "but, as her descendant, I hope there won't be any issue with this arrangement, as it was agreed to prior to any knowledge of your existence?"

"What? Why?" Tia asked in surprise.

"Well, the house represents a substantial financial loss, if you were anticipating—"

Tia stopped them with both hands. "Whoa, hold on, hold on. I see where you are going, and I absolutely understand the need to broach the subject, so I want to make my position, our position, very, very clear."

The others waited, looking hopeful, but obviously on edge.

"As I told you in our first meeting at the Starbucks, my mother and I have exactly zero expectation of financial, or any other kind of gain from our relationship to Vivian, other than personal, and informational. We want to get to know her, and vice-versa, learn about our heritage, share our lives with her, everything, but we never, ever hoped for, wanted, nor do we expect, any kind of monetary gain from this."

She waited, glad to see they looked relieved. Vivian actually beamed.

"So," Tia asked with a smile. "Are we clear?"

Stephanie grinned. "I think you passed every hurdle and wiped away every concern, all in one fell swoop."

Criss-crossing her heart, Tia raised her right hand. "And in case we are ever alone, I swear I will never use coercion, or any other diabolical method, to pry any worldly goods or money out of Vivian."

They all laughed.

"Okay, you've passed every test," Naomi said with a smile. "To continue, the deed will be signed and the transfer of ownership completed by the end of the month. The second story rooms on the north side will be offices, and closed to the public. The main floor and the gardens will be open to the public a couple of days a week, and available to rent for events. The upper bedrooms on the south side will be open for viewing, as well, and optional as a part of a special, overnight package. Some of the furniture will be Vivian's, some will come from the Museum. We want to re-create an antebellum home, yet one which has been a home to families for over one hundred and eighty years."

"That. Is. So. Cool," Tia said, and meant it. She sat back in her chair, then turned and patted Vivian's hand. "I love being related to such an awesome person. So cool."

The conversation went on, but the details were sailing over her head. This era, that era, plans, and etc. Tia was conversationally sidelined. Except for an exclamation here or there, she had no real input. This was their game.

After an hour, Tia was fading. She needed to stretch her legs, get her circulation jump-started. She raised her hand. "Uh, bathroom?"

Vivian grasped her hand. "I'm so sorry. Stephanie can show you. Naomi, can you give me a hand?"

The group split, and Tia asked her guide, "Is Vivian okay? She looked a little spent."

"She's feeling her age more and more," Stephanie answered. "All this moving and deciding what goes where, its taxing for anyone, and she's ninety-five, plus there's the emotional component. She's going to rest for a bit, and I'm heading back to work, but Naomi will still be here. No need to worry."

Tia stopped. "Wow, ninety-five. I knew, but once we met, well, I would've guessed, heck, I don't know, but younger, certainly. She's great. Sharp. I'm in awe."

"She is very sharp, but she tires easily these days. Come with me, I'll show you around."

She was shown the facilities nearest the sitting room, and couldn't believe her eyes. The toilet was small, had a wooden seat, and a delicate floral design covered the base. The tank was also floral, but it was mounted on the wall, a couple of feet above the base, with a pull chain. Affixed to the wall, the sink, a tiny, ceramic beauty with scalloped edges, had the same floral design. The mirror above was gilt.

Holy freakin'... Tia thought. A girl could have shy bladder syndrome in a place this pretty.

Stephanie was waiting a polite distance away when Tia came out. "Will we be meeting in the sitting room again? If you abandon me, I need to pay attention to be able to find my way back."

She grinned. "I won't abandon you, so no need for bread crumbs. The public rooms, as we think of them, form a square in the central portion of the building. The grand foyer with the double staircase is in the exact center. The smallest rooms on the ground floor are the parlor, on the right, which is where we had tea. It's twin, on the left, is the office, where formal business is conducted. The library is next to the office, with its counterpart on the right being the dining room." Stephanie gave her a glimpse of the office, then opened wide the double doors to the library. "This is the library, and back in the day was strictly off-limits to the ladies during social events. The men retired here after dinner to smoke, drink whisky, talk politics – nothing a woman would ever be interested in, right?"

Tia shook her head with a smile. It looked as though it had been patterned on Henry Higgins' library in *My Fair Lady*, and was filled with intriguing-looking books, floor to ceiling.

"We'll peek at the dining room and kitchen before going on to the ballroom." Stephanie headed back to the right side of the foyer, then along a short hallway between the parlor and the dining room. Doors opened to both rooms from the hall, and Tia saw a very long table in the dining room, many chairs, and another sparkling, though smaller, chandelier.

"Oh my..." Tia breathed when they entered the kitchen. Copper, brass, wood, crockery, and tile were everywhere. It was grand, and very, very, old school.

"This is a rather magnificent recreation Vivian and Thomas did shortly after they bought the house in the fifties. It's a period-style kitchen, for sure, however not one typical of the South. Actually, it is closer to something you might find in the grand estates in Europe, since they took their inspiration from the Royal Pavilion in Brighton. Everyone loves it."

They walked through the kitchen. Stephanie opened the back door and pointed to a small building several feet from the house. "You'll notice the porch does not wrap around this side of the house. That's because it's the working side of the house, and, for safety's sake, the kitchen fires were typically kept in a separate building. The original burned long ago, so Vivian and Thomas recreated this building, and turned it into a wine cellar."

So far, there were three rooms Tia would be happy to spend the rest of her days in – the parlor, the library, and now the kitchen, especially if there were access to the wine cellar. No need to go anywhere else, ever again.

Stephanie backtracked into the foyer, then walked

between the arms of the stairs. Underneath the apex, she slid open enormous double pocket doors.

"And this is the grand ballroom," she said with pride.

Tia drew a breath in amazement. The expansive room had a real wood parquet floor, three large chandeliers, and floor to ceiling windows graced the entire exterior wall, which looked out over a lawn and formal gardens.

"If a celebratory event was called for, there would be dancing in the ballroom after dinner," Stephanie explained. "These days, and for years, now, they've allowed historical conferences to be held in here, and we've managed a dance or two, as well. I met my husband at one of those. My brother, Seth, you met him at coffee, agreed to work security, and asked Rob to help out." Stephanie grinned and nudged her. "I forced my brother to let Rob shed his security persona so he could dance with me. We were both goners by the end of the evening."

Tia smiled at the story, and thought, *Romance is good. Romance is also...elusive.*

With another look beyond the windows, Tia noticed dusk was settling in. Like a hammer blow, she realized she was exhausted.

There were footsteps coming in from the foyer, and Vivian entered on Naomi's arm.

"I hope you liked the tour," she said. "I had thought to ask you to stay for dinner, but I must confess I'm very tired, and these two ladies need to get home to their husbands. Would you mind if we called it a day? Perhaps you could come back for breakfast in the morning?"

"Perfect. It's dawning on me how tired I am, too. I've been awake since the wee hours, and my head is spinning," Tia replied with relief. "When would you like me to come by?"

They made arrangements for breakfast, all four agreeing

to attend. Stephanie said she would bring food, Naomi, beverages, and they all departed before dusk turned to dark.

Tia punched in the hotel's address, and the GPS got her there in under fifteen minutes. Fifteen minutes after that, her head hit the pillow and she was out, completely forgetting she'd promised to call and update her mother.

CHAPTER SIX

READY FOR THE DAY, TIA LAY BACK AGAINST A PILE OF PILLOWS and dialed her mom. She'd done her hair in her signature 'cop do,' because she felt she needed to make an upgrade in her style game around these women. As for her clothing, she wasn't sure she owned a skirt, and she sure hadn't packed one. Black jeans, a black and white polka dot blouse, and black ankle boots were as good as she had.

"Hi, honey. How's it going?"

"Everything is awesome, Mom. Hope this isn't too early. I'm about to head back there for breakfast. I spent a couple of hours with them at Vivian's home as soon as I got in, yesterday. You wouldn't believe it," Tia said. "I have to remember to take pictures this time. I keep forgetting, so text me if you haven't gotten any by noon, your time. In the meantime, think Tara."

"Oh, my, I'm so intrigued, and it's not too early. I'm doing some redesign sketches before I head out. So, you're getting along? Everything's pleasant?"

"They are the nicest people. Vivian is ninety-five, and incredible. Funny, sharp, and hugely considerate and giving, if half of what everyone's telling me is true. You have got to get out here."

"Arrgh," Cherry groaned. "I will, I will,"

Tia rolled off the bed and grabbed her sweater and wallet. "I'm holding you to it. If I have to threaten to arrest your client for unlawful imprisonment, I will."

She heard her mom laugh at the weak joke.

"I'm heading out, so I'll call you later, full of details. Remind me if I forget to send pics." Tia ended the call and left her room, then dropped into the florist next door and bought a fragrant spring bouquet.

Her hotel was downtown, and Tia took in the sights as she left. Greenville was pretty, had a quaint feel, and was dotted with old buildings throughout. Everything seemed quiet and clean, and she saw no evidence of transient activity, unsavory corners, or tagging. They probably existed, she mused, just not in the touristy part. She crossed a bridge she didn't remember from her arrival in the dark the night before, and spotted a nice looking pub not far away. She vowed to remember the location for dinner.

Her mind drifted on as the GPS took her back to Altamont. Maybe she could suggest Stephanie and Rob join her at the pub. They were younger than she, in their twenties, she guessed, but Seth looked closer to her own age of thirty-three. Maybe she could drop a hint for Stephanie to invite her good-looking big brother along.

To round out the table conversation, she told herself.

When Tia arrived at the gate, she pushed the button and smiled into the camera. She was starving, but more interestingly, she was excited to see Vivian again.

She recalled a dream she'd had the night before, in which she and Vivian were both young, maybe eight, and full of giggles. They laughed when Tia called her Gramma Viv. They were on a floral chintz couch, much like the one in the parlor, but there had been lots of pillows they'd burrowed into as their laughter continued.

Tia knew nothing about dream interpretation, but hers had put her in a pleasant, warm mood nothing could dispel.

She pushed the button again, and once again got no response. A wave of disquiet pushed through her. Cop vibes.

Tia backed out of the driveway, parked the car to one side of the gate, then got out. She made an automatic check for her gun, concealed at the small of her back, then, skirting the gate, she climbed the drive on foot.

Before she got to the top, she could see flashing red lights – EMTs? – through the trees. *Oh, damn!* She started to run.

Coming into the open, Tia saw an aid unit parked at the front door. She holstered her weapon, and rushed inside.

She found an empty gurney in the foyer, then a crowd in the parlor. The scene before her filled her with a terror she'd never known before – a personal fear.

Vivian, pale and unresponsive, lay on the couch with a saline drip running into her arm. She had an oxygen mask over her nose and mouth, and an ugly knot on her forehead. She was propped on a pile of floral pillows Tia hadn't seen anywhere but in her dream, which sent a chill through her body.

Stephanie sat beside Vivian, holding her hand. The EMTs hovered near Vivian's head, looking grim, talking on their radios, monitoring her vitals, and giving feedback. Naomi stood at Vivian's feet, tears in her eyes.

Tia took her hand. "Naomi, what's happened? What's going on?"

Naomi turned unfocused eyes on her.

"What happened to Vivian?" Tia asked with a calm, but firmer voice. She knew shock when she saw it.

"Uh, oh, Tia." Naomi's tenuous hold on her emotions dissolved, and she put her arms around Tia.

Tia used the moment to assess the EMTs body, and verbal language, and felt a measure of assurance. They had Vivian stabilized. They were making plans to transport. Good.

She took Naomi by the shoulders and gently separated them, without letting her go. Tia looked her straight in the eyes. Direct. Calm. In control. Cop mode.

"Naomi, tell me what happened. What's going on? The facts. Can you do that for me?"

Naomi nodded, but remained speechless.

Choices. She needed choices.

"Was there an intruder? Did she fall? Cardiac? What is going on with her?" Tia tightened her grip and gave Naomi a little jolt. "You need to focus and tell me what happened. Okay?"

Naomi nodded again, and Tia was glad to see her eyes coming into focus.

"Good girl. Now, tell me what happened."

"We were getting everything ready for breakfast, when, when she just dropped," Naomi explained, her arms gesturing listlessly at her side. "We were both within feet of her, but neither of us could get there in time to stop her fall. She just dropped. No words, no groan. No unsteadiness, just...dropped."

"So, not intruders? Nothing external caused this?"

"No. She was so excited to see you again." Naomi was more focused, now. Sad, instead of lost. "Vivian wanted everything to be perfect. We set breakfast out in the library, because Stephanie said how impressed you were with it. She wanted everything to be perfect for you. We all did."

Tia swallowed hard. Stupid emotions. "Okay, thanks, Naomi. Gentlemen?" She let go and addressed the EMTs. "I'm family. She's my great grandmother. Can you please tell me what's happened?"

One of the medical techs stood. "Looks like a mild stroke.

We're transporting immediately. We're ten out from the hospital, and they'll assess and give her clot busters, if needed, as soon as we get there. Prognosis is fair. These ladies saw it happen and called immediately. The doctors will be able to give you more specifics, and a prognosis, at the hospital."

Tia and Stephanie helped get furniture out of the way, then stood by while Vivian was lifted onto the gurney. All three of them moved to the porch and watched helplessly as Vivian was wheeled out the door and into the rig.

As the aid car headed out, two police cruisers roared into view, giving way to let the rig pass.

Rob and Seth jumped out of their cars and hurried to the porch.

"Dispatch heard the call to Fire and let me know," Rob said, taking Stephanie in his arms. "Are you okay? How's Viv?"

Stephanie melted into her husband's arms and started crying.

Tia reached out and shook Seth's hand. "I'm so glad you're here. I arrived after the aid car. She's stable, possibly a small stroke." She glanced at Rob and saw he was taking in the details. "Stephanie and Naomi were on top of everything. Handled it. Saw her drop, called 911, did everything perfectly."

Rob gave his wife another hug, and Tia heard the mumble of his tender, reassuring words.

"I assume you ladies want to go to the hospital?" Tia asked.

Nods.

She turned back to Seth. "Are you two skipping school?"

He shrugged. "We're here for all of you, until another call comes in."

"I'll take the three of us to the hospital, if you'd like," Tia offered. "I don't want either of them driving, right now. Meet us there?"

"Sure, sounds great." Seth smiled, gave her a little squeeze on the elbow, then whacked Rob on the shoulder, and returned to his cruiser.

Within minutes, they were all in the ER, waiting for any news on Vivian.

CHAPTER SEVEN

ONE WEEK LATER, VIVIAN WAS STABLE, BUT VERY WEAK. HER senior living facility confirmed they could take her in on their medical floor, if needed, as soon as she was cleared. At the moment, her doctors couldn't say when that might be.

Tia spent every day by Vivian's side, holding her hand, talking to her, even though she rarely responded. Tia had asked for, and been granted, an extended family emergency leave from work. Naomi insisted she move into Altamont, and use Vivian's car, to save money, and after some weak protesting, Tia gladly accepted the offer. Together, they made a schedule for volunteers who wanted to stay by Vivian's side, when Tia or Stephanie couldn't be there.

The prognosis was encouraging, but barely. Vivian had indeed suffered a mild stroke.

The vibrant woman Tia had barely met, seemed anything but, these days. Regardless, Tia kept talking, whether Vivian was responsive, or not.

"Gramma Viv," Tia gave her hand a squeeze. "We've had so much fun starting our new life as family, and there is still so much to uncover. I have pictures of Grandma Barbie, er,

Opal, from my mom's childhood, and I'd so love to hear what she was like as a child. I'd like to know all about your childhood, too, and about my great grandfather. I don't even know his name. Oh, there's so much we still need to share."

Tia stopped, took a sip of the coffee she'd bought on the way in, and winced. Cold. She put it back on the bedside table, and returned her gaze to Vivian. So far this morning, she seemed to be sleeping. The nurse assured Tia Vivian's lack of response wasn't due to any permanent issues with her brain activity, but, at her advanced age, it was more difficult to regain the strength needed to stay awake, or converse, for long periods of time.

Even so, Tia worried. There was no indication Vivian was hearing any of her words, although she looked pretty good. Her breathing and color were much improved.

"I bet you had all the guys chasing after you, right?" Tia said with a smile. "How did my great grandfather, hmm, I think I'll call him Rhett, because he must have been very dashing, what made Rhett so different that he could win the hand of the prettiest girl in town?"

Did she detect a smile? Tia held her breath and waited. No, nothing.

With a sigh, Tia let go of Vivian's hand, grabbed her cup, and was about to go in search of a microwave.

"Cooper."

Tia stopped short and turned around. "Gramma Vivian? Did you say something?"

There was a smile, so Tia put the coffee aside, took Vivian's hand once again, and repeated, "Did you say Cooper?"

Vivian squeezed her hand, nodded, her smile broadening. "My first. Cooper. Best kisser."

Holy...first what? Not sure she wanted details, yet wanting

54

to coax Vivian out of her lethargy, Tia asked, "My great grandfather's name was Cooper?"

Vivian shook her head.

Perplexed, Tia tried again. "But, um, so this not-Cooper was a good kisser?"

Vivian grinned, pursed her lips as though she was puckering up for a good one, then wiggled her eyebrows, opened her eyes, and winked at Tia. "Best damn kisser."

Stunned, and ready to burst out laughing, Tia was glad when Vivian immediately closed her eyes again.

"Well, if I'd known talking about boys would get you cussing and divulging sexy secrets, I'd have started days ago. Those are two of my best subjects."

Vivian chuckled. "Raise the bed, please," she said in a weak voice. "Would love something to eat. And tea."

Tia did as she was asked, then buzzed the nurse's station.

Throughout the morning, Vivian talked in snatches, but her references weren't complete, as though she assumed Tia already knew the details and could follow along. Regardless, Tia was thrilled at her returning stamina, and delighted by this hilarious version of her very proper great grandmother. Tia suspected all of her usual Southern Lady buffers weren't working normally, which led to some great off-color jokes and stories.

Nevertheless, Vivian was fragile. She could barely manage one full sentence at a time. When she told a joke, it could take several minutes for her to manage all of the words. Finally, after two hours of conversation, Vivian drifted off to sleep. She looked happy.

Stephanie stopped in at eleven and gave her a hug. "Tia, let's go grab some lunch. The nurse says she's been talking all morning, so she could use the rest, and you could use a break. I'll drive, and when we get back I'll sit with her for a while."

Over lunch at a little bistro, Tia relayed the scope of the morning's conversation, hoping Stephanie could shed some light, or fill in gaps. Her eyes widened in surprise at some of the language Tia assured her Vivian had used, along with the reference to kissing, but Stephanie had no idea who Cooper might be.

"I know quite a bit about her history, her familial past, but not sentiments, or anything terribly personal, just facts. Anyway, I'd prefer she tell you of the more personal aspects," Stephanie said. "After all, it's her story to tell. But as for Cooper? I've no idea."

"I understand your position; but a few facts sure would be great. I'd love to have some idea my lineage, names, anything. I've researched her online, so at least I know my great grand-father's name was Thomas Weiss, and that he died in 2002, but the articles only cover their work together. I've tried to get information on his family, but there's not much there, either."

Stephanie eyes widened for a moment, then drifted away, as though she were considering her options. She chewed on her lip.

"That first day at the coffee shop," Tia persisted. "We all got caught up in the Barbara vs. Opal, but what about Weiss? She obviously dropper her father's surname, too. So, where did Henderson come from? That's the maiden name she gave us."

Stephanie heaved a sigh. "Okay, I guess you have a right to some basics. First, Thomas Weiss is not a blood relation of yours. He was Vivian's second husband. Opal's father was Vivian's first husband."

Surprised, Tia sat back in her chair and stared. "So, he was the Henderson? Was his first name Cooper?"

"No, I don't think so. As I said, I can't think where that name came from. Naomi, or some of the other women who've been there for years and years, might know more, so you should ask them, or ask Viv when she's better, of course. All I know is, Thomas was her second husband. She was widowed during World War II, when Opal was an infant. She married Thomas in the early fifties, so her daughter would have been ten-ish years old, or maybe less. He adopted her, gave her his name. We've always known the daughter as Opal Weiss. I'm not sure of the father's full name, only that Henderson was his last."

Stunned, Tia felt like her grandmother was becoming more mysterious, not less. No wonder Barbara Henderson had been impossible to trace. She hadn't used either of her legal names.

They finished lunch and drove back to the hospital. Once there, Stephanie turned to Tia and put a hand on her arm. "I'll take the afternoon watch. Naomi said she'd drop by after work and stay until visitor's hours are over."

"But—"

Stephanie smiled and shook her head. "No buts. You need some R&R, and you need to go shopping."

Perplexed, Tia frowned at her. "I do?"

"Yes. For one thing, you only brought clothes for a week. For another, it's too warm here for the things you brought. Plus, we're taking you out for beer and burgers, tonight. No arguments."

Tia laughed and raised her hands in surrender. "Okay, I give. Sounds great. I look forward to getting to know Naomi better. A more casual setting would be perfect."

"I'll come by at seven," Stephanie added. "And there's one more thing. Buy something cute. Naomi won't be there, because this was Seth's idea, and he and Rob are going to meet us there after their shift."

"Boy-howdy," Tia replied with a delighted grin. "We got a live one, Bernadette!"

. . .

DINNER WAS a fun change of scene. They met at an Irish Pub, and she and Seth hit it off like crazy. Stephanie was very proud of her match-making skills, and let everyone know it.

"But, wasn't this Seth's idea?" Rob asked.

"Those very words were on the tip of my tongue," Tia added, raising her beer to toast Stephanie, regardless.

Seth leaned over and mock-whispered in her ear. "She might've let some hints drop, like, 'ask her out, dammit.' I thought of the foursome-with-beer idea, though, all by myself."

Tia laughed and clinked glasses with him. "Well done."

The whole dinner was easy and pleasant, from beginning to end. She talked some cop shop with the men, but they kept it to a minimum for Stephanie's sake. Conversely, when she and Stephanie updated the guys on Vivian's progress, they were brief and to the point.

They asked for the check around nine-thirty, and Rob, Seth, and Tia all tossed their cards into the tray.

So fun. She hadn't had a casual night out in weeks, or maybe months. And she hadn't had anything resembling a date in over a year. She could get used to this. Easily.

"You ready?" Seth asked.

She smiled, and thought about how ready she might soon be, as she looked back at his dark, dark eyes.

Tia focused and realized everyone was looking at her. "Uh, sorry, I was drifting. Happily, though. Thinking about what a great night, what a great idea this was. Thank you all."

There were chuckles, and Tia blushed. *Hey, Prom Queen, get a grip!*

The checks came back, but there were only two slips to sign.

Seth handed her card back to her. "Ladies don't pay in the South, at least not on the first date."

About to protest, she knew it would be an empty gesture, so instead, she raised her glass and clinked it against Seth's once again. "Here's to first dates, then. Thank you for a great idea, a great night, and for covering the check."

They all finished what little was left in their glasses, and got up to leave.

Seth helped her on with her coat.

When was the last time anyone, besides her father, had done that?

"Wow, thanks," Tia said. "Chivalry sure isn't dead in the South. I think it died out mid-sixties on the West Coast. You'd better watch out. I might get used to this."

Seth grinned. "My life's ambition. By the way, I'm also a cad, so I'll tell you right now what the official line is: Rob has had a long, hard week, and misses his wife badly, so, gallant knight I am, I've offered to drive you home, since Stephanie cleverly got you here in her car."

Stephanie was grinning like a Cheshire cat. "You youngins be good now, y'hear?"

"Devious woman." Tia replied. "Will you be coming by tomorrow?"

"Yes, on my lunch break. There's a curator's meeting all morning. See you then."

Outside, Seth led her to his truck. It was a big, black, F-250. He opened her door, and she climbed inside to find leather seats, and all the bells and whistles. It was beautiful.

When Seth got in, she said, "I have an F-150. 2016. I love it."

Seth didn't respond, right away. He seemed to consider something, then turned and looked at her for a moment. He raised his hand slowly, and Tia thought he was going to touch her hair or something. Instead, he took her chin in a soft grip, leaned in, and kissed her. The kiss started as though he meant to give her a peck, but then it lengthened, soft and gentle, and Tia kissed back, utterly enveloped in the moment.

When Seth pulled away, he kept his light hold on her chin, and held her gaze. "I don't kiss at the door. Too much pressure, for both parties. Actually, I don't kiss at all on the first date. Hard rule. However, I'm hoping this is the first of many, so my perspective might be a bit skewed."

He gave her a soft smile, then let go, and started the truck.

Tia was speechless. And moved. She wanted this to be the first on many, too.

As promised, he did not try to kiss her when they arrived at Altamont. He got out, opened her door, and walked her onto the porch. He held back, letting her unlock the door.

"Thank you for a wonderful evening," she said. "And the kiss wasn't bad, either."

He grinned. "Hard to practice, but I wanted to make sure you had the best I have to offer."

"Duly noted. I think you did a fine job."

He laughed and backed off a step. "I'll give you call. Maybe we can do something, just the two of us."

"Ditch the old married couple? I'm all for it," Tia said. Then she made a decision. She stepped forward, took Seth's chin between her thumb and forefinger, as he'd done earlier, and gave him a quick kiss.

"Never fear. I did the kissing this time," she said. "So your rule is unbroken. My rule is, I haven't met anyone I've wanted to kiss in a very long time."

CHAPTER EIGHT

WHEN TIA ARRIVED AT THE HOSPITAL THE NEXT MORNING, SHE was surprised and delighted to find Vivian already sitting up and eating her breakfast.

Vivian reached out, and Tia took her hand, then gave her a hug. "You look great, Gramma Viv."

"They've got a room for me at a very nice rehab location. They don't want me to go to the senior living place quite yet, but this next place is lovely. I've visited friends there in the past, many times."

"That's wonderful news." Tia replied. "When will you be able to move?"

"This afternoon."

"Oh my gosh."

"Yes, and I want to have a serious talk with you before all the moving begins."

Taken aback, Tia raised her eyebrows. "Am I being sent to the principal's office?"

Vivian laughed, her eyes twinkling with mirth for the first time in days. "No, indeed, but I heard you say many things while I was unable to communicate, and it lit a fire in my soul. We need to talk about your heritage, about Opal, my past, all of it, and I know exactly where to begin – at the beginning!"

She looked at Tia with triumph.

"All this before you're moved?" Tia asked, feeling a bit flatfooted.

"No, of course not all. We'll cover the beginning this morning. That's all. I called Stephanie. I asked her to bring me a couple of things, and she's already dropped them by. We shall start when you are settled."

Tia took off her sweater, pulled a chair next to Vivian's bed, and sat.

Vivian tapped a button on the recorder Tia noticed on her tray table, then picked up a small, blue velvet bag with a draw string. She handed this to Tia.

It was surprisingly heavy, and made a little tinkling sound.

"First, I, Vivian Gardiner Henderson Weiss, am recording this for you, Cynthia Benson, my great granddaughter, so you will have both an accurate record of what I'm about to tell you, and a recording of my voice, which might be nice, later on. A copy will also be made and given to the Greenville Historical Society. Please, open the bag, dear."

Fascinated, exhilarated, Tia opened the bag and emptied the contents into her hand. She held a charm bracelet, but no modern version, this. The charms were intricate, finely wrought, nothing like the simple trinkets of today's versions. Most were silver in color, and by the weight, she was sure they were the real thing.

"Each tells a story," Vivian continued. "While I've been resting these past few days, it occurred to me this would be the ideal way to open my life's book for you to see, and hope-fully, understand. Now, to begin. I received the bracelet as a

62

gift from my parents, the Christmas of my eleventh year. It was 1935…"

~1935~

Vivian and her youngest sister leaned against the window sill of their hotel room in the Waldorf Astoria. New York City! They were so high in the air it made her dizzy. The streets below teamed with yellow taxicabs, and endless crowds of New Yorkers bustling along.

"Look at all those people," six-year-old Lucille exclaimed.

Vivian nodded. "And all those taxicabs. Where do they all need to go?"

Their oldest brother, seventeen-year-old Michael, leaned over and looked out. "I'd bet, if you counted all of the people on just one side of one block, there'd be more than the total number of people in all of Abbeville. By far."

Vivian looked at him and smiled. He was so smart. She would miss him terribly when he went off to college in the fall.

"We're leaving," Nanny Camille ordered. She allowed no disobedience or sloth in her world. "Girls, put on your gloves and hats. Everyone will carry their own suitcase."

They had three adjoining rooms in the hotel. Their parent's room was at one end, she and Lucille shared a room with Nanny Camille at the other end, and the five boys were in the middle room.

They all met in the hallway, while the rooms were checked and rechecked. Vivian's mother looked very beautiful, with a fitted wool suit, and a sharp little hat cocked to one side of her head. There was a pheasant feather sticking out of the band, which made her look very jaunty, and Vivian remembered when Papa had put it there. He'd taken the older boys out to hunt pheasant, and the feather was from one of the birds they'd dined on.

Once hats, gloves, suitcases, and children were all in place and accounted for, the hotel manager himself arrived, and personally escorted the large family to the lobby.

"I do hope your stay was a pleasant one," he said with a slight bow in the crowded elevator. "As the Waldorf Astoria's way of saying thank you for your visit, I've ordered special transportation for your short trip to the wharf. I do hope you enjoy it."

Goodie, Vivian thought with excitement. *We'll get to ride in a taxicab.*

Outside, the sun was blazing, and as Vivian looked at the blue sky overhead, she was astonished to see so little of it. Tall buildings surrounded them, and she realized the sun wouldn't be shining on them for long.

She put her hand in Michael's. "Does it get dark here, when the sun goes behind the buildings?"

"No, I shouldn't think so," he said, gazing upward. "It'll still be daytime. Like, when there's lots of clouds at home, you can't see the sun, but it's still daytime."

Three dark, fancy looking cars, and one yellow taxicab, pulled to the curb, and Vivian heard her parent's and older brothers' exclamations of delight.

"Too much!" "Keen!" "Wonderful!" "Aces!" "Thank you so much!"

Vivian dropped Michael's hand and headed for the lovely yellow taxicab, but the doorman stopped her. "The taxi is for the luggage, my dear. Your family will all be riding in the Rolls Royces."

Disappointed they were meant to ride in the black cars, Vivian waited to be told where she would sit. Her disappointment only increased when she and Lucille were made to sit on uncomfortable little seats that folded out from the rear of the front seat. Plus, they would be riding backwards. She didn't like much of anything about these special automobiles.

However, the ride didn't take long, and soon they were parked at the dock, where, once again, masses of people streamed back and forth, all in a hurry. But here, Vivian noticed a marked difference between this crowd, and the people outside the hotel. While the others had looked grim and unfriendly, these people looked excited. There was hugging, laughter, waves. They reminded her of the crowds at the Fourth of July parade. Everyone was happy.

The car doors opened, and she and Lucille got out first.

Light bulbs popped and flashed.

Vivian squinted, wondered at the attention, then looked away.

"How was it, little lady?" A man with a notepad asked her. "Are you excited to see Europe?"

"Yes, I am, but how was what?" she asked back.

"Why, the ride in the Rolls Royce, of course."

"Oh, well, it was a bit cramped, and I didn't like the fold out seat very much." Vivian got a nudge from Jonathan, her second oldest brother. "But, uh, it was all right. Fancy, I guess."

The cameraman and the note-taker both laughed.

Was she funny? She hadn't meant to be. She was trying to answer his question.

"Who are you? Why are you taking pictures of us?"

"We're with the New York Times newspaper, little lady, and you're a hot story. Such a big family, all travelling to Europe together. Pretty special, I'd say."

Nanny Camille came over and, pointedly ignoring the newspaper people, she gathered the girls to her. "Come along. Come along. We don't want to miss the ship."

With suitcases in hand, they all headed toward the dock and the boarding line.

The reporter was talking with her father, now, and Vivian thought she could see a little bit of grumpy behind Papa's polite exterior.

"No, we are not a wealthy family," she heard him say. "We are a farming family. I am simply affording my wife and children the opportunity to see the county where I was raised, and to meet their extended family."

The idea of wealth made her want to laugh. She doubted very much if wealthy people got out of bed before the sun to feed livestock, or – she glanced back at the Rolls Royce they'd climbed out of – drove cars like Papa's creaky old Model T truck.

Vivian enjoyed watching the bustle, until a looming darkness caught her eye. She looked up. Above her, seemingly right over her head, was the enormous, black hull of a ship. Her mouth dropped open.

Her youngest brothers, George and Mark, followed her gaze.

"Wow," ten-year-old George said.

Vivian read the name printed along its bow. "*Ile de France*."

"*La gloire de la France*," her father said with pride. The glory of France.

"Are we moving back to Papa's country?" Lucille asked, sounding worried.

"No, silly," Vivian assured her. "America is Papa's country, now. But we're going to visit his family, cousins and stuff, before we come home. It'll be swell."

They dropped off their luggage, had their tickets checked, and headed for the boarding ramp. Unfortunately, the reporter and photographer weren't left behind. Instead, they were able to obtain a temporary boarding pass, and moved along the ramp with the family.

There was such a mass of people on deck, their parents were hard-pressed to keep everyone together. The older children kept a tight grip on the younger's hands, while Lucille and Vivian linked arms with Nanny Camille.

The reporter caused a lot of commotion directing them into a tight group and shooing away those who did not belong. Once this was accomplished, the two mounted some steps and took several more pictures, with everyone waving and smiling at the camera.

After more taking more candid shops, and trying to extract yet more information, a bell clanged, and the loud speaker boomed.

"This is your ship's captain. The *Ile de France* will be departing shortly. All un-ticketed guests must disembark at once."

There were tears all around them, as loved-ones hugged each other, and those unfortunate enough not to have a ticket, made their way off the ship.

As the crowd thinned, uniformed men moved through the remaining passengers with platters of streamer ribbons and festive poppers. Everyone grabbed fists full, and pressed toward the railings.

Soon, a great claxon sounded three times, a bell rang continuously, and the three, towering smoke stacks belched out black smoke. Lines were loosened and pulled onboard. A gap appeared between the ship's hull and the dock full of waving relations.

They were underway.

All along the wharf-side railing, people cheered and colorful streamers filled the air. On the dock, far below, families waved to their loved-ones, and Vivian did likewise, although she knew no one there. It was thrilling, and she nearly wept for the joy she felt in the moment.

Later, she could recall little of the actual trans-Atlantic voyage, except it was beautiful. The staff were nice, and their waiter, Archie, became a good friend. Vivian prowled the ship with one sibling or the other, every day. She knew all of the nooks and crannies in every public area, and even made it into one of the galleys, before being politely escorted out.

But there was one memory that stood out – The Windy Deck.

She found it on the second day. It was a narrow deck overlooking the bow, where the winds were relentless. Nobody ever ventured out there. Except Vivian. She would go to the corner on the north, or port side, as she'd learned, and stand, gripping the railing at the point where it met the exterior wall. The wind whipped her hair and clothing in every direction. The air felt as though it was being torn from her lungs if she opened her mouth. And even in full sun, it was cold. Oh, but the things she saw; the force of the mighty bow as it crashed through the seas; the endless, rolling swells as far as she could see, crested with white streams of foaming ocean. She was sure they were going as fast as the stars that streaked across the heavens at night. And dolphins. Twice she saw dolphins. They seemed to be racing with the ship, and for a time, they kept pace with her, before finally diving out of sight.

MONTHS LATER, Vivian still thought about their trip every day. How she wished she could go back to see the mountains and charming, storybook buildings of Switzerland, the glorious Italian cathedrals, the smelly water channels of Venice, or the chateaux in the Loire Valley.

But it was the ancient ruins that lit a fire in Vivian's heart, especially those in and around Rome and Pompeii. All of the history they represented, and the people who'd lived so far back in time she could hardly grasp the concept. She wanted to learn everything about them, and checked out all the books she could find in the library.

That Christmas, when Vivian unwrapped her parent's special gift, tears sprang to her eyes. It was a lovely, silver, charm bracelet. On it hung an ocean liner, a tiny, tinkling, Swiss cowbell, a gondola, the Tower of Pisa, the Eiffel Tower, the Statue of Liberty, and a little shield with an enameled image of a fountain with one overarching word, Trevi. It was the wishing fountain in beautiful Rome they'd all tossed coins into.

With shouts of joy, Vivian launched into her parent's arms. "I love it, I love it, I love it," she exclaimed. "Thank you so much. I'll keep it forever."

"We had to be quite clever when we bought them," her mother said, laughing. "I sent Nanny Camille to give you some chore or other every time I wanted to duck into a shop, undetected. We felt quite clever you never caught on."

"Oh, Mother, I love it. I love it. Someday I'm going back," she promised. Sitting on her father's lap, Vivian looked at him. "Can I add to it, someday?"

"Certainly that would be fine, don't you think, Effie? These charms are only the beginning," her father assured her. "I've seen some fancy ladies with fifteen or twenty charms on their bracelets. You can add one to each loop, but this isn't a toy. You may not wear it to school, or for play. It's only for special occasions."

"We thought you were old enough to appreciate it, instead of getting a toy, or a doll?" her mother added, with a questioning note in her voice.

Vivian hugged the bracelet to her chest. "You were right. This is the best gift I've ever gotten, and I'll have it for my whole life, and it will always remind me of our big trip, and of the best parents in the whole world."

~2019~

With tears in her eyes at the poignant recollection, Vivian turned off the recorder, then looked at Tia, and smiled. "We made the return ocean crossing on the Queen Mary, which was much the prettier ship. It was all quite extraordinary, I can assure you. Now, we're about due for lunch, I'd say."

"What a wonderful memory." Tia returned the charm bracelet to its pouch, and handed it to Vivian "You're a great story teller. I could see everything, as though the scenes, the people, were all right in front of me. I feel as though I know them."

"Thank you. Now put it in your purse and take it home," she said. "It's safer with you than with me, here. You can bring it in for our little story times. Agreed?"

Tia hefted the pouch thoughtfully, then put it in her bag.

"Yes, I'd be delighted to keep it safe for you. Just give me the word, and I'll have it with me, whenever you're ready to tell another story."

CHAPTER NINE

IT TOOK SEVERAL DAYS FOR VIVIAN TO REGAIN HER STRENGTH after her move to the rehab facility. The place was clean, efficient, and the staff attentive. Tia had become very protective of Vivian, and made sure everything was of the highest quality.

Tia didn't press Vivian for more charm stories, although she was dying to continue.

In the meantime, she went on a couple of solo dates with Seth, and she had to admit she was smitten. He made her feel all weird, bubbly, and very un-cop-like when they were together. What had she suddenly become? A silly seventh grader? It was a very unusual and discomforting feeling. And oddly delicious.

They'd gone out to dinner both times, but afterward he'd taken her on walking tours of his hometown. They went under the bridge she'd seen the first day, and walked along the Reedy River, then through Falls Park. He pointed out historic neighborhoods, wealthy neighborhoods, and the questionable ones. His tours were informative, both from a homeboy's perspective, and from a cop's.

Everything was beautiful. Warm. Friendly.

Curiously, he never pushed for another kiss after the first night. She wondered about it, while trying to ignore the nagging voice in her head reminding her that her home, her job, and her life, were three thousand miles away. Because of that nasty little voice, she never sought to kiss him, either.

When Vivian announced she was ready to divulge the stories behind the next set of charms, Tia was more than ready to set her mind in a different direction.

The following morning, Tia arrived with a bouquet of flowers and a box of Vivian's favorite tea.

"Thank you, Tia, you are a dear to remember."

"My pleasure. You are in the custody of people who boss you around all day," Tia replied with a smile. "It was the least I could do."

The nurse brought them hot water in a thermos.

"Thank you," Tia said to the nurse. She put a tea bag in a cup, filled it, and put the travel lid on, before handing it to Vivian. "I know it's not exactly prison, Gramma, but I thought you might want a little luxury, a little taste of home, anyway. I also thought you might want to break free, if you feel up to it. There's a lovely garden here, and at least one empty bench."

"They will insist you wheel me out. Nevertheless, I shall be the envy of the cell block," Vivian chuckled. "Let's go."

"Are you sure you're ready for this? We can take a raincheck, if you'd prefer."

"Oh, no, I feel fine, though I must admit to some trep-idation."

"Why?"

"The next few charms belong to a very difficult part of

my life. One of great loves, and great losses, the brightest moments of my young life, and then the very darkest."

Tia took Vivian's hand and squeezed. "Well, I remembered the bracelet, but I only want you to tell whatever you feel you can handle. If it gets too hard to relive, we can stop, and begin again another day."

"Well then, bring my recorder along, and the tissue box, too, and let's get on with it. I believe we may both have need of its services before I'm done talking."

Once they were installed in the garden, Tia pulled out the bracelet, and put it on Vivian's lap.

She rummaged around and found an HH, a St. Christopher medallion, a wedding band and an engagement band with a small opal, soldered together, and two pair of baby booties. She was about to push the recording button when she noticed another charm, and made a little sound of delight.

With a smile of remembrance, Vivian pushed the record button.

~1941~

Vivian sat with her youngest brothers, George and Mark, and her sister, Lucille, on a shaded bench in the town square in Abbeville. Vivian had earned some money tutoring, and treated her siblings to ice cream during the stifling heatwave assaulting the South. Ice cream was a rare treat, since they lived on a farm, and trips to town were infrequent.

She'd also purchased a charm. She turned it over and over, admiring it as she worked on her cone.

"What is that?" Lucille asked.

"It's a Minute Man. My history teacher gave us an assignment to research our family ancestry. I had to interview Grandpa, to find out what he knows about our family. He said we came over from Ireland before the Revolutionary War. He said Grandma's side did too, but he couldn't say if they were married there, or here."

"Huh," Lucille said, as she worked on her treat, trying in vain to catch every melting drip before they landed on the ground.

"He said both sides of the family fought together at King's Mountain and Cowpens. Remember when we were there, last year?" Vivian paused to take a lick, savoring the taste of mint.

Lucille looked at her in horror. "They didn't fight for the British, did they?"

"No! They fought for us, of course. And this is a charm to represent them, and our family. I'm going to put it on my bracelet."

Lucille accepted the information, then returned to the business of her ice cream.

Vivian put the charm in her pocket, and let her mind wander. There were only the four youngest kids at home now, so the house was quiet. Too quiet. All her older brothers had left for college, or trade school. Michael was married, on his way to becoming both a doctor, and a father. Jonathan had graduated from an automobile and avionics mechanics school, and had a good job at the local airfield. Earl had no interest in school after the ninth grade, and remained happily ensconced on the farm, turning it into a prosperous business, once again.

The property had been in Vivian's mother's family for more than a century, but her father had never shown any more than a lackluster interest. He was a professor, after all, and preferred his academic studies, and nurturing the intellect of his students, to working the combine, or driving the hay wagon. But Earl loved it all, and the old farm thrived under his stewardship. Technically, he still lived on the farm, but he'd fixed the original homestead, and lived there. He'd wave from the field, but only came to the new house for Sunday dinners.

Vivian, at seventeen, was nearly graduated high school, and looked forward to secretarial school in the fall. She harbored a secret ambition to become a legal assistant to the most prestigious law firm in town. She had big dreams, and no other firm would do.

"Hey, y'all," came a familiar voice.

Harold Henderson. He lived on the neighboring farm to theirs, and they'd known each other all their lives.

Vivian had recently come to realize their friendship had turned into something more. She loved him, and he'd professed his love for her. They were officially sweethearts, now, and he'd even given her a promise ring – a slim gold band with a tiny opal, which was also her middle name. So pretty. So thoughtful. He'd even asked for her hand under the old Live Oak that straddled both properties. He felt it was the only proper location for such an event, since it joined the land, as they would one day be joined in marriage.

Both sets of parents had given their blessing to the union, but made it clear there would be no wedding until Harold graduated college.

She smiled at him before taking another lick. It seemed like forever off in the future.

Harold gave Lucille a tickle, punched the boys in the shoulder, and gave Vivian a kiss on the cheek, before sitting beside her. "I see y'all bought out every last drop of ice cream in town. How's a poor boy supposed to cool off in this heat?"

Vivian popped the last morsel of cone into her mouth, licked her fingers, and laughed. She nudged him with her shoulder. "Silly boy," she scoffed. "Go for a swim."

"You're telling me to go jump in a lake, are you?" He grabbed his chest dramatically. "You wound my heart."

George moaned. "Oh please."

Mark swung his feet, kicking at pebbles as he sat, then gave Harold a queer look. "You gonna go off to war, if Roosevelt jumps in?"

"He's not jumping in, Mark," George angrily butted in. "He's said as much a million times."

Mark shrugged. "I dunno. Churchill seems pretty persuasive."

"Well of course," George argued. "He's in the middle of a mess, and he wants allies. He wants us, but you're still a boy, and easily goaded, and Roosevelt, for all his dang faults, won't be goaded. He'll stand firm."

"Still," Mark mumbled, and looked at Harold again. "Would you go?"

They all looked at Harold, but he remained silent for a long moment.

"Well," he said at last. "I reckon if it comes to it, I won't have much of a choice. If America goes to war, I don't think they'll ask whether I want to go, or not. It'll be a command. Regardless, you won't find me cowering in some hidey hole. You better believe I'll go."

"I've tried pelting you with acorns most of my life," George said with a grin. "Don't think I've ever once hit you. You're damned good at duckin' and hidin', so I expect you'll come out all right. And if the welts you've given me are any indicator, you'll give *Herr Fritz* and them Jerries of his what for."

Everyone laughed, but there was an undercurrent of worry.

Vivian thought back, remembering many of the places they'd visited in Europe. She couldn't imagine such beauty being destroyed by war.

She looked around the town square that played such a central role in her life, and the lives of their family, since before the American Revolution. She wondered what it would be like to have war, literally, at your doorstep. She only vaguely recalled the faces of her French cousins, aunts, and uncles, and she knew her father worried about them. They hadn't answered letters since the fall of France, the year before.

A nudge. Harold was smiling at her. "Sailing past the moon?"

Vivian smiled back. Harold was so darned good looking, with his wavy dark hair, and gorgeous blue eyes. Her very own Gary Cooper. Better, even, since he wasn't on some screen. He was here, and she could hold his hand. Gosh, she wanted to give him a kiss, right now, in front of everybody.

"Uh-hem!" Harold theatrically cleared his throat. "I've got you a little something. Made a delivery to Greenville this morning and saw this."

He held out his hand and let a silver medallion on a chain drop from his palm.

It swung, tantalizingly, in front of her face. She reached out and took it.

"A St. Christopher medal?" she read. "It's beautiful, but you know I'm not Catholic."

Harold shrugged, an impish smile on his face. "I have it on good authority He works for everyone, regardless of denomination."

"Works?"

"It's for protection, I think, but mostly, to me, it means we're going steady, which is the latest and greatest way to be. I was told people who are going steady, well, the lucky guy gives it to his girl. I figured, since I already gave you a promise ring, this would seal the deal, doubly. Turn it over."

Vivian laughed, and turned the medallion over. 'Love always' was inscribed on the back.

Vivian was delighted. She put it around her neck, engraved side against her skin.

"I'll keep the message private, and I'll wear it forever. Thank you."

Harold leaned in for a kiss, but she had a sudden thought, and held him back with a hand to his chest. "Hold on, you said you first saw it this morning. Was it pre-inscribed?"

Harold smiled, and came closer still. "You caught me. I bought it last week and had it inscribed. Picked it up this morning. I wanted to surprise you."

With that, a delighted Vivian closed the distance between them.

Lucille made swooning sounds and collapsed against Mark, who mocked sticking his finger in his throat and gagging.

"Hey, I've got the horse and wagon parked 'round in the shade," Harold said, pulling away. "If y'all quit the antics, and don't mind riding in the back, I'll give you a lift home. Mother was making some sweet tea when I left. Maybe we can take some to the creek, and cool off at the rope swing."

Months later, in early December, the girls were in the kitchen washing dishes after returning from church. Their mother was already preparing for Sunday dinner, and their father dozed in the living room, beneath the front section of the *Greenville News*.

They were excited, because Earl was bringing his new girl, Carol, to meet the family.

"I'm grabbing Papa's ashtray while he's not paying attention," Vivian said quietly. "It's overflowing. Ick."

She tiptoed out, carefully avoiding the squeaky section of flooring near the radio. Music played softly. Vivian reached out and quietly took the heavy, crystal ashtray, and glanced at the front page headline.

FDR SENDS HIROHITO PEACE PLEA IN FINAL BID TO PREVENT WAR.

"From the front page to God's ears," she whispered.

The radio crackled noisily, and the music stopped.

"Shush!" Vivian hissed at the box, but Papa stirred. The damage was done.

"From the NBC newsroom in New York. President Roosevelt said in a statement today, that the Japanese have attacked Pearl Harbor, Hawaii, from the air. I repeat that..."

Vivian stood, riveted with horror at the significance of the words.

Her father pushed the newspaper away. "What'd he say?"

"Shhh, Dad!"

A short Jell-O ad interrupted the broadcast. When the announcer came back on, they both leaned forward. Terror filled Vivian's heart, and a strange roaring filled her hears. She heard only snatches; *"call for police and auxiliary personal to muster, citizen volunteers, call for calm. Go ahead Honolulu. Several planes shot down, heavy artillery fire, taken by surprise, incendiary, state of emergency..."*

Despite the graphic words, there was only one vision in her mind – Harold. She turned and ran for the front door, barely registering the sound of the ashtray as it hit the floor, or her father's exclamation – *"Que Diable!"*

TWO AND A HALF WEEKS LATER, on Friday, the twenty-sixth of December, their family, Harold's, and Carol's, arrived at the court house for a pair of weddings. Standing all in a row, Vivian and Harold were wed, and Earl married his sweetheart, Carol Atkinson.

Time was pressing. The US had entered the war, and

there was no telling when, or if, any of them would be together again. Make hay while the sun shines, everyone said. And so they did.

Vivian was three weeks shy of her eighteenth birthday, and over the moon to be Harold's wife, to be Mrs. Harold Henderson. Her new name had a glorious ring to it.

There was joy, but behind the facades, there was anguish. The newly minted husbands were to report for duty the following Monday, as would her two older brothers, Michael and Jonathan. George, four months shy of seventeen, secretly vowed to Vivian he would lie, cheat, or steal to get in on the action, and then swore her to silence.

After a luncheon at the Gardiner home, the newlyweds departed under a shower of tossed rice and well wishes. Earl took his bride back to the homestead house, and the Gardiner and Henderson families paid for a night at Abbeville's best hotel, the Eureka. It was their wedding present for Harold and Vivian. Afterward, the couple would live with the Hendersons.

Vivian gazed at the slim, gold band gracing her finger alongside the opal engagement right, then finished setting the dining room table. It was her one-month anniversary, and her in-laws had invited her parents to lunch in celebration. It was a nice gesture, since Harold couldn't be there. He, Jonathan, and George, who had indeed lied about his age, were all at boot camp, and nobody was sure if any of them would be able to visit home before shipping out.

Carol and Earl were with them, since it was also their one-month anniversary, as were Michael and Miriam. Michael had been given an exemption, since he was still studying to be a doctor, and had a young family. Earl was also exempted, since he was a farmer, and a plentiful food supply was critical to the war effort. With his French upbringing, Vivian's father offered his services, and spent a week every month, translating text and radio transmissions, or going over maps.

As they sipped coffee and made small talk after the meal, her mother handed her a tiny gift box.

She opened it and found her charm bracelet inside.

"You left it in my jewelry box at home," her mother explained. "I've also added a little something."

Vivian checked, and sure enough, next to her Minute Man, there was a silver disk with looped wedding bands on one side, and *H & V 12/26/41*, engraved on the other.

"Oh Mother, it's perfect," Vivian exclaimed with delight.

By her second-month anniversary, Vivian knew she was pregnant. She was terribly embarrassed to tell anyone, because it would mean she and Harold had...well, it was embarrassing!

She was only two months into her second term at secretarial school, as well, and she wondered if she'd be showing before the end of spring term, and thereby forced to drop out. So much to think about, yet she couldn't face her parents with the news. Not yet. But she had to talk to someone, so she made a date to have lunch with her sister-in-law.

After hearing the news, Carol forgot about her tuna melt, and stared at her, mouth open. "But, how, I mean when, oh, never mind, I guess I know all that. I'm so happy for you! Jeepers, I'm not. At least I don't think so. Your courses stop, right? And anyway, I thought it took longer."

"Yes, they stop, and I thought so, too, but apparently not," Vivian replied, her face a deep crimson, if the sudden flush of heat on her face was any indication. "I mean, did you ever get an in-depth talk about," she waved her hand vaguely, "all of that?"

"Oh gosh no. The only thing Mother told me was that the best sort of wife kept her husband happy by always remaining a lady, and keeping the lights off at night." Carol leaned in and spoke in a giggled whisper. "I've failed miserably on both fronts. We had fun, and not always at night. Scandalous, right? So, when are you due?"

"Well, end of December plus nine months, so," she counted on her fingers. "End of September, I guess."

"Ew, preggers all summer. Rough," Carol said with sympathy. "Hopefully, I won't get – you know, *that* way – before the start of summer, then it'll be cooler when I'm big."

Vivian liked Carol, but decided she'd bite the bullet and visit her mother after lunch, since, as it turned out, her sister-in-law wasn't much comfort, and no help at all. She certainly didn't have a wealth of knowledge to impart, and Vivian needed knowledge even more than she needed comfort.

Effie's response was not what Vivian expected. She looked shaken, even sorrowful.

"You're not helping, Mother," Vivian said, her voice sounding a bit strangled. "Actually, you're scaring me. What's wrong?"

"I'm fine. My girl has suddenly grown up, is all," she said. "I wish Harold didn't have to miss this. Your father was always so helpful, solicitous, whenever I was in a family way. I feel badly the two of you won't have this special time to share. In his stead, you may be sure both we, and Harold's parents, will support you every step of the way."

"Do you think I'll have to quite school?"

"Hmm, let me think," Effie mused. "During my first pregnancy, I don't believe I started showing until about the fourth month, but even then, it was easily disguised by clothing. No,

I don't believe it became obvious to outsiders until the fifth month, so you should be fine. Of course, you won't be able to attend class next fall, but perhaps you can return to class again next January? I'll babysit." By now, Effie was smiling, eager, and she gave her daughter a hug.

"I need to write to Harold right away," Vivian stated. "They'll let him come home before he deploys, won't they?"

"Surely, dear," Effie said with an excited smile. "Surely they will."

But it was not to be. Harold, delighted to know he was soon to be a father, deployed to the European Theater one month later, without getting any leave. Two months after later, Vivian, already big as a house, had to quit school three weeks before the end of term. Her pregnancy was too obvious, and even though she was married, the faculty did not see her 'situation' as 'fitting' around the unmarried women taking classes.

Every Monday, she wrote Harold of her progress, gave him tidbits of news from home, and asked for his preference in baby names.

His letters came less often. Every month or so. They were always heavily censored, with only a word or two, here or there, visible to read. It was impossible to make much sense out of them, and Vivian wondered if her letters reached him in the same condition.

By the end of July, Vivian's doctor was scratching his head at the size of her belly.

"You're quite certain," he asked delicately, "you did not engage in, eh, conjugal, eh, relations, before your wedding day?"

Effie stood behind the doctor, and Vivian could see her eyes go wide at the question. Vivian had gotten past her embarrassment months ago, so she looked him straight in the eye when she replied. "Absolutely, categorically, emphatically certain. No, we did not."

Effie nodded matter-of-factly. She looked both proud, and relieved.

The doctor cleared his throat, thought a moment, scratched his head, then pronounced, "Well, well, I see. First timers usually deliver a little later than term, which would push the date to early October. However, considering your size, I'm thinking mid-September. If what you swear to be true actually *is*," he lifted an eyebrow, and she glared back, "then I suppose we have no other choice than to entertain the notion of your having twins. Is there any history in either family?"

Vivian gaped at him. Effie dropped in a heap.

Vivian wasn't at all prepared, but by mid-August, she was certain she would have twins, because she could feel them duking it out, playing chase, and kicking her kidneys, separately, day and night.

There was no such thing as a comfortable position to lie in. Vivian had no recollection of what a cool breeze, or a cool anything, felt like. Every waking moment was filled with heat, and sweat, and trepidation. She stopped writing letters. They weren't getting answered, and her sweaty, sausage-fat fingers kept dropping the ink pen and making a mess.

On September 27, Vivian was jolted awake at 2:05 a.m., when the first contraction hit. Seconds later, as its potency became obvious, Vivian screamed from the pain and terror of it.

There were responding shouts in the Henderson home. The doctor was called. Her parents were called. Her father-in-law only had a horse wagon, so they waited for her father to arrive with his Model T truck. She was loaded in and taken to the county hospital, jolted unmercifully over dirt roads along the way.

Twenty-two hours after the initial contraction, exhausted, depleted, and beyond caring or the ability to push, the doctors used the forceps and brought forth a girl, Euphemia Opal Henderson. She was born at 12:15 a.m., and was whisked away by nurses, squalling her fury for all to hear.

But that was not the end of it. The contractions continued. After another half hour, Vivian noticed the grave looks on the faces of the doctors and nurses surrounding her bed. There was talk of C-Section. The baby wasn't moving. Bad position. Umbilical cord wrapped…

Her throat was raw. She was well beyond exhausted. Pushing was out of the question. She felt disembodied from herself, and she was utterly without strength.

The doctors checked her vitals and looked worried. There was mumbling, then came a decision for one more try before they opened her belly.

She didn't care anymore. She wanted the baby out, gone.

"Dearie," a nurse spoke close to her ear. "Your baby needs you to make one last effort, one more push. As hard as you can manage. I'll help, and it'll hurt, but you have to try. Okay? Are you with me? Let's save your baby, shall we?"

It took a few seconds for her to muster the wherewithal to nod.

Someone propped her against pillows, and then they waited for the next contraction to begin. When it did, the nurse leaned over her and pushed on her belly with all her force.

Once again, the forceps were introduced, which cause Vivian to scream.

Another contraction. The nurse pushed harder. The forceps probed.

Vivian screamed again, and this time the scream kept going, and going, and going, until darkness took her away.

. . .

"IT's A BOY," Vivian heard the doctor mumble from what seemed like miles away.

The nurse eased her back against the pillows and mopped her brow.

"You did good, honey, real good," she said, but Vivian could hear the hurt in her voice.

Afterward, the room was quiet. She didn't care. It was over.

Will they let me sleep, now? she wondered, as she drifted off.

David Harold Henderson, named for his grandfather and father, was born at 1:15 a.m. on September 28, 1942.

He was pronounced dead at 1:17a.m.

SUN SHONE THROUGH HER WINDOW, and Vivian turned her face to it, relishing the gentle warmth. She opened her eyes and smiled at her mother, who sat beside her.

"Hi, Mama. Am I late for breakfast?"

Effie shook her head, and tears sprang to her eyes.

"What's the matter?"

Her mother straightened, took her hand, and explained. "You are in the hospital, Vivi. We brought you in yesterday morning, and, uh, the children were born very early this morning. The doctors were correct, of course. You had twins. A girl and a boy."

Vivian smiled. "I remember now. I remember the girl, and I named her...I named her...after you, right? That was my first choice for a girl. All of the name choices for both were on the list I gave the nurse. I can't remember anything clearly. When will I get to see them?"

Effie took a deep breath. "The nurse will bring your

daughter in after you've had breakfast, and she'll teach you how to nurse."

"And then my boy?" Vivian queried. Her thoughts were fuzzy, scrambled. "One at a time? Will I have to wait for more milk before I can nurse him? I don't know how it works." Vivian giggled. She felt oddly euphoric, but couldn't place why that might be. "Did they give him the name on the list? Or do I still need to do it?"

Her mother swallowed hard, and twisted her hanky with an unsteady hand. "Your son, David Harold – we gave him your first choice for a boy from the list – did not... he did not survive." She paused to gauge Vivian's reaction. "He, it was a very difficult labor, for both of you, and he was pronounced dead within moments of his birth. I'm so sorry, Vivi."

Silence. Searing agony destroyed her euphoria. She was fully awake, fully aware, and wished she could die. Barely a mother, and she'd already lost a child. Vivian knew the horrible news must be true. Her mother hadn't called her Vivi since she was a child. Somehow, that made it more real. More awful.

She felt the pain as though a limb had been severed. A part of her was gone, a part she'd come to know through his movements, as his life took shape within her. She'd talked to him, loved him. And then, in the blink of an eye, a whole life she would never meet face-to-face, was gone, extinguished.

How could she go on, if she couldn't even manage giving birth?

"I want to see him, Mother," Vivian blurted. "I can't possibly say goodbye before I've had a chance to say hello. I must, I must see him. Tell them I want my baby!"

Effie looked anxious.

"Now! Go tell them," Vivian cried out, her voice reaching a hysterical pitch.

Startled, Effie hurried out to make the request.

When she returned, they both sat without speaking, empty and hurting, until a nurse tapped on the door.

"Do you want me to stay?" Effie quietly asked.

Vivian shook her head. "No. Thank you for the offer, Mama, but I'd prefer to have this time alone, just the two of us."

Effie nodded, motioned for the nurse to come in, and left the room.

The nurse placed the little bundle in her arms. "He'll be cold. I'm so sorry, but its...it's how we have to keep them until the funeral home arrives. You can open the blanket, or not, whatever you wish. I'll be right outside the door, if you need me."

Vivian waited until the door clicked shut, and then a little bit longer, before she folded back a corner of the soft, blue blanket.

A sob caught in her throat when she saw wisps of dark curls. He had his daddy's hair.

She steeled herself and drew back the blanket from his little face.

Peaceful. Sleeping. So beautiful. So absolutely beautiful.

Vivian leaned in and kissed her son's forehead.

He was cold, his skin unyielding, even to his mother's kiss.

Regardless, this was her child, her baby, not a doll. He'd been very much alive, within her, only twenty-four hours before. She knew his personality, the foods he liked, and those he hated. Her little boy.

"Hello, David," she said, as her tears dropped onto his face, anointing him. "I'm glad to meet you. I'm so sorry we won't have a chance to get to know one another better. Not just yet, anyway."

She touched his cheek, then unfolded the blanket a bit

further, in order to expose his little hand. She put her finger against his palm, and gently unfurled his little fist, until his fingers curled around hers. She kissed each miniscule nail.

"I promise I will tell your father all about you, about how strong you were, about how long and hard you fought. You were so brave, and he will be so proud of you."

She sat quietly with her son in her arms. Minutes became nothing as they slipped away, until, finally, she sensed their time together was drawing to a close. She started singing the first lullaby that came to mind.

Sleep my child and peace attend thee,
All through the night
Guardian angels God will send thee,
All through the night
Soft the drowsy hours are creeping,
Hill and dale in slumber sleeping
I my loved ones' watch am keeping,
All through the night...

CHAPTER TEN

Vivian turned off the recorder, and she and Tia wept together for Vivian's lost child.

Tia couldn't imagine, simply couldn't imagine. Had modern medicine been available, David probably would have had a full life, but now he was only a distant memory. A memory that still stung with the appalling pain of loss.

People would stroll by, gape at them, then change course to give them their space.

Several minutes later, after they'd gathered themselves, Tia wheeled Vivian back to her room.

"Can I get you anything, tea, before I go?" Tia asked. She was exhausted, wrung out by the raw emotions they'd shared.

"Do you have to go?" Vivian asked.

"No, but I thought you might like a rest. Hearing about David was terrible, the turmoil of emotions completely drained me. But you actually have those memories, and to relive them, well, I figured you'd had enough for the day."

"It has been excruciating, but would you mind staying a bit longer, Tia?" Vivian pleaded. "I want to get through this next bit, and I won't be able to sleep if I haven't gotten it out, and behind me, once and for all."

"Okay. If you are willing, I am able." Tia arranged the chairs, and they sat, side by side, in front of the window.

When she was ready, Vivian pushed the recorder once again, and continued her tale. "That Christmas, my mother gave me three new charms. Two sets of booties with initials and birth date inscribed, and one with a simple HH. I want to finish the segment with this."

~1942~

Opal was a beautiful child. She, too, had her father's hair and eyes, but no one could say where she got her temper. From the moment she was born, she was head-strong, frequently churlish, and obstinate as the day is long. Before she could stomp her feet in protest, she'd kick. It was her way, or no way at all. In public, she was the very image of serenity, even as an infant, but once in the privacy of their home, she could spend the day wailing, seemingly out of sheer spite.

One afternoon, Vivian was at her parent's home, heating some milk for the baby's bottle, and holding Opal on her hip while the child fidgeted and complained. Nursing hadn't lasted beyond the third month, since once Opal's first tooth came in, she learned to bite.

If there was a bright side, their struggles as mother and daughter took Vivian's mind off of her loss, and her loneliness. In the dark of night, she would remember David's beautiful face, then Harold's, and wish she could have introduced the two.

Harold. Even the censored letters had stopped.

Battle after battle after battle. The radios blared nonstop about Africa, Europe, The Orient, The Pacific. She knew he was somewhere in Europe. One of his rare, early letters, and even rarer string of uncensored words, had been, 'charm bracelet.' He knew her bracelet was from Europe, and she deduced the clue was his way of telling her where he was.

After the babies were born, she sent letters about once a month, and included lace-edged photos of Opal. She'd told him about both babies, but she'd only received one letter since their birth. It made no reference to fatherhood, or babies, at all, and he'd never given name suggestions, so she was left to wonder if he even remembered about any of it.

Somehow, thinking he might not recall made her feel alone, vulnerable, and lost.

Opal continued to fuss as Vivian plugged the nipple into the ring, screwed the top onto the bottle, then tested the liquid on her wrist before holding it for the baby to suckle.

Once Opal started feeding, Vivian's attention was pulled to her parent's conversation in the next room.

"That child would drive a wooden woman crazy," her mother muttered.

"Now, Effie," her father quietly cautioned.

"Well, it's true," her mother huffed. "If it were up to me, I'd keep that child gettin' up."

Vivian frowned. She'd never heard either turn of phrase before, but it was fairly clear what she meant.

"Effie, ma chere, I don't know what it means," her father said. "Why are you so upset?"

"It means her child needs discipline. It means, every time she gets on her high horse, I'd knock her right back off, again and again, and I'd keep her getting' up until she learned some manners."

Slack-jawed, Vivian couldn't believe her ears.

Her father started laughing, and sounded dang near fit to be tied. "But you are too small, *ma petit*. Even at only one year of age, the child is nearly as tall as you," he said. "Have patience, she will come around."

"She is ten months old, and certainly not as tall as me, and she absolutely needs discipline," her mother snapped, sounding more wounded than angry, this time.

Vivian could tell, despite her strong words, Effie was losing her own internal war. Her mother never raised her hand to anyone, unless she was praising Jesus. It had always been the death stare she gave misbehavers that kept them in their place. Vivian had seen it herself, many times. It put the fear of God in a child's heart, and Effie'd never needed to do anything more to keep a child in line.

Unfortunately, Vivian had to admit, it hadn't yet put the fear of God in Opal's heart.

Still, her words gave Vivian pause. Was her child so terrible she'd driven Effie beyond the pale?

She looked at Opal, who suckled noisily at her bottle and paid her no attention. The child was a handful, there was no doubt. Instead of coddling, should she try taking a stronger stand?

By early September, Vivian had to admit her renewed attempts at managing her daughter were largely futile. Still less than a year old, Opal knew her mind. If told to do something she didn't want to do, the child would look at her, take a deep breath, and scream.

The child was purely exhausting.

September 20 dawned crisp, bright, and clear, which worked out perfectly, since Mondays were also laundry days. Without a cloud in the sky, and humidity having released its summertime grip, everyone was outside. Vivian, visiting her family for the day, helped her mother hang the wash on the line. Her brothers were feeding the barn animals, and Lucille was in the side yard with Opal, trying to encourage her to walk. True to form, Opal was refusing her efforts. Seemingly, she didn't see the point, and preferred to be carried everywhere.

The child would be sorely disappointed the following week when Vivian returned to secretarial school classes in the mornings, and started work at the uniform manufacturing plant in the evenings. Gramma Effie would take charge, and there would be no more misbehaving after that.

Dust rose from the lane leading to the house, and Lucille started toward the front door.

"Lucille, stay with Opal, will you?" Vivian called. "I've got to go inside, anyway. I'll see who it is."

She went in through the back, wondering when her father was ever going to oil the hinges on the screen door. She got the last basket of laundry out of the machine and put it near the door in time to hear knocking.

Who's being so formal? She wondered. She wiped her wet hands on her apron, and went to greet their guest.

Walking across the front room, she saw his bike leaning against the porch rail, and felt a frisson of fear. She noted his cap, and a cold sweat broke out across her brow.

Western Union.

She stared at him through the door for a moment. Little Ricky Gunderson, from the other side of town. She recognized him from church. What was he? Ten? Twelve?

And why was he there? Dread washed over her. Was he bringing information about Jonathan? George?

Her knees felt weak as she reached out to open the screen door.

"Mrs. Henderson?" Ricky asked.

She was confused. Mrs. Henderson? Her mother-in-law? He'd gotten the wrong house, but, with a measure of relief, she took the telegram, fished a couple of coins out of her pocket, and handed them over. No need to send him to the right house. She'd take the telegram with her when she went home.

The poor kid looked anxious. "I'm supposed to ask. Uh, will there be any response?"

Response? For what?

"Well, I don't think so," she replied, and quickly opened the telegram, in case a reply, or a quick trip home, was needed.

Mrs. Vivian Henderson,

We regret to inform you your husband, Private First Class Harold Henderson, was killed on September 15, 1943, at the Battle of Salerno, Italy.

Blood roared in Vivian's ears. She could see nothing but stars floating before her eyes, and the pain, the incomprehensible familiarity of ruthless, bottomless pain.

She heard someone scream. The world darkened and swirled around her. There was a sudden, sharp pain in her head, but she paid it no mind.

It was nothing compared to the pain in her heart.

~2019~

Vivian stared out the window, her eyes once again filled with tears, and whispered, "I loved that man. I dearly loved my Harold. To this day, I have no idea if he ever learned he was a father."

CHAPTER ELEVEN

Exhausted after her emotional journey into the past, yet still subject to her rehab schedule, Vivian begged off story telling for a couple of days.

On Tia's first day off, she visited Vivian for lunch. Naomi and Stephanie both dropped by during the course of the afternoon for brief visits, but for the most part, they all gave her the space and quiet she needed.

That evening, Seth called and made a date for the following day, but would divulge nothing about where they were going. He only asked they get an early start.

He played tour guide once again, and took the opportunity to show her around his corner of the state, by visiting Cowpens and King's Mountain, where decisive battles had been fought during the Revolutionary War. By early afternoon they were done trekking the battlefields, and left for lunch in Spartanburg, and a lazy stroll through the historic downtown.

As they got back on the road in the late afternoon, their sights on a return to Greenville, Tia pointed to a roadside stand boasting boiled peanuts.

"What's the deal with boiled peanuts?" she asked. "I see those signs all over the place."

"You don't know about boiled peanuts?" Seth asked, sounding skeptical.

When she shook her head, Seth wrenched the wheel to the right, put the truck into a controlled, one-eighty-degree spin, and brought it to a stop beside the stand.

Dust wafted over everything, nearly obscuring their view. Nevertheless, she could see the stand-keeper grinning his approval.

"You going all *'Dukes of Hazard'* on me?" Tia asked, laughing, and loosening her death grip on the dash. "A warning before your next stunt driving move would be appreciated."

Seth gave her a look of utter seriousness.

"Y'all've never tasted boiled peanuts? Truly?" he asked, his Southern drawl suddenly thick.

Tia shook her head. "No, we don't do boiled anything in Seattle, as a rule. We do grilled salmon. Or poached, maybe. And wine. And beer. Nothing about peanuts, unless they come in a bag at the ball park."

"Girl," he replied. "Prepare yourself, because y'all have officially only scratched the surface of the meaning of life, until y'all've tasted boiled peanuts."

Tia started to giggle, which was highly unusual for her. She couldn't figure out if it was because of the adrenalin rush from the spin, the general intoxication she felt spending the day with Seth, or the fact he pronounced boiled as though he were saying 'balled.'

They got out of the truck and walked over to the stand.

"Hey," the stand-keeper said, amicably. "Nice parking job."

"Hey," Seth replied. "Got a crisis here. Girl's from out west. Never tasted boiled peanuts. Needs fixin', don't it?"

Tia could barely keep a straight face. Seth sounded like he was pulling out every bit of Southern he owned, and putting it into his speech. Where before, he, and everyone else she'd come to know, spoke with a soft drawl, Seth now sounded like he was straight out of the bayou.

Which was the real Seth? she wondered. *The polished city boy, or this down-home version?*

The boiled peanuts chef was about five-four, with a deep tan that probably didn't fade anymore, and gnarled hands. He looked at her with skepticism. "Out west, huh? She wantin' hot or plain?"

Seth grinned. "Better start her off slow. We'll take plain."

The guy took the ladle and scooped a mass of peanuts out of a slow cooker, then let the juice drain out before emptying it into a cone of wrapped newspaper.

"Being as this is her first go, I'll give it gratis as my Southern civic duty," the man offered. He handed it to Tia with a wink and a smile. "Welcome to heaven, out-west lady."

"Thanks," she replied, responding with a straight face. "As a Westerner, and virgin boiled peanuts eater, I shall do my best to do it justice."

The stand-keeper kept a passive expression, but he couldn't hide the dance of humor in his rheumy eyes.

Seth, having a harder time with a straight face, handed him a couple of bucks and whispered something about virgins in his ear, which made the man bark out a laugh.

They got back in the truck, and Seth got back on the road.

Dubious about being played, she looked to Seth for instruction. "Do I eat them as is, or take them out of the shell, first?"

A big grin spread across his face. He was enjoying this way too much.

"Shell'em, darlin'. Crack 'em with your teeth and start suckin', 'cause there's gonna be some sweet juice comin' your way. Then," his grin got even bigger. "Take them nuts into your mouth, pitch the shell, and enjoy."

Juice? Sucking? Nuts??

Seth was having so much fun he could barely drive.

This had all the hallmarks of a setup, so Tia approached with caution. Was this a Southern boy's way of introducing out-of-town women to the South?

She took a nut and bit the tip to break the shell.

Jeez, how had this suddenly become sexual??

Then, delicious, salty liquid spilled down her chin.

"Y'all should swallow, instead of making a mess of my truck," Seth said smoothly, his mirth under control, barely. "Now crack it open and eat, then open the window and chuck them shells outside."

Deeply skeptical, but enjoying it so far, Tia emptied the nuts into her mouth and bit.

O.M.G! Delicious. So delicious.

She flung the shells out the window, and grabbed another, then two more.

Instant addiction.

"Holy crap, they're freakin' awesome," she managed around a full mouth. "I'm a pig. I can't stop. I don't know what crack is like, but there's no way it's as good as this. You want any? Because I need to warn you, if you say yes I might have to shoot you."

"Damn, it's true, this girl got herself some bonafide Southern roots," Seth said, then laughed so hard she thought he might lose control of the truck.

A HALF-HOUR LATER, the peanuts long gone, Seth dropped her off at Altamont. After a shower and a change, Tia drove into town to meet him, Stephanie, and Rob, at a pre-arranged restaurant boasting Southern comfort food.

They all greeted one another, and everyone laughed as Tia raved about the wonders of boiled peanuts. After they gave their drink orders, things relaxed into a comfortable quiet.

After a moment, Seth leaned over and whispered, "I have never thought of boiled peanuts as being sexy, until you came along."

Tia, taking a sip of water, nearly spewed her mouthful across the table.

Seth howled with laughter, and the other two looked on with blank expressions, as though they simply couldn't fathom young love.

Their drinks arrived, and then, without preamble, Rob slid a manila folder across the table. "I was asked to give you this."

Tia shot him a questioning look and got nothing in response, then turned her gaze on the other two. Both seemed as clueless as she, as to the contents.

She opened the envelope and pulled out a packet of paperwork. With a second questioning glance at Rob, she focused on the heading and read.

APPLICATION FOR EMPLOYMENT, GREENVILLE, SC PD OFFICER - LATERAL.

Stunned, Tia looked at each one in turn, but nobody had anything to say. She put the paperwork back in the envelope, and tucked it next to her jacket, choosing to ignore it for the moment. So did everyone else.

The dinner was fun, but she, at least, felt an undercurrent of tension. Was it her? Or was everyone feeling the same thing?

The following morning, Tia went in early to visit Vivian. She found her sitting by the window, drinking tea.

Tia kissed her on the temple, and sat beside her. "I need guidance, and since you are my great grandmother, and the official family matriarch, I'm putting this all on you."

Vivian chuckled. "I'm all ears."

After describing the previous day, and then the envelope she received, Vivian shook her head and smiled.

"Don't smile. What am I supposed to think?" Tia asked. "I mean, does everyone think I'll just uproot, leave home, and move out here? And who's idea was it? Not Rob. Jeez, was it Seth? Don't get me wrong, I like him, and I'm pretty sure it's mutual, but still, I hardly know him. It's a big step when you don't even know the person. Too big."

Vivian started to chuckle, then reached out and patted Tia's hand. "My, my, for such a solid, put together person, you certainly have cornered the market on worry this morning. First of all, it was my idea. I asked Rob to bring you the paperwork, but I never asked him to be secretive about it. I wanted to pique your interest, give you something to think about. And it's not such a wild idea."

Vivian placed her tea cup aside and rose. With her back to Tia, she gazed out the window and continued. "This, after all, is also your home. Your ancestral home. You already have family and friends here, and if you began the application process, it would give you a chance to see if your mutual interest with Seth wants to turn into something more. You don't have to accept a job offer if the fit isn't right. I simply thought of it as a way of opening a door you hadn't previously considered. Take a good look at what lies beyond the door, Tia, and make your decision based upon knowledge. That's all I meant by asking Rob to give you the envelope."

Tia didn't answer right away. Instead, she let the idea sink in.

. . .

ON HER THIRD DAY OFF, both Seth and Rob were on duty, so Naomi invited her to the Cultural Heritage Museum offices. She was introduced around, and then Naomi took her to the genealogical research room.

"Because of the bequeathal of the house, and the whole wing we're devoting to her, we've done a very thorough background on Vivian, as you might imagine. So, with her permission already given, I'm going to give you a bit of a family tour. We'll call it – beyond the bracelet. Are you game?"

"I am. Totally." Tia was continually amazed by everyone's hospitality and kindness. "You know, my grandmother was an enigma, even to my mother. To me, family meant those I could reach out and touch. Nothing more. Certainly nothing further back. This is incredible."

"Well, here goes. Through Vivian's line, the family first set foot in the colonies in the 1750's. They came from County Donegal, in Ireland. There were four generations who owned land in and around Abbeville, but the family splintered in the 1830's, over the issue of slavery. Politically, tensions were already on the rise. Your family was among the few who refused to own slaves, because of what they'd suffered in the old country. Under British rule, the Irish were treated as slaves, without the moniker. So, to get away from the institution and the strife it caused, some of the children decided to move their families to a free state. The elder folks were too old to leave, so one of the daughters stayed with them. That was your family's branch."

"How many other branches are there?" Tia asked.

"The elder couple had four children. Two went west, and settled in Illinois. You know about the daughter. The fourth was the catalyst for the family splintering, instead of simply moving. He'd purchased two slaves as soon as he got married. It was considered so egregious, none of them ever spoke to him again. He eventually sold his stake in the family land and moved to Arkansas."

Naomi explained so much, gave so many names and dates, Tia's head was starting to spin with data overload. When she couldn't suppress a face-splitting yawn, Naomi chuckled. "I'm killing you with information, aren't I?"

"I'm sorry, truly," Tia replied. "It's a lot to take in all at once, I guess. I love hearing every detail, though, don't get me wrong."

"I have information on Vivian's paternal side, too, but we'll go over that another day. Suffice it to say, her father's family immigrated from France in his early teens. At any rate, I'll have everything printed out for you, so you can go through it at your leisure. In the meantime, how about we grab a quick lunch, and then I'll take you to Abbeville, show you the family homestead, and take you out to your family's church? It's about an hour from here."

"I'm all yours," Tia replied.

They ate their lunch at a nearby sandwich shop, and headed out of town.

"The original property is located in the Abbeville Historic District," Naomi explained as they drove. "Your maternal side was one of the original settlers, as well as founding members of their church. The church isn't open today, but we can call and make an appointment to tour the inside at some later date, if you'd like."

A little over an hour later, after passing signs to downtown Abbeville, Naomi pulled to the side of the road in a densely treed area, and pointed to what looked like a ATV access trail.

"This all used to be farmland, but a paper company bought it years ago, and now they grow these trees to harvest for paper goods. You'll come to what is left of the remains of your family's original homestead in about thirty yards. Want to have a look?"

This was incredible. Tia had never envisioned a moment like this, and her heart raced with anticipation.

As Tia got out, Naomi honked the horn, then came around to her side with a grin. "I'm not a big fan of snakes. Want to make sure that if the car noise didn't shoo them away, then the horn would."

Snakes?

Together they carefully followed the overgrown track. The air was still and heavy. The humidity, thick in the grove of trees, wetted her skin, and she felt as though she were in a sauna. They'd only gone about twenty yards, when Tia saw the silhouette in the dim, green light the canopy of leaves allowed in.

The old chimney was mostly intact, and stood about ten feet high. From its base, she could make out the tumbledown remains of a stone foundation, and right in front, three stone steps.

She stopped to gaze at it, filled with the wonder of it all. She continued forward, and Naomi let her go on alone.

Tia took one stone step, and paused. Her ancestors had trod these steps. Visitors would be knocking on the door from this point. She looked around, and could imagine a pair of rocking chairs outside the front of the house, could almost smell the wood fire, and hear the soft, Irish/Carolina drawl as they talked about current events, or the mundane things of their day to day.

A frisson swept over her spine. Why? What was it? Cellular recognition? Memory? A poignant sensation that, at long last, she'd found her true home? Tia didn't believe in past lives, but she sure felt a connection to this place.

She wanted to take a memento, and reached for a small

stone, but decided not to. It belonged here, and there was little enough left as it was.

No, she would have to come back. Often. Maybe have a chat with her forebears, now and then.

Tia turned to Naomi. "You'll have to map this out, so I can find my way back. I want to sit here. I want to talk with these people. Is that weird?"

"Not at all," Naomi reassured her. "Y'all have a lot to catch up on."

The red brick church was less than a mile from the homestead. It sat back on its fenced property, surrounded by an extensive graveyard.

The iron entry gate was unlocked during daylight hours, and Naomi led her across the grass, weaving between headstones and markers of all sizes, styles, and age.

She stopped and pointed at a pair of headstones about four feet apart from each other. They were not new, but newer than most.

One read, Harold Henderson, 1921-1943, Beloved Son, Husband, Father. Just below on the same stone, David Harold Henderson, 9/28/42, Beloved Son and Brother. The second stone read, Thomas Weiss, 1920-2002, Beloved Son, Husband, Father.

"Those are Vivian's husbands, and the twin that died at birth. Harold isn't actually here. They buried him in Italy, but she put up the stone, anyway, and had the baby buried in his spot. She is to be buried in between the two, when the time comes."

After a moment, they continued on.

Several paces away, they stopped beside two more headstones, both very weathered. They read; Euphemia McClinton Gardiner, 1901-1944, and Thierry Gardiner, 1899-1956.

"These are your great-great grandparents," Naomi said.

"Vivian's parents."

Emotions running hard, Tia reached out and touched Effie's headstone. "Hi," she whispered.

Naomi gave her some time, then indicated there was more to see. As they neared the farthest corner of the grave-yard, the modern headstones were left behind, and the grave markers were more crudely wrought.

Naomi stopped once again, and pointed at a pair of natural-looking rock, each about a foot wide, by ten or so inches tall. They were dark, blotchy, and unremarkable.

Tia looked at her guide with a questioning glance.

"Come over this way," she said. "You have to be at the correct angle to see it"

Tia moved sideways a step or two, then crouched. There was something scratched onto the face of each stone, but she couldn't make it out. She cast Stephanie another questioning glance.

Stephanie knelt and slowly traced her hands over each letter.

Suddenly, Tia could see it.

Wm McClinton on one stone.

S McClinton on its neighbor.

Tia gave her a third questioning glance.

"William and Sarah McClinton. They are your forebears. The very first to land on these shores. They are your founding American ancestors."

Tia couldn't name her emotions, but when she reached out and ran her finger over the rough edge of the headstones, tears blurred her vision.

Before leaving, she found four pebbles, and placed one on top of each of the family headstones. Thomas and Harold already had several little stones, and Tia knew Vivian had visited many times. It was a way to say – 'You are loved. You are not forgotten.'

CHAPTER TWELVE

"HOW ARE YOU, DEAR?" VIVIAN ASKED WITH A SMILE, WHEN TIA arrived the next morning.

Instead of kissing her on the temple, as she'd come to do, Tia sat, facing Vivian, and held both her hands.

"Naomi took me to the homestead and the church, yesterday," she began. "I cannot find words to describe the emotions that overwhelmed me, the connections I felt. I...I wasn't prepared for any of this. I imagined we'd get to know one another, and we have, but I thought, I don't know, I thought I'd get to know a delightful woman who was my great grandmother, and hear a bit about her past. I never once thought I'd acquire an entire lineage, or that I could feel such an emotional attachment to it, or them, or even to you."

Vivian laughed with delight. "Oh, my dear, I'm so very glad to hear it. You've filled my heart with such unlooked for joy. I can't tell you the immense happiness you've brought into my life."

Tia embraced Vivian, and the both held on for a long moment.

Once re-seated, Vivian dabbed at the corners of her eyes

with a tissue, then took a deep breath and smiled. "Do you have the bracelet?'

Tia drew it out, and put it in Vivian's hand.

She had her recorder set to go beside her, and pushed the button. "Today, I thought I'd tell you about college, and my first jobs, and how I got started in this business."

"Can we stop and back up for a minute?" Tia asked. "You've made everyone come alive for me, and, if it's not too much to ask, I'd like to hear how everyone got through the war, before we move on to the aftermath."

Vivian's gaze drifted. "Oh, yes, the war…"

~1944~

Looking back, Vivian later realized she spent several months in a state of shock, before clarity and purpose gave her the will to build a different life than the one she had envisioned with Harold. She would finish secretarial school by summer, and enroll in college in Greenville, in the fall. She could do secretarial work on the weekends to make some money, and she might even be able to continue working at the uniform factory one day each weekend. She would have to live on campus and come home on the weekends – Greenville was much too far to take the bus every day. Poor Opal was going to have to stay with her grandparents until Vivian was on her feet. She simply didn't have the means to keep Opal with her, and pay for a sitter.

They weren't the only family living in hardship and deprivation. Many neighbors were scrambling for extra work, and growing their own food. Many, too, had lost loved ones overseas. People all over town, and around the county, wore black clothing, or had black armbands made. Those who hadn't yet received a telegram, kept their eyes lowered as though fearing what they might see, if they dared look into the faces of the grieving.

Rationing was in full swing. The Gardiners and the Hendersons were luckier than some, since they grew food as a business. Still, there was rarely enough gas to fill the old truck for trips to market, so the two families doubled their loads, and went to market in the horse-drawn wagon.

Vivian took morning classes, and worked weekday afternoons at the law firm, and Saturday's at the uniform factory outside of town. Opal was two-and-a-half, and loved to spend time underfoot in both family kitchens.

It was early spring, and dawn lit the sky. Vivian left the Henderson's while it was still dark, and dropped the child with her mother before heading into work. She had her lunch bag slung over her shoulder, and was already halfway to town. She didn't mind the factory work, and especially enjoyed the walk. It gave her the quiet she craved, and she let her mind wander.

She split her time between her old and new families these days, not wanting to overburden either them with herself or Opal, even though both houses were much quieter than they'd been used to.

The Henderson's second son, Robert, went off to war in the Pacific the moment he turned eighteen, but he was very good at getting letters home, so his parents bore the stress well. Still, Vivian knew they enjoyed having a house full of family noise and bustle.

Her oldest brother, Michael, now a father of two, was doing his internship in the hospital in Spartanburg, caring for injured soldiers. He was able to come home every weekend.

Jonathan was proud as a peacock when he earned his wings. He was a Navy aviator, fighting the Japs.

Earl was still at home, tending the farm, but it was

looking more and more likely he would be called up. In the meantime, he and Carol were still trying to have a child.

Not to be outdone, George earned his wings, as well, but they had him flying out of England to harass the Jerries, a half-world away from his big brother.

Mark, the youngest, bless his heart, wanted to go so badly, but he had such a baby face, he couldn't even lie his way in. He'd have to wait.

Vivian heard a truck approaching from behind, and stepped to the side of the dirt road to let it pass. Instead of passing, the driver slammed on his brakes as he neared, causing dust to billow everywhere. She covered her mouth and nose with one hand, and tried to wave away the cloud with the other, when she saw the driver jump out.

It was Earl. He looked...awful, stunned, and fear gripped Vivian's heart.

"What is... who is it?" she asked, not wanting to hear the answer.

"I've come to get you," he blurted. "I'm not to say another word. Just get in. They'll have to do without you at work today."

His voice was choked with pain.

Oh, God, no.

Vivian grabbed the front of his shirt, "Tell me! Who?"

Tears soaked Earl's dusty face, leaving little trails. He grabbed Vivian to him and sobbed, and she heard his muffled words.

"Shot down. Never recovered."

NO!

"Who? Who was shot down?" Vivian started to sob, as well.

"Jonny."

Vivian screamed, and would have collapsed, if her brother hadn't held her so tightly.

"He, they said… shot down on his approach to the ship… plane burst into flames… went into the Pacific. Nothing recovered. He went to the bottom with his plane."

They held onto one another, in the middle of a dusty road, and wept for their lost brother.

~2019~

Tia watched the painful memories wreak havoc on the old woman's face, and realized two things. She loved this woman with all her heart, and, the tears on her own face were genuine, and not just for Vivian. They were also for the family, her family, that had sacrificed so much.

Vivian sat straighter, and smiled through her tears. "Life is not for the faint of heart, my dear."

Tia smiled. "And yet you can, for all the heartache, make a little joke."

Vivian shrugged. "*De tristitiae, laetitiae.* Out of sorrow, joy. In this life there will be sorrow. The trick is, we must work our way through sorrow, to find the joy which surely lies beyond," Vivian explained. "If we do not, then we will have very little joy at all. You bring me untold joy, Tia, and yet to have you, I had to lose my Opal. Sacrifices. There are always sacrifices. Now, let me tell you in brief about the others, for a long story would take what little strength I have left."

"I want to do whatever you think best, GG," Tia said. "By the way, I decided to call you GG, short for Great Grand-mother. To call you Vivian seems too formal anymore, too impersonal. And Great Gramma Vivian sounds so clunky. So I thought of GG. Does that work for you?"

"Perfectly. Gigi, like the movie. I adore it." Vivian laughed, then straightened, and got serious. "Now, as for the others, and I'm sorry for giving you short shrift, dear ones," she looked to the heavens, "but my old heart can't take the long version."

She settled back into her chair and counted on her fingers to tick off the names. "Michael and Miriam survived the war. They had five children, and became quite well-to-do. They both died later in life, and lived long enough to know their own great grandchildren."

She moved to the next finger. "As I told you, Jonathan was shot out of the skies over the Pacific. I can't remember where or what battle, but Naomi could probably find out for you, if you're interested."

Finger three. "Earl was eventually called up, and was part of the D-Day invasion. He never made it off the beach, and is buried over there. He'd only been gone three months when Carol received her telegram. It was the same week she found out she was finally with child. She had a lovely boy, and named him after his father."

Oh my God, Tia thought, stunned. *Two brothers gone.*

Vivian took a deep breath and bent finger number four. "George. I think his was the worst fate of all. A few weeks after D-Day, George's plane was hit. He parachuted, landed without injury, and was able to radio his position, but was quickly captured and sent to the *Dulag Luft* at Frankfurt. He survived, too, but came home a broken man. He never married, rarely spoke, and spent his time working the farm and avoiding people, or getting quietly drunk in a local bar. It was awful. I never saw him smile after he came home. He just…existed."

Tia was looking at her lap, afraid to ask. "Is he still alive?"

"Oh, no. He died in the early seventies. He didn't wake one morning. When he wasn't seen in the fields, somebody went and checked on him. He looked as though he was sleeping, but he'd passed. Thankfully, at least his last moments seemed to have been peaceful."

"Finally," she bent her fifth finger. "There was Mark, my youngest brother. He ran off and enlisted as soon as we got word about Jonathan," Vivian continued. "They needed men, so I think they overlooked his obvious youth. He was there at the D-Day invasion, as well, but he had a lucky star shining over him, or perhaps the Good Lord thought we'd given enough. He survived the landing, went on to fight in the Battle of the Bulge, and eventually was part of the groups that liberated a couple of gulags, although not the one where his brother was kept. Later, they liberated Bergen-Belsen. So horrible, the things he saw. But he was able to put it away, somehow. He came home, met a girl from Virginia, and moved there. They had, let me see, they had three boys. He lived a long, good life, and we saw him often. He passed away in the mid-nineties."

"And Lucille?" Tia asked.

"Oh, yes, Lucille," Vivian said with a broad smile. "I was only counting brothers, silly me. Well, she became a WAC, was shipped off to work in England, and met a dashing RAF pilot. She stayed there, married him, and they had seven children of their own. He was a distant blueblood of some sort, and they lived a very ritzy life. Bless her heart, she raised her kids right, though. Taught them to fear only two things in life, herself and God, and she never forgot her humble roots. Their kids were half-American, so they spent plenty of time here, too, and she made sure they learned to cherish their American heritage. She also made sure they knew how to slop hogs."

Vivian shook her head and grinned at her memories. "She died in the mid-nineties, also, but she had a good, long life."

Vivian stopped talking, and Tia let her rest. After a few minutes, Tia patted her hand. "Shall we call it a day? You look tired."

Vivian shook her head. "No, I'm fine. I was looking

forward. Let me get you through my college years." She separated out a tiny shield, and a year charm – 1949, then pushed the button on her trusty recorder once again.

Knowing what she now knew, Tia noticed a pair of bands soldered together, one of them adorned with an opal. Vivian had originally separated them out, but pushed them back, which sent a flood of sadness through Tia's heart.

~1944~

It was late August, and Vivian's heart was divided. With two brothers dead, another unaccounted for, Lucille off working in England, and the youngest still marching across the battlefields of Europe, Vivian no longer wished to pursue her plans for college in Greenville, thereby leaving her mother alone.

Vivian thought Effie looked pale. She was unusually listless, and walked with a stoop. Her mother's poor heart was broken, it was obvious, and Vivian didn't think she could take another child leaving her side.

As the war intensified, her father spent weeks at a time in Washington DC, going over French documents, and translating radio broadcasts.

On a rare weekend her father was home, he pulled her aside for a talk.

"Viv," he said. "All our hearts are broken. We can't fix what's done. But you must not put your life on hold for us. You have things to do, and I want you to go out and do them. Live your life. Make us proud."

"But Mama," she pleaded.

"But Mama nothing," he replied. "I've put in for leave to return to teaching this fall, and they have granted it. With France liberated, they don't need me anymore, so I'll be here with your mother. And we'll have Opal to keep us busy."

Vivian couldn't help smiling. "A very kind understatement, Papa."

He chuckled. "Mama loves her *petit choux,* however busy and obstinate the child is. Now," he took her hand. "You go on to college, and come home on weekends. Think of it, two of my children gone to college. You make us so proud."

Two weeks later, Vivian was packed and on the train to Greenville. She would study history, and languages, and maybe even some philosophy. She was excited to see the world, and the University of Greenville would be her starting point.

Upon her arrival, Vivian was handed a welcoming packet complete with information about class locations, activities on campus, student organizations, and fraternal clubs. The women's fraternal societies, called sororities, intrigued her, and she agreed to participate in the 'rush,' which would determine her selection.

There were teas, and visits to each membership house, and several invited Vivian to join their ranks. But for her, only one stood out, and by the end of the week she'd pledged Alpha Chi Omega, which seemed to be the best fit.

Vivian had never spent so much time in close proximity to so many women, and found it both thrilling, and a little bit silly. None of these girls, as she thought of them, were married, certainly none were mothers, and they couldn't even imagine widowhood. Most of the girl's goals seemed to center around garnering a good man after the war, rather than a good education, and one or two tried to pry the secrets of the bedroom out of her, but she refused to play along. Those few days she'd spent as a new wife were precious memories, not to be shared, and most assuredly not to be giggled over.

Regardless of their differences in age, which wasn't much, and experience, which was vast, Vivian grew very fond of a few of the girls, and knew their special friendships would endure a lifetime. Overall, she was happy at U of G, and delighted with her choice of sorority.

Vivian dove into her Classical Studies, Western Philosophical Thought, and American History classes, and returned home every weekend to extol the wonders of college life. Her father listened avidly, but her mother hardly seemed to hear what she had to say.

One Sunday morning, Vivian rose early, leaving Opal to sleep. She tiptoed downstairs, and found her mother standing at the back door, sipping coffee and staring into the yard.

"Mama?" Vivian quietly said.

Effie took a deep breath, and let it go, but said nothing in response.

"Are you mad at me for going to college? I need to know," Vivian pleaded. "I would do anything to see you smile again. To have our chats again. To have my mama again." Vivian did all she could to hold back tears. "I miss you, Mama. I miss us. So much."

Where before, Effie's shoulders had been high and tight with tension, her shoulders suddenly sagged. With a deep breath, she turned and took Vivian's hand. Her eyes were filled with despair, something Vivian had never seen before.

"I have been wrong to keep you at arm's length, and I'm so sorry, but I was trying to protect you, to protect everyone."

Dread filled Vivian at her mother's words. She drew her mother to the kitchen table and they sat, facing each other.

"Everyone is devastated over the losses we've suffered from this war, and I understand a mother would suffer more than all, but," Vivian tightened her grip on her mother's hands, "but there's something more, isn't there?"

Effie took her time to answer, then finally, almost imperceptibly, she nodded. She wouldn't look at Vivian. Instead, she kept her eyes fixed on their joined hands.

"Yes," came the whispered answer, at last. "I suspected. My mother...I made an excuse to go into town, and visited the doctor. He confirmed what I most feared."

Waves of horror hit Vivian, but she refused to succumb. She had to be strong, as strong as her mother, and shoulder this for everyone's sake, whatever it was.

Her grandmother. What had happened? Did she have a disease? She'd died when Vivian was only eleven, shortly after the family's return from Europe, and all she could remember was she had been physically weak, and terribly sweet, and then she was gone. And she remembered her grandfather crying. It was the only time she'd seen such a thing.

"What about your mother?" Vivian asked.

Effie shrugged. "She had lumps on her breast, but breasts are lumpy things, so who pays attention? Then, when she lost her strength, and the pain radiated throughout her body, Daddy called the doctor. It happened while we were away in Europe."

Effie shook her head. "The doctor said the cancerous growth had begun in the breasts, but had spread to the rest of her body. There was nothing anyone could do, and it was only a matter of time. Very little time, as it turned out."

"Oh, Mama, you don't think...?"

"Vivian, I saw the doctor last week. I was quite sure before I went, and the doctor only confirmed my worst suspicions."

Effie heaved a sigh and turned her face away. "I may well have gotten this from my mother, but I will tell you this: I have lost so many babies my heart has no will to carry on. My heart is broken beyond repair. If the doctor wishes to call it cancer, then so be it. For myself, I believe it is the result of a mother's broken heart."

She turned a harsh gaze on Vivian. "And you are not to fret. You and Lucille are strong. You will be fine, and you must be strong for your dear father. My boys are, or were, strong, as well, and I pray for my remaining boys, and their futures, every day. But I know in my heart I will not be a part of it. And truly, I don't want to be. Life is hard, but it has been especially cruel to us. I want to see my lost boys. I want to be free of this cancer. I want to lay my burdens down, and rest in the arms of my savior."

She squeezed her daughter's hands. "Vivian, I am so very tired. I want to go. I welcome the release. But for now, you must finish your semester. You must not let your future escape your grasp. Don't worry about me. I'll still be here when you return for Christmas. I promise. And the doctor assures me it will be so."

True to her word, Effie held on until Vivian's Christmas vacation from school. Two days after her return home, Effie, surrounded by her loving family, drew her last breath.

~2019~

Vivian looked at Tia and smiled a sad smile. "It was a long time ago."

Tia nodded. "You know, not knowing anything about our past, both Mom and I have done some testing, and neither one of us carries the genetic marker. That's not to say it can't happen, but we're both very careful, and will be especially vigilant from now on."

Vivian smiled. "As I said, without sorrow, there is no joy. They are linked. I am filled with joy that my own sorrows have filled you with vigilance in this regard. I am also joyful that neither of you carry the same dark seed."

They sat in silence for a few minutes, and then Vivian added, "And now you know how my mother's wedding band came to be on the bracelet. If you look closely, you'll see her name engraved along the interior rim. On the bracelet you'll also see my sorority crest, and the year I graduated with a double degree in Classical Studies and American History, and a minor in Philosophy, 1949."

CHAPTER THIRTEEN

Tia spent the rest of the afternoon wandering aimlessly through Altamont, thinking about what Vivian had said, and the people she'd spoken of.

So much tragedy. So many lives lost, or uprooted, and yet, she'd managed to find joy through it all.

Tia couldn't help making a comparison with her own life, which had been pretty close to perfect. She thought of herself as tough, worldly, a cop's cop, but was she actually wearing Pollyanna glasses in regards to her personal life? Her mother had lost a parent at a fairly tender age, but then, they hadn't been close. A stunning thought occurred to her – had she only assumed the loss hadn't caused her mother much pain, because she herself felt no emotional connection to it?

Suddenly, a strong sense of her own selfishness swept over her. She pulled out her phone and called her mother.

"Hi, honey!" her mom's cheerful voice always soothed Tia's jangled nerves. "How's it going? How's Vivian doing? I've got about ten minutes. Tell me absolutely everything."

"Vivian's doing great. She's been in rehab for four days, and they're doing wonders with her. She'll probably move straight into her new residence sometime next week. There's talk we'll be moving furniture this weekend, to try and get it ready before she arrives."

"I'm so glad to hear it. Sounds like you're making friends."

Tia smiled at her mother's fishing expedition. "I have," she replied vaguely. "I, uh, wanted to ask you something sort of personal. Do you mind?"

"Not at all. I'm at a Starbucks for lunch. Had to get away from my very best client for a breather," Cherry said with a chuckle. "What's up?"

"I, well, Vivian has been telling me so much about her, our family, and it suddenly dawned on me you've never talked about how you felt when Grandma Barbie died," she said, then paused. When her mother kept quiet, Tia tried to explain. "I guess I thought since you weren't close, it didn't affect you much, almost like it was just another day. Now I realize it was me thinking that way, not you, and, and I wanted to talk to you about it."

The continued silence on the other end of the line opened like a chasm, and Tia worried she'd overstepped her bounds. There was a cough, and some rustling, and finally, her mother's somewhat strangled voice.

"Tia, this isn't the best time, and over the phone isn't exactly how I'd like to do this, either." Another pause. "But I guess there's never a good time, so here goes. Heavens above, if you make me cry in Starbucks, you're going to owe me forever, got it?"

"Got it."

"Okay, in a nutshell, I was devastated. I was about to graduate college when I got the call. At first my mind didn't take it in. I remember thinking *what the heck is she doing on the Oregon Coast?'* I mean, last I'd heard, they were supposed to come for the ceremony, but that was weeks away, and anyway, they were going to fly, not drive." Cherry covered the phone and mumbled something to someone, before coming back to Tia. "Now you've done it. A nice lady sitting next to me saw my blotchy face and asked if I was okay. So anyway, honestly, it was horrible. When it really hit me, all I could think of was how selfish I'd been, how I'd always intended to bridge the gap, get to know her, try to find a connection, but it always seemed insurmountable, so I always put it off for another day. And then there weren't any more days left. I spent a lot of next year hating myself."

"You shouldn't have, though," Tia argued. "She was the adult, the mother. Why in the world did she hold you at arm's length in the first place? There should never have been a gap to bridge."

"I know, I know. I spent the year after that with a therapist to get that through my head, but you can't help a broken heart. It has to heal on its own."

Tia let her words sink in, then her mind went back to her mother's earlier comment. "Did you ever find out why she was in Oregon?"

There was a short, bitter, bark of a laugh. "Yes, Dad finally came clean, and frankly, it helped a lot to heal my wounds. She was trying to reclaim her hippie days, it turned out. She'd had enough of her 'pedestrian life,' as she called it, so she left Dad that spring. Said she'd be gone for the summer, maybe longer, and he simply needed to deal with it. Turned out she wasn't even going to make the graduation. She was living in some nudist colony commune, having sex with anything with a pulse, I imagine. High as a kite and having a ball reliving her glory days. She was always a very self-centered person, always wanted all the attention. All I can say is, I hope she died happy."

Shocked, Tia had no words. Then, finally, when the silence became too heavy, she said, "I'm so sorry, Mom. And I'm sorry I've opened old wounds. But I'm glad to hear it, too, because now I know how strong you have been all these years, how much you had to endure. And you never once spoke ill of her, even though you would have been justified."

"Thanks. I guess I looked at it, at her, like a great role model for how never, ever, to behave. Especially as a mother. I think Dad took it that way, too. He changed afterward."

"Grandpa was very sweet, and you've been an awesome mom," Tia said. "Truly."

"Thank you." Tia heard Cherry clear her throat. "Okay then, now that we've dealt with that sordid bit of history, and given my kind-hearted coffee neighbor an ear full, may I call for a subject change? Who are you dating? What's his name?" The humor was back in her mom's voice. "You've been evasive, which means you're hiding something, which means there's a guy, which means you don't want me to worry you might decide to move to South Carolina."

Tia burst out laughing. "You know me too well. His name is Seth, he's a cop, and yes, I like him. He's funny, strong, serious when needed. Keeps close, without crowding. His brother is married to a woman Vivian works with. We've been on a couple of dates, nothing too serious, yet, and Vivian has also asked me to consider a lateral move to the local police department. She thinks I belong here, and that I should at least give the idea a good look."

"What does Mr. Seth think?"

"Don't know. He knows I have the paperwork, but he hasn't mentioned it."

"But he's still hanging around?"

"Yep. We're meeting tonight for dinner when his shift is over."

"My guess is," Cherry said, "if he hasn't headed for the hills, then he isn't opposed to the idea. He likes you, too."

"We'll see, I guess."

"Tia?"

"Yes, Mom?"

"Your sister, Audrey, got married and moved to Texas with her own Mr. Wonderful, and I didn't fall apart. We talk all the time, and I have a free place to stay whenever I want a warm getaway. All bonus."

"Which means what, exactly?"

"It means, if you decide South Carolina is where you are happy, then by all means, move. Just be sure to keep a room with my name on it. I have to get back to work. Wish me well."

"Love you, Mom." Tia hung up and slipped the phone into her back pocket. She went into the kitchen, grabbed the application packet she'd left there the night before, and went to sit on the front porch.

The afternoon heat and humidity were already far more intense than anything she experienced in Seattle.

It'll take some getting used to, she thought, as she started to fill out the paperwork. *Especially in uniform.* Startled, she stopped writing mid-word. Was she already thinking of a move in terms of *fait accompli*?

She needed to make a pro's and con's list, in order to see things clearly. Tia put the packet aside, pulled out a piece of paper, and made her list. Under pro's, she wrote, *GG, Seth, beautiful area, great cost of living, warm.* On the con's side she wrote, *GG 95 yrs – not going to be here forever. Seth – might tank. Humidity – not going to change.* Back on the pro's side, she added, *Family,* which then led her to add, *history, roots, belonging.*

Tia heaved a sigh and drew circles around the names. If those two people were taken out of the equation, would she still want to be here? Her heart was screaming at her, but she needed to be sure. Uprooting one's life on an insubstantial whim was not a good idea. And it had the potential to become a very expensive bad idea.

Her mother had essentially already advised her to follow her heart. If she called her sisters, she'd get the same advice. She knew her brother and father would support her decision, but would holler "caution, caution, caution," until she made it.

Antsy, and wanting something more to do, she had an idea and texted Seth.

Feel like cooking. Dinner here?

Tia rose and headed back inside. She dropped the paperwork on the kitchen counter, and grabbed her wallet. Her phone buzzed with a return text.

Great! Off at 6. See you at 7. Should I bring food, or can you actually cook?

She grinned, and sent him a single emoji as a reply. She could almost hear him laughing as she headed for the car.

By 7p.m., Tia had dinner ready. Amazingly, she'd found a lovely 2017 Malbec from Brook & Bull, a top notch winery from the Walla Walla region of Washington State. To go with it, she brought a pair of filets she'd marinated, asparagus, a Caesar salad ready to toss, and vanilla ice cream with peach chunks blended in.

The gate buzzer sounded, and Seth smiled for the camera. Tia let him in, and soon she heard the sound of tires on the gravel drive. She met him at the door.

"Hey."

"Hey," he replied with a grin. "Sounds like you're learning some Southern lingo."

Tia grinned, and led him into the kitchen. "Nah, we say 'hey' out West, too."

"Still, I think I heard the beginning of a drawl in there. Probably them boiled peanuts got you goin'."

He had his way-Southern twang going again. Tia laughed, and turned to playfully shove him for his silliness, but stopped short.

"A Southern gentleman don't come empty handed," he said, and offered her a beautiful bouquet he must have been hiding behind his back.

"Seth, thank you," Tia said. "They're beautiful. Help me find a vase."

Before she could turn away, Seth put a hand on her waist, and gently pulled her close. He paused before making his move, giving her time to disengage. She nestled against him, smiled into his eyes, then dropped her gaze to his lips, just before they touched hers.

They were soft, full, and talented. When he pulled away, he left her wanting.

"I can't smell a thing in this kitchen," he said, his voice gravelly. "Are we ordering pizza?"

Tia laughed and stepped away. "No. I've got some beautiful steaks and veggies all ready to go, and we can start with some wine, and a salad, while the grill heats."

Seth walked over to the counter and put the tips of his fingers on the packet. He swirled it around, then looked at her. "Have you filled it out yet?"

Tia didn't answer right away. She opened the wine, poured two glasses, and handed one to him. They clinked glasses.

"I'm going to shoot as straight as I can with you, okay?"

Seth raised his eyebrows, and nodded.

"I have filled it out, and I plan on turning it in tomorrow." When a grin spread across his face, she put out a hand. "Hold on. I'm not done. I like it here. I feel like I'm home, even though I never felt not at home in Seattle. And, I like you. A lot. But I don't want this to imply anything. If we become a 'we,' I don't want it to be because I moved here. I don't want either one of us to feel obligated because of this decision. I want us to become an 'us' because that's what we want, what we feel, regardless of any other decisions I may make." She stopped speaking and waited for a response. When he didn't, she asked, "Did I make sense? I didn't mean to offend, I just didn't—"

Seth was against her in an instant, holding her close, and kissing her hard. When he backed off, his expression was serious. He touched her cheek, then ran the pad of his thumb over her lips. "I want you to stay. I want to have you in my life. I want to see where this goes, just like you. No pressure. No obligations. We're pursuing a relationship, and we'll be honest about where it's going, or not going. If we end up working together, and not being together, we'll be adult enough to end it, and treat each other respectfully."

Tia let a slow smile form, and whispered, as her lips touched his. "Deal."

After a few more minutes of tenderness, they backed off and started looking for a vase. Once the flowers were arranged, they turned to fixing dinner. Their conversation was easy and far reaching, although they both chose to let their earlier conversation alone. They'd each said what they needed to, and that was good enough for the time being.

Later, stuffed after polishing off the peach ice cream, Seth gathered his things.

"Thank you, Tia," he said. "It was great. All of it."

There were warring factions inside Tia. One wanted him to stay, and the voice was screaming. The other side whispered, and warned her to set a slower pace, a pace that wasn't about the physical. A pace that allowed their spirits to connect, before their bodies did.

"Damn if the whisper isn't winning," Tia said with some surprise, and rose on tiptoes to lightly kiss Seth goodnight.

He looked at her quizzically, then shrugged. "I guess my quieter voice is winning the day, too." He took her hand, then stepped back until their arms were outstretched, the fingers barely touching. "If we go there, it won't be for a jump in the hay, I promise. We will take our time, and we'll go there together, with a lot more in our hearts than a quickie. Sound good?"

"Sounds perfect."

"I guess I need to go now. Say goodnight, Tia."

Bemused, Tia answered with the first reply that came to mind. "Goodnight, George."

She could hear him laughing until he rounded the curve on the driveway.

The following morning, Tia dropped the packet at the station before visiting Vivian, and when she got to her room, she found Vivian sitting on the edge of her bed, fully clothed and ready for the day. Her hair was styled, she wore a lovely pink sweater combination, and gray slacks. Her nails were even done.

"GG, you look wonderful!" Tia exclaimed.

"I feel wonderful," Vivian replied. "Naomi treated me to a makeover yesterday, and this morning the doctor said I can move to my new home on Monday."

Tia hugged her. "That's wonderful news, and I have even more for you. I've taken your advice. I thought about it, and it felt right, so I filled out the paperwork and turned it in before coming here this morning."

Vivian threw out her arms with an exclamation of delight, then stood and embraced Tia.

"That is so…oh heavens, I'm so happy," she said. "We should have some champagne. Do you think they have any here?"

"I like the way you think," Tia laughed. "But maybe we should wait and have the champagne when you move in to your new place?"

"Certainly the wiser plan, I'm sure," Vivian said. "Besides, if we had any now, I'd forget what I wanted to tell you."

"I am all ears."

"It's about my first job, the summer after I graduated," Vivian explained.

They chatted as Tia arranged the chairs by the window, then went to the nurses' station to procure some hot water. Soon, they were seated, tea and coffee in hand, respectively.

"Okay, we're ready," Tia said. She pulled out the bracelet and put it next to the recorder.

Vivian cleared her throat, and separated out another shield charm with three keys emblazoned.

"I went on my first dig the summer after graduation. We, the group of us, lived in Avignon, in southern France."

~1949~

Vivian and her father were greeted at the docks in Le Havre by one of his cousins. Opal was spending the time between her paternal grandparent's home, and that of her Uncle Michael.

Father was to stay with his relatives for the summer, and they would all meet again before returning to Abbeville in September. Vivian stayed with her French relatives for week, hearing stories about her father's youth, and fine-tuning her French, before catching the southbound train.

She spoke French with her father throughout her childhood, and in college she'd studied Ancient Greek and Latin. She looked forward to putting all three to good use in the coming months.

When she disembarked in Avignon, she found a very handsome, dark-haired man, holding a sign with several names listed. Hers was among them.

She stuck out her hand. *"Bonjour monsieur. Je suis Mademoiselle* Gardiner, *de l'universite de Greenville, USA."*

"Ah, bonjour mademoiselle. Enchanter…"

He went on to introduce himself as Patrick Joachim, director of Ancient Studies, University of Avignon.

She would find out later he spoke excellent English, but between the two of them, it turned out French was all they ever needed.

Soon, there was a group of fifteen or so individuals, the rest from France, Canada, or the UK. She was the only American, and one of only two women.

They were all housed in the university dormitory, where she and the other woman shared a room.

Her roommate seemed very personable, was cute as a button, with masses of dark, curly hair, and freckles scattered across her nose and cheeks. She also had a distinctively husky voice. Vivian noticed she was prone to giggling, and wondered how serious she was, or if she was simply here on a lark.

Once they claimed their beds and dropped their luggage, the girl stuck out her hand.

"Sondra Knight. University of Lincoln. Twenty-three. Born and raised in London. Working on my Master's in ancient art and document restoration and conservation," she said brusquely. "I like boys and wine and cigarettes, not always in that order. My mother is from the West Indies, my father, London, so I'm half negro. I hope this will not be a problem for you. Okay, what about you?"

"Hold on," Vivian replied, mentally going through everything she'd said in reverse order. "No problem with the negro thing, half or whole. Father French, mother American, um, no cigarettes or boys, but want to learn about wine, and…oh, yes, recent graduate University of Greenville, double degree in Classical Studies, American History, and a minor in Philosophy. Don't know yet if I'll pursue a Master's."

She looked triumphantly at Sondra, who seemed to be waiting.

"Oh, yes! I'm Vivian Gardiner Henderson, born and raised in South Carolina, married, war widow, mother of a little girl."

Sondra's eyes rounded. "Oh, wow. I'm sorry. How old?"

"Also Twenty-three."

"I meant your daughter."

Vivian laughed. "She'll be four in September."

"You must miss her terribly," Sondra offered, shaking her head. "I can't imagine. Not any of it."

Vivian shrugged. "It's okay. So far, anyway. She's with family, and it's a nice break from, well, everything, to spend the summer here."

"Bloody hell," was all Sondra could say.

"We don't have orientation until morning," Vivian said. "What's say we begin our wine education right away, and leave off decorating until tomorrow?"

Sondra grinned, then slung her purse over her shoulder, and they linked elbows. "Brilliant. Let's get out of here."

Within minutes, she and Sondra had become fast, and life-long friends. And just as it'd happened with Sondra, it didn't take long for Vivian to realize she and Patrick also had something special going on.

Sondra was perfectly aware, but nobody else in the group ever suspected. They kept their public lives professional, but Vivian couldn't help the frisson of electricity that passed between them, if he happened to lean in for a closer look at the work she was doing.

He was romantic, and a true gentleman. He never pushed her toward anything, and despite her insistence their relationship remain platonic, it didn't stop her desire for more.

One night in mid-July, sitting on their dorm room beds and surrounded by books, Sondra broached the subject for the millionth time.

"You guys love each other. Go for it," she coaxed. "I mean, it's obvious he's going to propose soon, so what harm?"

"Sondra, stop," Vivian pleaded. "I'm way too fertile. I lived as a married woman for three whole days, and I got pregnant. With twins. I can't chance it. Not without a ring in place. And, honestly, I love him, but I'm not at all sure I want him to propose. His life is here, and mine is five thousand miles west of here."

"So, move," Sondra said, grumpily. "He's too good looking to turn away."

Vivian laughed. "He is."

"So?"

"Drop it."

Sondra rolled her eyes, but let her be.

The group traveled throughout Provençe all summer, visiting Roman and medieval sites, as well as those related to the Papal Schism, the Cathars, and the Visigoths. As a working group, they split their archeological efforts between digs in the towns of Orange, and Arles, where Romans had been heavily concentrated. However, for the most part, Sondra remained in Avignon, and applied her expertise in the archival backrooms of the Palais des Papes, the beautiful, medieval home of the Popes during the schism. It dominated the highpoint in town, and overlooked the entire region, including a broad swath of the Rhône River.

Eventually, the first week of September arrived, bringing with it all the locals who'd been away on vacation for the month of August. Avignon was crowded, the atmosphere hot and grumpy.

Late on their last night together, Vivian and Sondra wove through the crowd on their way to the Papal gardens that crowned the hill the beside the palace. It was their favorite location, and she needed air.

Her bags were packed, and they would all be on the morning train to Paris. There had been no proposal, and she was glad she'd not given in to her romantic desires.

Still, it hurt. Terribly. She'd come to realize Patrick did indeed love her, but love, in his world, was transitory, and in no way involved a ring, or commitment beyond the end of the semester. He was a serial monogamist.

The nail in their romantic coffin had come earlier in the evening. The entire group gathered for a final meal together. When he rose to give a toast, he pointed out the achievements of several, and congratulated everyone. He vowed he would miss them all, and was terribly sorry he would not be able to see them off in the morning. It was all very generic. He shook everyone's hand, and gave Vivian and Sondra a perfunctory double cheek kiss, before leaving the room.

Vivian felt hollow.

Sondra looked confused. She leaned in and whispered. "Are you meeting him after this?"

"No. I haven't seen him one on one since yesterday, and he never mentioned anything," Vivian replied, near tears. "I think we're done. I think he's gone for good."

"Without a real goodbye?" Sondra was shocked. "After all you had?"

"After all we had. Romantic dinners. Walks." Vivian looked at Sondra. "He introduced me to his family. We spent many evenings with them, and they couldn't have been nicer."

"We need to remedy this."

Vivian shook her head. "I am not running after him. Don't even suggest such a thing."

"No, girl," Sondra looped her arm over Vivian's shoulder.

"We're going to the garden and getting rip-roaring drunk. Are you game?"

Vivian laughed. "I certainly am!"

~2019~

"So." Vivian flicked at the little shield with Avignon's three key papal crest, then turned off the recorder. "My instincts were good, and I left with my virtue intact. And that is how I took to heart the old saying – 'Tis better to have loved and lost, than never to have loved at all."

"Hmm," Tia said. "I've heard the saying, of course. Shakespeare?"

"Tennyson, dear."

"So I guess I shouldn't go looking for love in France, huh?" Tia asked with a grin.

"No, dear." Vivian smiled at her. "I believe you've already found everything you need, just as I did, right here in South Carolina."

CHAPTER FOURTEEN

TIA BOUGHT SOME GROCERIES ON HER WAY BACK TO Altamont. She made herself a salad, gathered a glass and a bottle of wine, then went upstairs and sat in the bay window that graced the room she'd chosen to stay in. The window looked north, over tree tops, to the city beyond, and she could see the sparkle of lights winking in the dusk.

This was Seth's Friday, but they hadn't made any plans, and Tia had to remind herself spending time together was not yet a given. Still, she was disappointed.

She finished her salad, then opened the wine, and poured herself a glass. As dusk turned to night, she turned on her Kindle, which she hadn't touched since her flight.

Trying in vain to concentrate on the words, she kept getting distracted by flashing lights in the distance. The cops were busy tonight. Sobriety check point? Thinking of Seth, she cranked open a little window and could hear the faint wail of sirens. She glanced at her watch. He'd gone off duty an hour before, and was probably already on his way home.

The thought gave her pause.

Knock it off, she scolded herself.

She took a sip of wine.

The wail of sirens continued. She glanced up, and the hair at the base of her neck stood on end. There were so many lights, so many sirens, Tia's instincts told her something big was going on. Something more than a routine check point. She didn't know the town well enough to have any idea where the lights were concentrated, and she had to stop herself from hopping in her car and running toward the situation.

"Boy howdy…"

Isn't your town, she reminded herself. *Isn't your concern. Not yet.*

Still, every cop fiber she owned screamed at her to go.

When her phone rang, Tia nearly dropped her forgotten glass of wine. She hurried to the bed, recognized Seth's work cell, and answered. "Hey."

"Hey." Seth's voice was low, determined, and under tight control.

Immediately, Tia knew there was a problem. "What do you need?"

"I need you to get Stephanie and come to the hospital."

Damn. "Done. Her addresses and name of the hospital?"

Seth rattled them off and hung up. Tia grabbed her wallet and a jacket, and headed out the door.

She arrived at Stephanie's home twenty minutes later, parked, and knocked on the front door. When Stephanie answered, her smile dropped, and fear filled her eyes.

"Don't go there. I don't know anything," Tia explained quickly. "Seth called and asked me to get you, and, and get to the hospital."

Stephanie clapped a hand over her mouth, and tears spilled over the tops of her fingers.

Tia took hold of her elbow, and steered them both inside. "Jacket. Purse."

Stephanie stumbled toward the items. She wasn't functioning, so Tia helped her into her jacket and shoved her purse into her arms.

"Where's your cell?"

Stephanie looked toward the sofa table. Tia grabbed it, and then guided her out the door and into her car.

She plugged the name of the hospital into her GPS, and hit the gas. There were no words worthy of the moment. She wasn't going to try falsely comforting platitudes. They were worthless, and neither of them knew what lay ahead. Instead, she took Stephanie's hand and held on.

She hoped it helped her new friend. She knew she felt better for it.

They pulled into the emergency parking area fifteen minutes later.

There were cruisers everywhere outside, and a lot of commotion inside, but the physical floor plan of the emergency department didn't allow Tia to see where anyone was. At the desk, Tia took charge. "This is Mrs. Rob O'Connor. Officer O'Connor's wife. Officer Lowe called and asked me to bring her in."

The nurse held up a finger, quickly shuffled through some paperwork, scanned one page, then nodded toward the visitor chairs. "Why don't you have a seat. I'll go check, uh, and I'll be back in a minute. Hold on."

She hurried away, but Tia stayed put, and wrapped an arm around a badly shaking Stephanie. Tia made soothing tones, trying to help her friend keep a hold on any remaining threads of sanity.

Suddenly, Seth was coming their way. He took his sister by the shoulders and looked her in the eye. "He's okay. He's going to be fine. Understand?"

Stephanie's shoulders relaxed, and she almost hit the floor when her knees gave way.

Seth held on until she regained her footing, then guided them to some chairs. He took Stephanie's hands in his. "I'm going to tell you straight, Stephanie, but listen to me, hear me, okay? Rob was hit, but he'll be fine. You got that?"

Stephanie nodded.

"I'm sorry I didn't spell it out when I talked to Tia, but I had no idea at the time how bad it might be."

"Okay, no worries," she responded rather automatically.

Tia wasn't sure how much her friend had absorbed since hearing 'he's okay.' "What happened?"

"There was a gas station robbery in progress, and Rob was about two blocks away. He went in with lights and sirens. Backup was close, barely a block away and coming. The suspect heard the noise, and came out shooting as soon as Rob arrived. The bastard wasn't trying to get away. He stood there and aimed for the cruiser's windshield. Three rounds hit their mark, but only one hit Rob. In the shoulder, the left shoulder. He's a lucky son-of-a-bitch, your husband. A lucky son-of-a-bitch."

Stephanie, who's eyes had been fixed on her brother during his explanation, let her gaze slip away. She looked exhausted.

"It's a through and through, and he's already been seen. He'll need time off, and plenty of rehab, but he should be fine. He'll probably be released tomorrow, or maybe the day after, and then you'll have an angry bitch of a husband for a couple of weeks, but I know you can handle a whiny, crybaby patient, right? Look at me. You can handle it, right?"

Stephanie's color was better, and the last string of comments forced a smile. "Oh crap. I'm gonna need a lot of Jack to get through this."

Seth started laughing, and belatedly, Tia realized she meant Jack Daniel's whisky. Yep, the girl was coming around. She'd be fine.

"You be sure to tell Rob I called it right when he starts complaining, okay?"

"Officer?"

Seth turned to the reception nurse with a questioning look.

"Y'all can go on back now. He's in the recovery room. I couldn't help but overhear, and you did nail it. Word has it, he's bitchin' already, just like you predicted."

Everyone laughed, and the women followed Seth's lead.

When they got to Rob's room, they let Stephanie go in alone. Seth put his arm around Tia's shoulder and pulled her close. Without a word, he rested his lips against her forehead.

Silently, she held on to him, knowing he needed this time to re-center. He'd been all cop, handling the situation and ignoring his emotions, but now he needed a release, if only for a moment, in the arms of quiet understanding.

After a few moments, he relaxed his grip, but didn't let her go. "You still want to move out here? Join the department?"

"More than ever," she whispered.

"Be with me?"

She smiled and nestled in closer, her cheek on his chest. "Like I said, more than ever."

"You're gonna key my mic if you keep hugging me on that side. Then everyone on duty will hear us."

Tia burst out laughing, her own emotions finding a much-needed release.

They let go, backed off, and smiled at each other.

Being with Seth was so easy, so…right.

Tia reclaimed some serious, and had to ask. "Rob's good?"

"Yea, he's good. It's not his shooting arm, and nothing vital was hit. It's going to take a lengthy period of rehab, and he's going to be unbearable, for sure. After a while they might put him behind a desk, or something else light-duty, until he can get back into the field."

"A lot better than dead."

"Damn straight."

"What about at the scene? How'd that end?"

"Suspect's dead," Seth said quietly. "He was still shooting when backup arrived, and he got plenty of return fire. That was it. Suicide by cop, maybe. At any rate, it was a miracle nobody in the surrounding area was hit. The paramedics spent some time on him, but he was gone, or almost, when they loaded him in the rig."

"Stupid piece of shit."

"Well, yea. Needed money to buy a fix. He was well known. Frequent flyer. Robbed his mama blind before she finally kicked him out. Robbed everyone, stole everything he could get his hands on for years, to buy his dope. Tonight, price was higher than he figured. It was either this, or death by self-injection. Only a matter of time. But like I said, he came out gunning. He wasn't ever violent, before tonight. Don't know what he was thinking. He should have known it'd be a death sentence."

"When are you off?"

"I was heading in when the call came through. I was the second on scene, actually, so someone'll want my statement. I don't expect I'll get out of there before midnight, and only then if I'm lucky."

Tia let his words sink in, then put her hand on his chest and looked him in the eye. "So, you were Rob's backup? Ballistics gonna show it was your gun?"

His gaze faltered as he looked away. "That'd be my guess, yes."

"You saved Rob's life. Don't lose sight of the good you did."

There was a faint smile on his lips, but it didn't reach his eyes. "Technically, he was done with Rob by then. He was shooting at every set of flashing lights coming in on him. My windshield's toast, too," Seth paused. "But I was first on scene after Rob, and my shots were the first to impact, or maybe simultaneous, with the third on scene."

Tia put both of her hands on his cheeks, and forced him to look at her. "You. Saved. Rob's. Life. And your own, I might add."

He heaved a sigh, then nodded. "Is it too early to say I love you?"

Tia smiled. "Boy howdy, Bernadette, I'd say it's about damn time."

THE NEXT MORNING, Tia went to see Vivian earlier than usual, and found her busy with rehab, so she sat by the window and waited. She needed to be near someone she loved, and Vivian was a wonderful choice. Once the rehab was completed, Vivian sat beside her, and took her hand.

"What's wrong, dear?"

Tia smiled. This woman knew things like a mind reader.

"Everyone is fine, but there was some police stuff involving Rob and Seth last night."

The elderly woman's grip tightened. "Tell me everything."

Tia filled her in on the evening's events, including Seth's declaration of love.

Both women grinned like school girls.

"Seth had to get back to the station, and I stayed until they kicked Stephanie out." Tia heaved a bone deep sigh of fatigue. "I took her home, then stayed with her. She had a hard time sleeping. She kept waking with a start, or a scream. It was pretty bad. She finally went lights-out around four."

Tia shifted, took a sip of coffee, then rubbed the back of her neck. "I called work for her, left her a note, and then left her sleeping soundly, after daylight broke. Didn't want her waking up alone in the dark. Anyway, I haven't been home yet."

"Don't you think you should go and get some rest?" Vivian asked.

Tia laughed. "I don't sleep well during the day. The early months on night shift were a disaster. No, I don't think I could sleep. I'd either be jerking awake trying to get in on last night's action, or jerking awake out of a stone-cold fear caused by Seth's declaration."

Vivian giggled until tears sparkled on her eyelashes. "Love will do that to you. Have you got the bracelet with you?"

"No. It's tucked away safe and sound, back at the house," Tia replied. "Sorry."

"Not to worry. I think you have need of a story. A happy story. So I'm going to tell you about my second true love, and beginning of the very happiest time of my life…"

CHAPTER FIFTEEN

Vivian and her father returned home from Europe in late September. She busied herself putting out feelers for jobs, and soon landed one at the Greenville Historical Society, as a research assistant and file clerk. With nowhere to live in town anymore, she arranged to clean the offices at work after hours, and was allowed to live in a tiny, studio apartment in the basement, in lieu of payment.

Opal continued to live with one or the other of her grandparents, and, as she'd done during college, Vivian took the ninety-minute bus ride into Greenville on Mondays, and returned home on Fridays.

By January, she had been able to demonstrate such a talent for research, she was promoted and moved to the genealogical section, and then field research.

She kept in touch with Sondra, and learned she was making progress with her Master's, had a good job at university, and a serious boyfriend, to boot.

Vivian thought a lot about getting her Master's, but between office work, field work, caring for her daughter and her father, plus the long commute, there wasn't any time.

She'd saved some money, and over the weekend she bought a new, lightweight suit for spring. It was a soft, gray flannel wool, nicely tailored to fit her slim form. She'd also bought three silk blouses in rich jewel tones, to change her look from day to day.

Proud of her investment as she was, by Friday afternoon, Vivian wished she were in her dungarees and plaid shirt and working in the garden, instead of finishing a paper, straight-laced into her pretty suit.

She glanced at the clock. She would be off in an hour, and home in three.

"Vivian?"

She looked around at her supervisor's voice. "Yes, Miss Bastier?" Vivian thought the poor woman looked as though she'd never, ever been kissed. Not even by her mother. She was thirty-ish, and wore her hair slicked back in a tight bun at the base of her skull. So tight, in fact, Vivian could swear it pulled at the corners of her mouth, causing her thin lips to unintentionally form a sort of a grim smile, allowing her buck teeth to peek through.

Despite her severe appearance, she was very nice, and Vivian wanted to give her a hug every time she saw her.

"Mr. Wexler wants to see you in his office. Now."

Vivian's eyes went wide. "Mr. Wexler? Am I in trouble? Oh my God, am I going to get canned?"

Miss Bastier actually giggled. "Heavens no. If you were to get the boot, I'd be the one to do it. I have no idea why Mr. Wexler wants to see you. He didn't tell me."

Minutes later, anxious and jittery, Vivian arrived at Mr. Wexler's secretary's desk.

The woman was beautiful, if a bit impersonal. She simply nodded when Vivian gave her name, pushed a buzzer, and told a voice box Mrs. Henderson had arrived.

"Send her in," came the scratchy reply.

Vivian started for the door behind the secretary, but the secretary shook her head, and used her pencil to point at the door opposite her desk.

With trepidation, Vivian spun around, took a deep breath, and pushed the conference room door open.

She knew it from cleaning, but never in daylight. She noted wood paneling, and paintings depicting hunt scenes along the walls. There were crystal decanters in a nook to the left, and a silver coffee and tea service in a nook on the right, but she couldn't make out much directly in front of her. The far wall was floor to ceiling windows, and in the late afternoon sun, the entire center of the room was back lit and blinding.

"Uh...," she said, and shaded her eyes with her hand.

"Come in, come in, my dear."

Vivian was pretty sure the voice came from Mr. Wexler. She'd seen him give talks at office meetings.

"I'm sorry, it's, I can't see," Vivian stuttered. "I'm sure my eyes will adjust in a minute."

She moved forward cautiously, until she saw the desk, some chairs, and perhaps a form or two on each side.

She heard chuckling, and a buzzing sound, and realized Wexler, or someone else, was closing the blinds electronically.

The room darkened, her eyes adjusted, and suddenly, she saw the large conference desk with several chairs surrounding it, and three serious-looking men facing her.

Had she forgotten to dust in here? Vacuum? No, they're smiling, she thought. "Thank you. How may I be of help, Mr. Wexler?" she asked politely.

"Mrs. Henderson," he began. "I have need of a linguist. I've searched high and low for over a year, and come to find out, I have one in my very building. You! Is this correct?"

"I, well, if you have need of a French linguist, then yes.

My father is French, and I am fluent in reading, writing, and speaking the language," she responded. This was great. She only hoped French was one of the languages he was looking for. "If you need documents in ancient Greek or Latin translated, I'm your girl there, too. I also speak and write those languages, but I've been hard-pressed to find anyone to have a conversation with, let alone a pen-pal."

She tried to laugh at her little joke, but her throat felt like it was closing. What was she thinking, making jokes with her boss's, boss's, boss?? He was so many levels above her, it made her dizzy and terrified thinking about it.

There was more chuckling, and shifting in chairs.

"Exactly," Mr. Wexler said. "Although I'm not looking for that sort of work, per se. What I'd like to ask, is whether or not you'd be able, and willing, mind you, to be a part of a panel whose objective it is to persuade the Board of Regents to put forth the funds necessary to enable the Society to pursue historical research on an international level, as relates to the historical writings that influenced our Founding Fathers, and their resulting influence on Southern Culture."

Confused, Vivian looked from man, to man, to Wexler.

Huh?

"Um..." Vivian shifted from one foot to the other. Random images flooded her mind, as though bolstering her; Harold. Her mother. Sondra. Strong, independent, Sondra. Suddenly she remembered she had a backbone.

She squared her shoulders.

"Mr. Wexler, I don't mean to be rude, but, first of all, I have not been introduced. Further, You've obviously caught me off guard, and I do hope it was unintentional. I must say, I understand your words, but I don't know what you're talking about, exactly, or precisely why I'm here. Can you please be more clear?"

She saw three sets of eyebrows rise simultaneously.

Oh boy.

Wexler smiled, seemingly in triumph, and looked to one, and then the other gentleman, to confirm the fact. They both nodded and smiled back at him.

Feeling irritated, Vivian was having trouble keeping her emotions in check. "If you please. I realize I may be jeopardizing my position here, but unless this is some sort of game, I think you owe me the courtesy of an explanation, instead of letting me self-immolate."

The older of the two unknown gentlemen burst out laughing.

"Mrs. Henderson," Wexler said as he came around the table. "There is no need to self-immolate, or to take any other drastic measure." He shook her hand. "A belated welcome, and please forgive this little test. Rest assured, you did not jeopardize your position here. Far from it. Your position is not only secure, based on the outcome of this meeting, it may well be enhanced."

He gestured to the man on the right, the one who'd burst out laughing. He stood and approached. "Dr. Carl McCarthy, Senior Fellow for the Study of Antiquities, Cambridge University, UK. He is a friend of long date, and visiting in an advisory role to help us move forward with some very interesting plans, which we will discuss, if you agree to consider our offer."

Vivian shook the man's hand, and held his gaze. Short and balding, she noted, with a paunch. His teeth were certainly wonky enough for him to pass as a Brit. Her suspicions were on high alert, but he showed no signs of anything but relaxed affability.

"And my other distinguished guest," Wexler said, turning to his left. "Mr. Thomas Weiss is a local businessman with substantial holdings, and a passion for history, both US, and Western Antiquities, Greece, Rome, and the like. In cooperation with the Society, he would like to establish a top-rate antiquities research wing at the Greenville Historical Society, with internships available to students at University of Greenville, and farther afield."

Mr. Thomas Weiss, making notes on a legal pad, stood abruptly and stuck out his hand. "Hello. So nice to meet you, Mrs. Henderson."

Vivian felt like a physical wave struck her when they locked eyes. Mr. Weiss was tall, handsome, and self-assured, without, seemingly, the above-your-paygrade aloofness she might have expected.

Vivian opened her mouth to reply, then shut it when the words refused to come. Her ears felt hot. Oh lord, was she blushing? Finally, she took his hand, which sent an additional jolt through her. "Sir."

Vivian let go and quickly turned back to Wexler. The ghost of a frown passed over Wexler's face, and he glanced between the two of them.

He quickly recovered a neutral expression, and swept his arm toward an empty chair. "Please, take a seat. Allow me to explain what we have in mind, and why I thought to call you into this meeting, today."

The rest of the hour was a little fuzzy, when she looked back on it. Vivian got on the bus that evening, and tried to focus on the plan Wexler was suggesting, but her mind kept veering back to Weiss.

Heavens above, she'd never had such a visceral response to anyone before. The feeling was so pronounced, she couldn't even look at him during the rest of the meeting. Her traitorous brain kept wondering if he was married, but she'd refused to let herself glance at his left hand.

She leaned her forehead against the window, thinking, and absently fiddling with her wedding band. She looked at it, and wondered if it might be time to put it in a drawer.

Harold had been gone over seven years. He wouldn't want her to remain alone forever. Nor would he want Opal, now eight, to go through life without a father.

"Arrgh!" She pounded her fist on her knee. "Stupid school girl emotions," she muttered. "You're better than that."

The lady across the aisle pretended to fix her hair, and shot her a not-so-covert glance.

Great. Now she was making a scene.

Later, once dinner was done and the dishes washed, Vivian met her father in the living room. As usual, he was softly snoring beneath the front page of the *Greenville News*.

"Papa, *peût-on parler?*"

"*Je ne dors pas,*" he mumbled, then pushed the paper away and yawned. "*Qu'es qu'il y a?*"

"You have so much more experience in these things, Papa. I need to tell you what happened today, and see what you think."

They talked for over an hour, and by the time she needed to put Opal to bed, her father was not only genuinely excited about the plans Wexler and the others had laid out, he was excited for her future.

Vivian was glad he saw things so clearly, but her mind was still in a muddle. She thanked him, and rose to leave the room.

"Vivian," he said.

She stopped in the hallway and looked back. "Yes?'

"I can see it on your face. You are interested in this Mr. Weiss, beyond just working with him, aren't you?"

She heaved a sigh. "Yes, but—"

He wagged his finger and stopped her mid-sentence. "I know of him. It's said he has political ambitions. I also know he is very well thought of in academic circles. He owns several firms, and is worth many millions, I would imagine. Regardless, he is very charitable. He sponsors education. He has endowments. From all accounts, he is quite an extraordinary fellow."

Vivian nodded. "Okay."

"And his wife passed away about a year ago. The ladies at work were all gossiping about it, about what a great catch he would be."

"Papa," she warned.

"I'm simply saying you should remain wise and circumspect, as you always are. In short, a lady," he said. "I also want to remind you that you are young, he is a good man, so far as I know, and Opal could use a father."

They looked at one another for a long while, so many memories passing between them.

Something crashed upstairs, and Opal hollered in anger. Vivian gave her dad a soft smile, and went to investigate.

The following Monday, Vivian caught an earlier bus, and did a little personal research into the three men attending Friday's meeting. Everything she could find before reporting to work was good, although limited. On her way to her desk, she tried a more informal route, and asked a few more questions around the office. To a woman, her co-workers had nothing but praise for Wexler. Importantly, there didn't seem to be any hint of impropriety. As for Weiss, all the women smiled and cooed and had no clear thought one way or another about the man, other than what they'd read in the paper. And the common thread they all took away from the articles was, the man was loaded, and he was single.

When Vivian got to her desk, Miss Bastier was loitering nearby.

"I'm curious to know how your meeting went, last Friday," she said, sitting at the next desk. "Am I going to lose a good employee?"

"I'm not sure," Vivian honestly replied. "Mr. Wexler was there with two men; Mr. Weiss, a local big-wig, and Dr.

McCarthy, an antiquities expert from England. They have some big plans for the Society, in conjunction with U of G, and they are interested in including me on their preliminary planning panel. Wexler was going to make sure I received the prospectus this morning, so I could read it."

"Sure sounds like you'll be moving on," Miss Bastier observed.

"I don't think so. It sounded more like the occasional meeting, and a lot of head-scratching. What I can't figure out is, why me? I haven't been graduated a year. I can't boast a Master's, and certainly not a PhD. There have to be other, more credentialed people they could ask."

"The more credentialed folk already have full-time positions and affiliations." Bastier shrugged. "Maybe they were looking for someone with the ability, and without the baggage, or the divided loyalties."

"Or easily manipulated? Should I be cautious?"

"Caution is always good, but I don't think you need to worry about motives," Bastier assured her. "Wexler's a straight arr…"

Her voice faded off as her eyes fixed on something over Vivian's shoulder.

"I'll leave you to it," Bastier said abruptly, and rose.

Vivian frowned, then turned around.

Mr. Thomas Weiss.

"Good morning," he said, his voice all low and sexy. He was looking at Bastier.

Vivian cleared her throat, stood, smoothed her skirt, and stuck out her hand. "Mr. Weiss. I, uh, this is unexpected. This is my supervisor, Miss Bastier."

They all shook, and it occurred to her he'd held on to hers a bit longer than strictly necessary. Had he done the same with Miss Bastier? She hadn't noticed.

"Miss Bastier," he said. "May I borrow Mrs. Henderson

for, say, a half hour? I promise I will get her back to her desk as quickly as possible."

"I, well, yes, of course," Bastier said. "Please, by all means."

Vivian slipped into her suit jacket and grabbed her purse, giving Miss Bastier a wide-eyed hunch of her shoulders while out of his line of sight.

They left the building, and Vivian noticed several pairs of eyes watching their progress through the office.

He took her to the diner across the street. "I plan on having a pastry with my coffee. Please, order whatever you'd like."

"Thank you. I'll have whatever you have."

He ordered, then turned his full attention, and a smile, on her. "Do you know anything about me? Have you made any inquiries since we met last week?"

Startled, Vivian answered as forthrightly as he asked. "I asked around. Mostly, the women swooned. My father was able to give me a clearer sketch, although his knowledge was limited, since he doesn't read the gossip columns. This morning I was able to locate some factual information at work on all three of you."

"Then you know I am a widower?" he said, a look of sadness passing, almost imperceptivity, across his face.

Uncomfortable, Vivian frowned and straightened her back. "I am aware. That was the first point every single woman made to me. It was, however, not why I made inquiries. Is your situation in some way pertinent to the job?"

"No." He made a wave of dismissal.

The waitress arrived with two coffees, and two hot Danish pasties, a pat of butter melting on top of each.

Despite her misgivings over the direction of their conversation, Vivian's mouth began to water. She decided to give him the time it took her to eat her Danish, before calling it quits.

"In answer to your last question, please allow me to amend my last statement," he said around a bite of pastry. "As to my being a widower, I mean, uh, yes, it is pertinent, but not as far as the job goes." He put his fork on the plate and looked perplexed. "I may well be making a hash out of this."

Vivian bristled, pushed her plate away, and looked at him frankly. "I'm not sure what you mean, but I'm not available, if you think I'm looking for a sugar daddy. Also, I doubt very much you have any need to go slumming for a date. I certainly hope you're not thinking I'll just fall into your arms, because I won't. I was raised to think better of myself. Are we clear?"

He sat back and looked genuinely stunned. Then he started laughing,

Angry, confused, Vivian dropped her gaze and stared at the pastry. She had completely lost her appetite.

He swept a hand under one eye, then took a deep breath. "If you would please give me a few more minutes, I beg you, I would like the opportunity to start again. Agreed?"

She refused to look at him, but gave a sharp nod.

"Thank you, Vivian," he said. "First, I have indeed made a hash out of this, because I feel awkward and…bashful, I guess. I'm not used to feeling bashful. I haven't done this in a while."

Done what in a while?

Still not wanting to look him in the eye, Vivian took a sip of her coffee.

"There are two subjects on the table," he explained. "The first is the project, and my being a widower has no bearing on it, whatsoever. Neither does our group's interest in you being hired for it."

He rummaged in his briefcase, and slid a thick envelope toward her. "This is the project information. I think you are ideal for the position, regardless of what I'm about to say next. Are we clear?" he ended, echoing her earlier comment.

"So far, yes," she replied, and put her purse on top of the packet. "Thank you."

"Great. Now for the awkward part. I knew of your qualifications, your name, the basics, before you walked into the room, yesterday." He paused, and Vivian glanced at him out of the corner of her eye.

He's blushing!

"To be blunt, I would like to ask you out, and let me explain why. You were radiant when you first stepped in, but it wasn't that. I see beautiful women all the time. But when you stood up to Wexler and demanded, very politely mind you, he pay you the respect you deserved, well, that bowled me over. I know McCarthy saw the stupid grin on my face, and I didn't care. If I wasn't 100% smitten then, I certainly was by the time we shook hands. And I think you felt something, then, too. Am I right?"

Vivian had never, ever heard such twaddle. She looked at him with consternation, and was stunned to see an open, sincere expression on his face.

"I don't like pedestals, or fawning," she said. "And as I mentioned, I'm not available."

Weiss tipped his head to one side and smiled. "I did some digging, too. You're a war widow with a little girl. You live with your father, and you're not currently seeing anyone. So, if I'm not mistaken, your lack of availability is personal, not legal."

Vivian did not respond. Dating. The idea of dating hadn't entered her mind. Not until Friday. Not until she met this man.

"May I ask you out?" He pushed her pastry toward her. "After one date, if you still think I'm a bum, we'll call it quits and I promise you, your new position on this project will not be affected. I will not bother you again."

She looked at him and shrugged. "I suppose we might go out. Once."

He grinned. "Great. Now, please call me Thomas, and please don't let your Danish go waste."

~2019~

"Tia?" Vivian asked.

She shifted and tore her eyes away from the pattern on the floor. "Yes?"

"You've been up all night, and look ready to fall out of your chair, my dear. You should go home and get some rest."

"It wasn't the fatigue that was getting to me," Tia said, and reached over to squeeze her hand. "No, it was your love story. I was blissfully daydreaming of Thomas. He sounds wonderful."

"He was. We were engaged less than a year later, and married the following June."

"I never told you, but right after the stroke, when you were barely lucid, you assured me Harold was your Gary Cooper. *And* a great kisser."

Vivian sputtered with mirth. "Oh dear."

"So, who and how was Thomas?"

"You are the very devil, you are," Vivian hedged. "I will tell you this much. Thomas was himself. Better by far than any matinee idol. And yes, he too was a very able kisser."

"So, which charms did we take care of?" Tia ventured.

"Let me see," she said, her eyes cast skyward. "Just the Gemini medallion, for now. His birthday was in late May. I'll tell your about our courtship and marriage next time. Now run home and get some rest."

CHAPTER SIXTEEN

Tᴵᴬ sᴛᴏᴘᴘᴇᴅ ʙʏ ᴀ ꜰᴀsᴛ-ꜰᴏᴏᴅ ʀᴇsᴛᴀᴜʀᴀɴᴛ ᴏɴ ʜᴇʀ ᴡᴀʏ ʙᴀᴄᴋ to Altamont. While she waited, she took out her phone and dialed her mother.

"Tia!"

"Hey, Mom."

"What's up? How's is going?"

Tia took her order and headed for her car. "Nothing. I just wanted to hear your voice. There was some stuff last night. Everyone's okay, or will be, but I spent the night sitting with the officer's wife, and I'm exhausted."

"Too close to home?"

"Yea, sort of." She started the car and pulled into traffic. "For sure too close to Seth. So close, it prompted a declaration of love out of him."

"Oh, wow," her mother said. "Sincere?"

"Actually, yes."

"And how did you respond?"

"He asked if it was too early to say it, and I told him it was about damn time."

"Was that all you said?" her observant mother asked. "No reciprocal declaration?"

"I, uh, no. It would have seemed sort of knee jerk, don't you think?" Tia responded.

There was silence on the other end.

"And I chickened out," she admitted.

Her mother chuckled. "That's what I figured. Doesn't mean it's not so, though. It's just not yet. How do you think he took your non-response?"

"I think he took it fine." Tia arrived at the gate and entered the code. "I mean, I certainly welcomed him saying it."

"Do I need to come out there and help you house shop?"

Tia smiled. "Nah, not yet. Like I said, I just wanted to hear my mama's voice. I'm headed for bed right now, and a good, long nap."

"Okay. I love you. Let me know when I need to book the flight. Bye."

Tia laughed and tucked her phone away as she rounded the corner in front of Altamont. She never got used to the view of the house as she came around the final bend, and stopped to take a picture. She sent it to her mother, then continued on and parked.

Once inside, Tia shrugged off her jacket, dropped it on a settee near the front entry, and headed upstairs, eating her meal on the way.

Too tired to remain standing for a shower, Tia decided a bath was the best option, because going straight to bed like she was would be disgusting.

So, bath, then bed.

She started filling the claw foot tub, then went into her room, dropped her clothes on the floor, and grabbed Vivian's bathrobe. It was a quilted, blue-green, floor length floral affair, and it made her feel like fifties royalty.

The first time Tia tried it on, she was surprised to find it fit well. Vivian was so small, Tia hadn't expected to get it over her shoulders, but Vivian must have been a similar size to her, back in the day.

Tia went to the bath and tested the water, then poured in some lavender bath oil. She turned off the faucet, untied the robe, and was about to drop it on the floor, when she heard her phone ring.

She hurried back into the room and grabbed it off the bed. It was Seth. "Hey."

"Hey. Um, two things," he said.

He didn't sound too serious, so Tia smiled. "Yes?"

"One, Stephanie gave me the gate code."

"Okay, great," she said with a grin. "Are you angling for another dinner invitation?"

"If you're offering, sure, but number two is, despite the security of the gate, you should lock your front door."

Tia quickly retied her robe, went into the hall, and looked over the banister. Seth stood in the foyer, door ajar behind him.

He gave her a little wave. "Bad time?"

"No," she replied with a slow smile and a wink. She put her phone away. "But still too soon for a good time. I went to see Vivian right after I left Stephanie. This is the first I've been back to Altamont since you called last night."

"Right," he shrugged. "Got home around 2:30a.m. myself, and just woke up. I wanted some company, and you, uh, I wanted to be with you."

Tia made an executive decision. She pointed to her room. "Come on. I've gotta take a shower, but you go ahead and hang out. I'll be done in a sec."

As Seth trudged up the stairs, Tia grabbed some leggings and a loose top, and disappeared into the bathroom. She pulled the plug on the bath and started the shower, a bit nervous about being naked and having Seth only feet away.

She hurried, then wrapped her hair in a towel, got dressed, and opened the bathroom door.

Seth was on the bed, sound asleep. Tia watched him for a moment, then kissed his cheek, and grabbed a blanket out of the closet. She tucked herself in beside him, and covered them both.

She thought for a moment about how right it felt...

"TIA," Seth whispered. "We need to start moving if we want to sleep at all tonight. Tia."

Her groggy mind clearing, Tia rolled toward the sound of his voice and snuggled against his warmth.

"Tia."

She sighed and opened her eyes, to find Seth looking at her from about three inches away. She drew back so she could focus, then looked toward the ceiling. It was getting dark outside.

"What time is it?"

"Almost seven," he replied. "You hungry?"

"How long have you been awake?"

"About thirty seconds longer than you." He leaned in and kissed her forehead. "Dinner?"

"No food here. I haven't done any shopping recently."

"I have a place in mind. Loud enough to drown out our conversation, not so loud we can't hear each other." He got off the bed and stretched. "Plus, it's got a kill—, eh, it's got a great view. And we can smoke."

Tia got off the bed. "You smoke?"

"Cigars. Once in a while. I'm feeling the need."

Tia could hear the grin in his voice and turned with a questioning look.

"Nice hair," he said.

Shit. Her long hair had dried in the towel, which was now lying on the floor. Had to be a nice look. She flipped him off and went into the bathroom, closing the door on the sound of his laughter.

A half hour later they arrived at a rustic-looking restaurant overlooking the city. There were two broad decks, one on the north side, the other facing east, with tables, umbrellas, and gas-fed fire pits. The north deck was the cigar section, and they were seated against the railing on the far side.

They ordered steaks, then settled in over a bottle of wine. "How's Rob?"

"Good. Bitching. He'll get released in the morning, and start rehab on Monday. He is pissed off about being shot."

"Better than being pissed off about being dead."

Seth raised his glass, and they toasted truth.

"Look, I want you to know, this is the first time I've had someone shoot at me," Seth said earnestly. "I can't think of a time a full-on shootout actually happened here, okay? I wanted you to know this is way out of the ordinary. Way out."

"Duly noted. How are you? Ballistics back yet?"

He shook his head. "Autopsy says he was hit six times. Two forty-fives, the rest nines." He looked at her. "My duty weapon is a forty-five."

Tia nodded. The next question was difficult. "Kill shot?"

"There were two. Pretty sure my second shot hit his heart. A nine took a chunk out of his throat. Simultaneous, or nearly. Either one would have done the job. He was moving pretty fast when I first fired on him. Six of my shots hit the brick wall behind him. He was still shooting. My first strike to hit him got him in the leg, and he stumbled, but didn't stop. Son-of-a-bitch actually dropped his mag and reloaded. He was aiming at another patrol car by then, so I took a breath with the next shot. That's when he stopped moving."

"You're on administrative leave?" Tia asked, though she knew the answer.

Seth nodded. "Me, Rob, and the other two guys who fired shots."

"How much time will it take?"

The waiter delivered their food, and refilled their glasses. They waited until he was gone.

"Two weeks mandatory, maybe more."

"Can you be seen having fun during that time?" Tia asked as she cut into her steak.

He looked at her, his fork hovering mid-way to his mouth. "Well, I wouldn't want to make a production out of it, but I don't have to live like a hermit. Did you have something in mind?"

"I've heard the low country is pretty. I was thinking Charleston, actually," she said calmly, and popped a bite into her mouth. "Know any good restaurants there?"

"Several," he replied carefully, a little smile playing across his lips. "It could take a couple of days to get to them all."

Tia grinned and clinked her glass against his. "My calendar is wide open, as it turns out. How about tomorrow? I have a date with Vivian in the morning, but I'll be ready by early afternoon."

Seth's smile broadened. "That works. You'll find I'm a helluva good tour guide."

"I'll bet," Tia grinned.

After dinner and a cigar, Seth dropped her at the house, but didn't come inside. Still, they'd graduated beyond his first-date rule, and the kiss he gave her on the front porch kept her warm all night long.

. . .

THE FOLLOWING MORNING, packed and ready, Tia dropped in to see Vivian. Stephanie was already there, having stopped by on her way to get her husband from the hospital. They all spent time talking about the events that had so shook their lives.

Stephanie, still emotional, was very thankful, and before she left she hugged Tia hard. "Have a wonderful trip."

When she was gone, Vivian's eyebrows rose. "You're going on a trip? Alone?"

Tia smiled. "No, not alone. I have a very special tour guide who agreed to introduce me to Charleston's finest restaurants."

Vivian nodded her approval. "Seth, I'm guessing. And apparently, you asked him?"

Tia didn't answer directly, but smiled as she pulled out the blue velvet pouch, and placed it on Vivian's lap. "We'll be back in time to get your new place ready for your move-in on Monday. He won't be by until one, so I have enough time for another couple of charms. Are you game?"

"Indeed." Vivian separated out a tall building, a trolley car, a medallion with the letters *BMI*, and the smallest of the three St. Christopher medallions.

~1950~

One week after their initial meeting, Thomas and Vivian went on their first date. He was waiting for her outside work, standing beside a shiny, tan-colored Buick. It looked brand new.

Nervous, she climbed inside the luxurious vehicle when Thomas opened her door. Her father still drove a 1935 Chevy Suburban he'd bought right after the war. Her father's car was clean and tidy, but the two vehicles were absolute worlds apart.

The Buick's interior had a wood dash, and chrome instruments. The seats were a medium brown suede, with wide bands of dark brown leather trim.

Vivian ran her hand over the leather. She'd never imagined automobiles could be this fancy.

"Your car is beautiful," she said, as he got in behind the wheel.

"Thank you. I got it last year," he said. "I spend a lot of time on the road, and it's a very comfortable drive. You'll see when I take you home tonight."

"Oh, Thomas, that's not necessary," Vivian exclaimed. "It's too long a drive."

Thomas put the car in gear, but kept his foot on the brake, and looked at her earnestly. "I wouldn't dream of making you ride the bus. I know you live in Abbeville, and I'm perfectly happy driving you there. No arguments."

"Thank you. I, I wasn't looking forward to the bus," Vivian admitted. "After the commuters are gone, the clientele on the buses can get a bit dicey."

"Well, tonight you needn't worry."

They had a lovely dinner by candlelight, and found conversation to be easy between them. They talked of the plans Thomas and Wexler were putting together. Vivian was thrilled to be a part of the project, and thanked Thomas for their willingness to listen to her input.

After Thomas paid and they were about to leave, he put his hand over hers. "I asked Wexler to find someone with your background, and we needed a person with enough backbone to deal with us. What none of us anticipated, was that our powerhouse would be a tiny slip of a girl. We were all as impressed by your poise and strength, as by your knowledge. I want you to understand that you more than earned the spot, and everyone is duly impressed."

"Thank you. I can't imagine how Mr. Wexler ever even heard of me. I was so surprised."

"He hadn't heard of you," Thomas admitted. "When your supervisor heard about our search, she recommended you. In the strongest terms."

Stunned, Vivian stared at Thomas. "Miss Bastier?"

Thomas nodded. "I'd forgotten her name, but yes, the very one. She championed you for weeks, until Wexler finally gave in and called you in. I'm forever indebted to her."

Vivian was amazed. Miss Bastier had never said a thing, never intimated Vivian's new position was in large part due to her.

"I am indebted, too. I'll be sure to thank her on Monday. I had no idea."

The drive to Abbeville seemed to take minutes, instead of the usual hour plus. When they pulled into the driveway, they found the front porch, and living room lights blazing.

Vivian grinned. Her father had waited up for her.

"Please, come in and meet Papa," Vivian said.

"I'd be pleased to. Let me get your door," Thomas said. He jumped out and hurried to her side, opening her door with a flourish and a bow.

Vivian laughed. "You know he's watching. He's going to think you're a nut."

"He'll know I treat his daughter as she deserves – like a princess."

Vivian laughed as she got out of the car. "He'll know you're crazy, mark my word. He makes sure this princess mucks out the stalls, slops the pigs, and feeds all the animals every Saturday, right before I cook breakfast for him and my daughter."

They walked toward the front door.

"That's good, though. He keeps you humble, because a

woman with your rare beauty could get princess airs if her feet weren't firmly planted on the ground."

"Now I know you're a nut." Vivian opened the door, and called to her father, as though she wasn't aware he was in the next room.

"Yes, yes, who is there?" her father said, playing his part.

"Papa, I'm back from my date. I'd like you to meet Mr. Thomas Weiss, of Greenville. He drove me all the way home."

"Then he's a man worth his salt," her father said, as he came into the small foyer and shook Thomas' hand. "Glad to meet you, Sir. Thierry Gardiner."

"I am very glad to make your acquaintance," Thomas replied. "I've gotten her home before nine. I hope we're not too late?"

"Not at all, not at all. May I offer you a drink?"

Thomas shook his head and smiled. "No, thank you very much. I don't mind the drive, but I do have to make the return trip, and would be better off with a clear head."

"Wise man, wise man," her father replied.

Vivian was bemused by their formal niceties at this first encounter, like two knights of old, stumbling over one another to make sure courtesy and honor were held to the highest standard.

When Thomas left, with a kiss to her hand, she and her father stood side by side and watched his tail lights disappear.

"He is a good man, *ma petite*," her father said. "I approve. And now I'm going to bed."

THE FOLLOWING MONDAY MORNING, Vivian asked to see Miss Bastier in private.

"What can I do for you, Mrs. Henderson?" she asked, closing her office door and skipping the preliminaries.

Vivian faced her. "Mr. Weiss said you suggested Wexler consider me for the position. Thank you."

Her boss looked taken aback, then shrugged and retreated behind the safety of her desk.

"You're quite welcome. I saw a good candidate and put your name in the hat. It's just that simple."

"But he said you did a lot more. He said you went to bat for me, over an extended period of time, until Wexler decided to give me a chance," Vivian countered. Something was going on, and she wanted to get to the bottom of it. "That's more than submitting my name. I truly appreciate it, but honestly, I'm confused, and want to understand what's going on. I didn't think you even knew my name before all this came about. Don't missunderstand, I truly appreciate what you did, but why go to bat? I work hard, but hardly more than anyone else. Hardly enough to warrant such a kind gesture on your part."

Truth be told, Vivian had a horrible feeling Thomas asked Miss Bastier to submit Vivian's name, to make it look legitimate. She felt heartsick, but had to admit it was the most logical answer. "Did someone put you up to this to get me onboard?"

"Good heavens, no, and I would never be a part of something so low," Miss Bastier answered sharply. "It's just..." She heaved an exasperated sigh and went quiet. She seemed to be weighing her options. "Okay. If this goes outside these walls, well, it can't. Understood?"

"Understood."

"I've watched you since you started here. I assumed you would be average, at best, because pretty girls don't usually have to put forth the effort the rest of us do."

Vivian opened her mouth to protest, but Miss Bastier wagged a finger at her. "I have also noted you are kind, and you help others with whatever they need, be it work related, or personal. And, most importantly, I have seen you defend those who are too weak to defend themselves. That is a very important quality. And a rare one."

Vivian felt humbled. She didn't feel deserving of all this praise. "Well, thank you, again. I do what seems right, and I don't like bullies, but I'm still not sure I'm deserving. I do appreciate your kindness, though, and I'll be sure to earn every ounce of confidence you've put in me."

She was about to leave, but somehow felt the conversation wasn't yet over. She waited, then gave Miss Bastier a questioning look. "There's more, isn't there?"

"The reason…" Miss Bastier started, then paused, and heaved a sigh. "Nobody knows my past, because I don't talk about it. I am Jewish. From Poland. When the Nazis invaded Poland in 1939, I was fifteen years of age. I lived with my parents, two brothers and a sister, in a nice neighborhood in Warsaw. My father had political friends, and their unease led my father to make certain arraignments with people outside of Poland, one full year prior to the invasion, in case the need to escape should come about. Well, it did come about. The evil arrived in early September, but, despite his plans, my father grew angry and refused to abandon his homeland to them. He wanted to stay and fight. Of course my mother refused to leave my father, and then my brothers refused to leave our parents. I tried to refuse, too, but they insisted. It would not be safe for my little sister to travel alone, they said. So, we two were sent off to Sweden, and then to England. My father assured us he knew the names and locations, and when all was safe again, they would join us, or send word for our return."

Vivian was stunned. This is not what she'd anticipated, and had no idea how it pertained to her situation. With crushing horror, she wasn't sure she wanted to hear what happened to Miss Bastier's family, but knew she needed to hear the entirety of this woman's story.

"I had no idea," Vivian said. "I thought your accent, which is very slight, sounded British. I figured you were from England, or maybe Boston, or something. If you can, I'd very much like to hear…the rest."

Miss Bastier straightened in her chair, her eyes red. "Our name was Baszynska. I was born Tuviah Baszynska. They changed our names and gave us papers. Suddenly, in London, I became Talia Bastier. They assured me the information would get back to my family when they asked for it. I am still in contact with those who sheltered us. To date, no one has ever made any inquiries."

Frozen with sorrow, Vivian could only stare. "I'm so sorry, so very sorry. I lost two brothers and my husband, and a third brother will never be well again, but at least I *know* how their story ended. Do you, do you know anything about your family?"

"I heard rumors, but most is supposition. They would have been forced into the ghetto, of course, and either died there, or were put on the trains to Treblinka. Personally, I like to hope they remained together, and died before the death camp could claim them."

"Oh my God. And your sister?"

The first hint of a smile brightened Miss Bastier's face. "She was thirteen when we left, met a very dashing Englishman, and married him the minute the war ended. She has two children, and one more on the way. She is giving them our family names."

"That's wonderful. Do you…have someone special? Someone to share all this with?" Vivian asked hopefully.

For the first time since entering the office, Miss Bastier looked directly at Vivian, her expression hard.

"I do not. Nor will I. Ever."

Confused, Vivian gestured toward Miss Bastier's hairdo. "But, you shouldn't feel that way. A softer hairdo, a little blush and some lipstick…"

Vivian wisely shut her mouth, knowing, by the hostility in her boss's expression, that she'd overstepped. By a lot.

"I thank you for your vote of confidence, but you misunderstand. I present myself like this because I don't want a man. My trust was shattered long ago. People who claimed friendship pointed us out, made us wear stars, and refused to speak to us afterward. No one stood up for us. When it came to it, everyone we thought we could count on, turned against us in hopes of saving themselves. Neighbors spoke against neighbors without a shred of guilt, and then they would move in and take our homes, steal the belongings of the families who were forced to leave everything behind. That is why I will never extend my trust to another living soul, excepting my sister. Ever."

"I see, and it's very understandable. So, why me? Why did you put my name in? Why did you fight for me?"

"Because you are intelligent, honest, and very hard working. And because of what I said before. You stand up for others, even if it could put you in a bad light. You aren't working simply to find a man. You have integrity, and if I were to put my trust in anyone again, it would be you. Perhaps I already have. And perhaps it is my way to deflect the evil done to me – by doing good – where it is deserved."

The two women sat silently for a time. When it felt right, Vivian stood and put out her hand. "Thank you, from the bottom of my heart."

When their hands clasped, Vivian made a decision and held on, then looked her in the face. "No one will ever know about your story. Not from me, I swear."

Miss Bastier nodded, then made to pull away, but Vivian held on. "I'm so sorry for you and your family, and I'm sorry for the hurt. I want you to know that, well, I care, deeply, and I love who you have made yourself into, and I will always honor the memory of your family. You have my deepest respect, and I treasure the confidence you have shown me, for the job, and for this visit. Thank you, Tuviah Baszynska."

Miss Bastier's eyes were sparkling with unshed tears. Vivian released her grip and left the office, softly closing the door behind her.

~2019~

"My goodness, it's already lunch time," Vivian said with a sigh. "And I still haven't gotten to the charms."

"You don't have one for Tuviah?"

Vivian gazed at the bracelet. "No. We remained close friends. She went back to England to live with her sister after she retired. Never married. She sent many pictures of the two of them, and of her nieces and nephews. She was happy there. Very happy. But giving her a charm seemed like a betrayal of the trust she'd put in me, so long ago. I hadn't intended to tell you about her, but it just came out. Ah well. She passed over twenty years ago, so I guess she wouldn't mind."

"I'm very glad you did tell me."

Vivian smiled. "You have a sightseeing date, if I'm not mistaken. Go, Tia. I'll tell you about the next batch of charms when you get back."

CHAPTER SEVENTEEN

SETH ARRIVED AT ALTAMONT AS THE CLOCK STRUCK ONE, AND they were on their way by 1:05p.m.

For some reason she couldn't quite place, Tia felt nervous. She sensed Seth did, too, since he was as quiet as she. She hated to go with a fallback topic – cop stories – but by the time they passed Columbia an hour later, she was feeling desperate.

"So, uh, any updates on the other night?" she asked.

"Not really. Ballistics are in, though."

"And?"

"One of the guys with a nine landed three shots, the other guy, one. The three-shots guys had the neck shot."

"And your .45?"

He was quiet for a moment, then, softly, "Heart. Like I thought."

Tia absorbed the information. "And brass? What're they saying?"

"Justified. No question. There's all kinds of film. Three cruisers with dash cams, the convenience store cameras, plus the clerk on duty. Also security film and an eye witness from a business across the street."

"When are you back on duty?"

"Still two weeks. That's the minimum," Seth said. "I have to do a mandatory one on one with a shrink. You know the drill."

Tia nodded and looked out her window. "Dotting i's, crossing t's."

What was going on? Why were they so tense?

"Tia?"

"Yes?"

"I feel like we're having first date jitters," Seth admitted. "What's going on?"

Tia faced him. "I agree, and I have no idea. Why so awkward? This is ridiculous."

Seth grinned. "So, I'm going to guess, okay? I mean, we might as well attack this."

"Please do," Tia agreed. "I'll give bonus points for every right answer, and huge demerits any time you're off base, or blame it on me. Agreed?"

Seth laughed, then took her hand, squeezed, and held on. "I think it's because the hot-n-heavy didn't, hasn't occurred naturally, and its sort of like, here we go, and we're going to mark it off our to-do list. So, not exactly romantic."

"Or spontaneous," Tia said with a grin. "Damn, you're good. Bonus points, for sure. Anything else?"

"Maybe we both want it to be special," he said quietly. "Meaningful. Not a fling, but...the official beginning of something more. Something bigger."

He nailed it, and the revelation was stunning. And terrifying.

Tia swallowed hard. *The first day of the rest of our lives?*

She looked at their hands laying in her lap. "You're right,

it is like that. What do you suggest we do to get over the awkward?"

"Let's not put any pressure on. If the timing isn't right, then it isn't right," he said. "Nothing's mandatory. No need to check such an important box in haste."

"You're absolutely right. We're going to Charleston for good food, good wine, and the best company, right?" Tia offered.

Seth smiled, brought her hand to his lips, kissed it, and then let go. "The very best. All I need."

Her heart squeezed, and she smiled. She felt the same way.

The rest of the drive passed smoothly, their earlier unease forgotten. When they arrived in Charleston, Seth drove along a lovely, historic street, and Tia was in awe. Every building looked as though it held a thousand stories, all waiting to be told.

"It's beautiful," Tia said. "I want to visit every single art gallery, restaurant, antiques shop, and museum. Everything."

Seth pulled to the curb and a bell hop was at her door in and instant.

"We're staying here?" she said, in surprise. "Holy cow, I thought you were giving me a tour."

The bell hop smiled and gestured toward the entry. "Welcome to The Vendue, Madam. *Bienvenue á* Charleston."

"*Merci, monsieur,*" she replied automatically.

Seth ushered her inside, and Tia looked around in awe while he checked in. The place was exquisite. Wrought iron grill work, white tile flooring with black accents, furniture and art to die for.

Seth took her elbow, and they followed the bell hop into the elevator.

Once they were alone in their room, Tia turned to Seth.

"Seriously, I was thinking Holiday Inn. This place is incredible, and ...expensive?"

Seth smiled shrugged. "Not so bad, and it's one night. I wanted something beautiful for you, for us, to remember."

Tia was overwhelmed. She wrapped her arms around Seth's waist and rested her head on his chest. "It is beautiful. Thank you."

His arms enveloped her, his cheek against her head.

Tia wasn't feeling nervous anymore. Far from it. "Two questions. Do we have a dinner reservation, and is there a tub?"

Seth checked his watch. "Dinner rez is for 8:00p.m. It's 5:15, so you have time, and yes, there's a bathtub, and a complimentary bottle of champagne. Would her ladyship like some bubbly while she bathes?"

He was holding to their earlier bargain. No boxes automatically checked, unless...

"Seth," Tia said, looking at him. "The other day, when you showed up unannounced at Altamont, you interrupted a bath I had planned."

"Sor—"

Tia stopped him with a finger pressed against his lips. "You owe me a bath. We can have champagne later."

The smile she got in reply was everything she'd hoped for.

The rest of their visit was a sweet blur. And they actually managed to tour the charming city before heading home.

Tia's cell phone woke her early. It was Wednesday, and she didn't have anywhere she needed, or wanted to be, except right where she was – Altamont. She rolled over and smiled at Seth, who didn't seem pleased by the noisy intrusion.

She put the phone to her ear. "Cynthia Benson."

"Hello. This is Lieutenant Hollings at Greenville Police Department. We've gotten your application, plus some unsolicited recommendations from a couple of our people, and we'd love to set a time for an initial chat. Do you have any free time this week, or early next, to come in?"

Tia was already sitting, and turned startled eyes on Seth. "Yes, Lieutenant Hollings." She said his name on purpose, so Seth would know who she was talking to, and saw an eyebrow raise.

"Yes sir. I appreciate the call. I have time. I'm on an extended leave, as you may have heard, so any time that fits your schedule will work for me."

"Is this afternoon too soon? Say, 2:00p.m.?"

"Fine. I look forward to meeting you then, Lieutenant."

Tia put her phone on the bedside table and looked at Seth. "Is it odd that my very orderly world has been turned on its head since getting the DNA kit back, and yet I'm not freaked out?"

Seth crooked his arm around her neck and gave her a warm kiss. "Not if it feels right, Tia. Not if it feels right."

Later that morning, Tia tapped on Vivian's door. They had moved her into her new place on Monday, but there were still plenty of boxes to unpack.

"Come in."

"Good morning, GG." Tia entered with the groceries Vivian had requested, gave her a kiss on the temple, then went into the tiny kitchen to begin putting everything away. "How do you like your apartment so far?"

"There are a lot of people with white hair in the dining room," Vivian called from the living room.

Tia laughed. "Latest fashion statement."

"It must be quite the craze. Everyone's on board, including me, although I don't remember giving it the okay."

"Would you like me to dye your hair?" Tia asked. "Maybe

a nice sexy red, or maybe brunette? Hey, bright pink Mohawks are in right now."

"Oh no," Vivian said, coming into the kitchen. "I'd make everyone too jealous with my new-found hotness. I simply couldn't."

Tia folded the grocery bag and tucked it away. "But otherwise, are you okay here?"

Vivian shrugged. "It's small, and I miss Altamont terribly, but I also feel safe here, and not so…alone. I've always had an independent nature, but I find community is the better call for me now. So yes, I like it."

They linked arms and went to sit in the living room. Vivian had a large, plate-glass window overlooking a garden and a small patio.

"I have some exciting news for you," Tia offered.

"Do tell! If it's good enough, I'll gift you with another story," Vivian countered with a smile. "If I can share your news with the white-hairs, it'll be even better. I have a feeling the residents here thrive on gossip."

"It'll have to be a quick story, and yes, you can share, since I have an interview at the police department at two o'clock today."

Vivian clapped. "Oh, good, good, good!"

Tia grinned. "I got the call this morning. Woke me up, in fact."

"What does Seth think about this?"

"Well, actually, he was right there when I got the call. He was all grins."

Vivian absorbed the information, then turned to Tia with a devilish look in her eyes. "It would seem quickies are the order of the day, then."

~1950~

Vivian and Thomas dated for three months before she admitted it to her coworkers. She was surprised to find out it was already old news around the office.

She split her time between her regular job, cleaning, the fledgling foundation, Thomas, and Abbeville. It was a lot to juggle, but she was passionate about all of it, and her life took on a fast-paced, rosy sort of glow.

Thomas' birthday came around in late May, and Vivian engaged her daughter in planning his birthday party. He wasn't a country boy, and she wanted to give him a taste of life on the farm.

He arrived at noon to find balloons tied along the fence line, all the way to the house. Vivian had a table set in the yard, and plenty of sweet tea ready to go. Later in the afternoon, there would be fried chicken, barbequed pork ribs, corn on the cob, grits, green beans, potato salad...in short, everything she could think of, plus homemade peach cobbler with ice cream, for dessert.

In a heartwarming gesture, Harold's family came, as well as extended friends and neighbors.

Opal was smitten with Thomas, and loved showing him how to feed the horse, the chickens, and swing on the two-man seat that hung from the old oak. Days earlier, she had thrown a tantrum when she learned the party would not be for her, but once it started, and she realized she had his full attention, she was all smiles.

After dinner, after everyone had drifted home, and after Opal was tucked in bed, Vivian and Thomas sat on the back porch, enjoying the quiet in the coming dusk.

"Vivian, thank you for today," he said. "I can truly say I've never had such a wonderful birthday."

"You're welcome. We had fun putting it all together for you," Vivian replied.

"There's, uh, something I'd like to give you, if you'll have it," Thomas said.

"But, you're supposed to get gifts on your birthday, not give them," Vivian said, surprised, and a little nervous.

"It's just a little thing, but it would mean a great deal to me if you'd accept it," he said, his expression earnest.

Vivian shifted, more nervous than ever. "Okay."

He held forth a little box, and Vivian took it, her pulse nearly shooting off the charts.

She opened the box, and there, lying on a bit of cotton, was a small St. Christopher's medal, with delicate scroll work along the edges. There was no chain.

Vivian looked at him, confused. "It's lovely."

Thomas took one of her hands in his. "You've shown me your bracelet, and told me about each of the charms. I, uh, well, I figured Harold started a tradition with the one he gave you, and I thought I'd follow suit."

Tears sprang to Vivian's eyes.

Thomas looked horrified, and hurried on with his explanation. "I felt like it was my nod to him, actually, because I would never want to pretend he wasn't a big part of your heart, and I also didn't want you to think it was intended to overshadow, or usurp, or anything. That's why mine is smaller. I, I hoped, because of us, you might consider putting it on your bracelet, too."

Barely breathing, he looked at her, anxiety written all over his face.

Vivian stared at the medallion in her lap, and let the tears fall. How was she so lucky as to have found two such wonderful men?

Thomas was in such a state, she almost started to laugh.

"I love it, Thomas," she whispered. "And I have a gift for you, too, as it turns out."

She took a small square of birthday wrap and handed it to him.

"You needn't, I mean, the whole day was enough—"

"Shush," she said. "Open it."

He opened the tiny package to find a small disk with a pair of smiling children on its face.

Vivian put a hand on his wrist. "It's the symbol for Gemini. I know you don't put any store by such stuff, and neither do I, but I thought it would be a nice way to commemorate you. And us. By the way, you can't keep it, because I'm going to put it right next to your St. Christopher."

VIVIAN WAS aware from the outset Thomas was a wealthy man. Wexler had said as much at the first meeting, her father had confirmed it, and every female in the office talked about how lovely it would be to have all those millions.

Thomas never boasted about a thing, though. Even his Buick, as lovely as it was, was not ostentatious, or even terribly high-end. When he was in town, he took her to nice restaurants on Fridays, but when he came to visit on the weekends, they enjoyed walks around the farm, or an ice cream in town.

However many millions he had, Vivian knew he worked hard for it. His grandfather had started the Blue Mountain Insurance Company at the turn of the century, and Thomas was running it now. Their home office, in Spartanburg, was in a lovely, thirty-story Art Deco building his grandfather had built during the depression, providing much-needed jobs for the community. They also had corporate offices in the Delaware Building in Chicago, and San Francisco's Chronical Building. He promised to show her all of them, but for now, he was the only one making the business trips.

. . .

I<small>T WAS</small> A<small>UGUST</small>. It was hot. And it was humid. Every office window was open, and fans were propped in most of them.

Trudy, a new co-worker who sat in the desk next to hers, undid another button on her blouse and pushed her chair close to a fan. "You should have that boyfriend of yours buy some air conditioning for this old dump of a building. Bring it into the modern age."

Vivian ignored her.

"I mean, the man's eyeball-deep in money," she went on. "He probably wouldn't even notice the outlay."

"Trudy, shut up," somebody mumbled.

"Speaking of outlay, I bet his house has air conditioning in every room. I'd do about anything for cool sheets, tonight."

Trudy chuckled at her own crude joke. Nobody else said a word.

Vivian heard Trudy's chair squeak, and knew she'd turned away from the fan.

"You giving him some sweet outlay, Viv?" Trudy ambled over and grinned at her. "You sorta seem like a prude, so I'll give you some free advice. Your charms ain't gonna last forever, so if I were you, I'd outlay right quick, and plenty often, and lock in those millions with a baby. That way you'll have a ring, and a wholelota happily ever after, in the form of a blank check boo—"

The sound of the slap echoed like a thunderclap, and all eyes turned Trudy's way.

Miss Bastier stood there, bristling with fury.

Trudy's cheek was bright red, shock and anger glinting in her eyes.

"You are a filthy pervert," Miss Bastier hissed. "You are fired. Clear your desk and be out of this office in five minutes."

Stunned, Vivian looked on in amazement. Wide eyes

from all around the office turned back to their work. There wasn't even any whispering.

Miss Bastier stood her ground until Trudy was gone, then turned and met Vivian's gaze.

Vivian stood and held Miss Bastier's swollen hand.

"Tuviah Baszynska," Vivian whispered. "You honor your past, once again. Thank you. I'll get you some ice."

~2019~

"So, there you go," Vivian said. "We've covered the Delaware Building, the Blue Mountain Insurance medallion, and the San Francisco trolley car, which I thought was much cuter than getting a second building. We visited each of them, many times."

Vivian suddenly clapped a hand to her forehead. "Oh, heavens, I'm all out of order. We didn't visit any of those places until after we were married. We were very proper, despite Trudy's crude suggestions. We didn't visit *anything* until after we were married."

She looked to Tia with a sentimental smile, her hands fiddling with her ring finger.

"He was a gentleman. Very proper." She sighed. "And kind. And funny."

"He sounds like quite a guy, GG," Tia offered.

"He was. And Seth seems very like him. Now, go on to your interview. When you're done, you may tell me all about it, and all about Charleston. I suspect you fell in love while there. Charleston will do that."

CHAPTER EIGHTEEN

AFTER THE INTERVIEW, SETH DROVE TIA BACK TO VIVIAN'S, and stuck his head in to say hello.

"Seth, I'm so happy to see you again," Vivian said as they shook hands.

"It's nice to see you, too, Vivian," Seth replied. "You're looking much better than the last time I was with you, which was when you were trundling down your driveway in the back of the aid car."

"I've given my traitorous brain a stern talking-to since then, and we've made peace."

"Good to hear," he said. "Tia has told me all about your charm bracelet, and about the stories each one represents. I think she's ready for more."

Vivian smiled at Tia. "I do hope I haven't been boring her to death, especially when she has so many other exciting things happening in her own life right now, such as yourself."

Tia was about to protest, but Seth held her off. "Vivian, I assure you she is thrilled. Not only about the stories, either, but about each minute she spends with you."

"Thank you," Vivian said with emotion. "I have cherished every moment, as well."

"Okay, then." Seth kissed both women on the cheek. "I'll be on my way. Tia, just give me a call when you're ready to head home."

Vivian took his hand and held on. "Where are you going?"

Seth looked a bit flustered. "I was going to have a beer. You know, let you two have your talk."

"I have beer, and you have an open invitation," Vivian said. "Your choice."

A big grin spread across Seth's face. "My daddy once told me, 'never refuse a beer offered by a pretty lady.'"

~1951~

Thomas and Vivian were married in early spring, in the observatory of the company building in Spartanburg. They were eager to add to their family, and Vivian anticipated seeing the first signs within a few weeks.

Thomas kept his apartment in Greenville, but it was too small for the three of them, so, at her father's request, Opal continued to live in Abbeville, attend her usual school, and be around friends and familiar surroundings. Vivian and Thomas spent every weekend with them on the farm.

Thomas presented Vivian with a pale blue Buick as a wedding present, so she could make the trip on her own, if needed, instead of taking the bus, or being locked into his schedule.

By July, Vivian was telling herself she wasn't pregnant because her fertility had finally slowed to normal, now she was a little older. No longer 'Fertile Myrtle,' she forced calm by reminding herself of the months her sister-in-law, Carol, had taken to get pregnant.

That fall, the grand opening of the Foundation for the

Study of Antiquities and American Heritage was announced at the University of Greenville. Thomas dedicated it to his grandparents, Richard and Elisa Thomas, founders of the Blue Mountain Insurance Company.

There was a lot of smiling and shaking of hands. It was exciting, but Vivian was relieved when it was over, and they were in their car on their way to the celebratory dinner. Vivian had a lot weighing on her mind, but she shoved it aside, and decided on a lighter, more timely subject. "Thomas, I never thought to ask," she ventured. "Why is the foundation here in Greenville, when the company, your family's whole life, is in Spartanburg?"

"My grandparents were both born and raised in Greenville, but felt Spartanburg was the better spot to start the company. More people, more commerce. He wanted to build something big, and at the time, that meant a bigger city, or moving toward the coast. He was always a mountain man at heart, so he stayed as close to home as he could. They moved there in '02 to start the company."

"I see," she smiled at him, then sighed and looked out the window. "You are a wonderful man, Thomas."

Vivian could feel his eyes upon her, but she didn't want to face it, face him. Within moments, he pulled to the side of the road and put the car in park.

"Vivian, what is it?" he crooked a finger under her chin and compelled her to turn her head. He looked at her, his brow wrinkled with concern. "Something is wrong, and I'm worried. You – how can I describe this? You seem to be fading before my eyes. Where once everything about you was sunshine, lately, you seem sad, worried. Have I done something to upset you?"

And here she thought she'd covered it so well. Silly girl. Poor Thomas' eyes were rimmed with worry.

Vivian looked at her clasped hands, humiliation washing

over her. "I am worried, but it's nothing you've done. I love you so much. You are the dearest man, and I am so blessed to have you, but…"

"But what?" he leaned toward her and grasped her hands with one of his. "What is it? Tell me, please."

Vivian swallowed, then nodded, her eyes downcast. "Harold and I were married three days when he shipped out, and he left me…in a family way."

"Yes, dear, I know," Thomas said. "Uh, but, I still don't understand. That was a long time ago. What does that have to do with us?"

"Three days, Thomas, and I was pregnant." Vivian looked at him. "We've been married nearly six months. I expected, I thought, by now…"

"Honey," Thomas cupped her cheek with his other hand, and she saw his concern melt into understanding. "I'm in no hurry, and sometimes it takes longer than expected. That's all."

Vivian shook her head. "I had a very difficult delivery. So difficult, it cost my little David his life. I think I need to see a doctor. I'm so afraid I may not be able to conceive anymore."

Thomas kissed her several times, on her eyes, her lips, the tip of her nose.

"Honey, I'll find the best doctor for you, and we'll discover the truth together, one way or the other. Okay?"

Vivian nodded, tears dripping.

"Honey," Thomas repeated, and gently held her face until she focused on him once again. "You know I want to adopt Opal. She can take my name, or keep her father's. I'm fine, either way. But hear me. We are already a family. We, you and I, already have a child. If that is all God wants to give us, then that's all we'll have, and that's all right."

~2019~

"The doctor confirmed my worst suspicions," Vivian said quietly. "He said I'd been injured during the birthing process with the twins, and would never likely conceive again. He cautioned me if I did conceive, I should be prepared to lose the babe, for my womb would never take it to term. I was distraught. I so wanted to give Thomas a child of his own, one we'd made together. But it wasn't to be."

Seth sat without speaking, his elbows on his knees, his gaze cast somewhere between his knees and his ankles.

"Oh, GG, I'm so sorry." Tia sat beside Vivian and hugged her.

Vivian straightened, smiled at Tia, then rose and went into the kitchen.

"I'm getting us more beer, so sit tight," she said. "My apologies for such a sad story. Sometimes I forget where things may lead. It seems I've blocked those things out of my mind until the point when they're coming out of my mouth."

She returned, handed Seth two beers, and Tia one, and asked Seth to open one for her.

They all clinked bottles, and took a long drink.

"So," Vivian said matter-of-factly, after a short break. "I never conceived with Thomas, which was a blessing, in a way, because I would have lost it, and once was hard enough. Thomas did adopt Opal, and gave her his name. And now I must back-track on the charms, where before I'd leapt forward a bit too far. Our marriage retired my first wedding band, of course, so I had that one soldered to the engagement ring with the opal. For our honeymoon, we chose to take the Trans-Canadian Railroad from Halifax to Vancouver, BC., then took the ferry across and spent a final few days in Victoria, before flying home. It was my first time on an airplane. Very exciting. Anyway, that is how the Maple leaf and the Victoria shield came to be."

"It must have been a beautiful trip."

"In so many ways," Vivian said with a twinkle in her eye. "Now, if you have a bit more time, I'll tell you one more story. A happy story, before you go."

~1952~

On their first anniversary, Thomas gifted Vivian with an extended trip across Europe, finishing in Athens, where they would participate in a dig sponsored by their newly-formed foundation. They would meet with three post-graduate students who'd been the first to receive grants, as well as Dr. McCarthy, who would head the research department.

Thomas had booked them on the maiden voyage of the SS United States, which departed July 3. There were fireworks and celebrating, but the fog was so dense, they could barely make out the receding coastline as they made their way to open waters. The first day out to sea, the wind was fierce, the seas rough, and very unlike the calm sailing Vivian remembered as a child.

Thomas, Vivian, and Opal stood near the windows in an enclosed promenade area, and gazed out as they kept tight grips on the railing.

"Want to try a walk outside?" Thomas joked.

"Don't you dare," Vivian said. She was tense, and didn't find his comment funny. "You'll be blown right over the rails, and I doubt the captain will want to ruin breaking the speed record in order to turn around and fish for you."

Thomas put an arm around her shoulder and kissed her temple. "We'll be fine, honey."

"I bet that's what everyone said on the Titanic."

Thomas tilted his head back and started laughing.

Nine-year-old Opal burst into tears. "I hate this. Why didn't we go on an airplane? Why do we have to go to stupid

Europe? I want to go home." She stomped her foot several times.

Vivian and Thomas exchanged a knowing look. They'd considered the eleven-plus hour flight, but quickly chose the slower sea route to give Opal a chance to move about. It was incomprehensible to think she'd endure the length of the flight without throwing a tantrum.

She made eye contact with Nanny Anna, whom they'd hired to accompany them and watch over Opal. There would be times they'd be in the field, and children, in general, weren't a good fit. Opal would be a terror.

After arriving in Southampton, England, they spent a week in London and its surrounds, then moved on to Paris, before taking a train to Frankfurt. From there, they hired a car and drove to the hamlet of Burg Hornberg. Thomas wanted to see the town his ancestors had left behind when they moved to America in the 1870's.

This was not a portion of the trip Vivian relished. She found she couldn't look anyone in the eye, remembering all too well the pain and horror these people had purposefully brought on the world, and on her and Tuviah's families.

Harold. Jonathan. Earl. George. The Baszynskas. So many millions more.

Thomas had also fought, in the Pacific Theater, but he'd been able to forgive, if not forget. Vivian hadn't yet found it in her heart to follow suit.

She didn't say anything about her suspicions, but she sensed by Thomas' grim demeanor he guessed well enough what he would find. Having a Jewish surname didn't bode well for any of his ancestral family having survived the war, or if any did, that they'd still reside in Germany.

After two days of searching and finding no trace whatsoever, they booked passage to Athens.

Thomas never again mentioned his failed search. They left Burg Hornberg behind them, and didn't return.

Their train rolled into Athens on the first of August. Greece was experiencing a heat wave, even by Greek standards. The mercury rose to an incredibly dangerous forty-two degrees Celsius, every day for two weeks running. Everyone was short tempered, people were dying, and the fragile power grid was stretched to breaking, which it did, frequently.

Thomas made sure plenty of water and tents were brought to the dig site, and insisted on short work rotations, to help the onsite field workers. It helped, some, but everyone was grateful when the heat wave broke, three days into their stay.

"I hate this!" Opal stomped her foot and glared at her mother.

"Don't say hate, dear," Vivian reprimanded. "You don't hate being here."

"I do too!" She stomped her foot again, her dark curls bouncing, her blue eyes flashing anger. "And I hate Anna. And I want to go home!" This last comment ended in a screech.

Vivian took hold of her daughter by the upper arm and marched her out of the hotel lobby and into the elevator. Once the door closed, she crouched and got eye to eye with Opal.

"News flash, the world does not revolve around you. You do not get to act like a spoiled brat because you aren't getting your way," Vivian scolded. "Daddy and I wanted to spend a special day with you. We were going to take you horseback riding as a treat, then the beach, but no longer. When we get to the room, you may sit and color all day, or look out the window all day. Or pout all day. You will be bored, but because of your bad behavior, I don't care."

The door opened, and a young couple stood back to allow them to leave. Opal looked at her mother, defiance oozing out of every pore, then looked at them. She opened her mouth and started screaming.

'I'd keep her getting up.' Vivian could hear her mother's voice clearly, and wished she could match whatever her mother had possessed that kept five sons and two daughters under tight control. If only.

They entered their room, and Opal skipped off as though nothing had happened. She'd embarrassed her mother, and so, she'd won. Again.

I should never have brought the child on this trip.

Thomas came in and raised his eyebrows in question.

"I'm so sorry, Thomas." Vivian grumbled. "The child is insufferable. Papa said once she has a pre-Copernican world view, and sadly, it's all too true."

Her husband gave her a quizzical look, so Vivian explained.

"She thinks the heavens revolve around her, and I refuse to take her out for a treat with her behaving like this. Anna's long gone. Even if we could find her, she deserves her day off too much to call her back."

"Then I have a solution," he said, drawing her near. "One of the staff offered to take care of her for the day."

"Hand her off to a stranger?" Vivian looked doubtful. "That wouldn't be fair to the stranger."

Thomas grinned. "The hotel manager vouched for the woman, says she babysits for hotel guests all the time. Plus, she saw Opal's little tantrum and still wants to do it."

"Will this woman insist on giving her back before she turns eighteen?"

Her husband laughed. "She was very specific about only watching Opal until this evening. Sorry. I have already canceled the horses, and have a surprise in store. The manager is a miracle worker, and he has arranged a special day for the two of us."

Within minutes, they had a picnic lunch packed, and a taxi waiting at the hotel entry.

"Hello, hello," the driver said, with broad swipes of his arms. "I am best taxi driver in Athens. Best also tour guide. Famous guide. I am George. I take you now. Come on, come on."

George hustled them into his cab – an American Willys, left over from WWII, still Khaki green, with the circled star on the hood.

They bounced along for hours, stopping here and there for Famous-George-the-Tour-Guide to show them the wonders of Greece. There were many such spots, but they finally reached their destination in the late afternoon.

As they rounded a bend, George grew quiet, his constant stream of conversation muted. To their left, the island of Kia, and the sea stretching on to the horizon. To their right, the Peloponnese lay in the hazy distance, majestic in its grandeur and deep history. They were coming to the most southern tip of the Attic peninsula – Cape Sounion.

Thomas took her hand and squeezed. In front of them, rising against the blue backdrop of the Aegean Sea, the mighty Temple of Poseidon perched on the high, craggy cliff, overlooking the sea god's vast domain.

When George parked, he handed them their picnic basket. "Stay for sunset. Very romantic. I go to beach and wait. No problem. I have friends to wait. You go. You go."

Thomas and Vivian sat on a boulder, not far from the car, and soaked in their surroundings, while George tromped off to places unknown.

Before they started exploring, Vivian rummaged through the contents of the basket, and realized there was more than enough to cover a snack and dinner, plus plenty of water, and a bottle of wine.

They spent the afternoon and evening weaving among the tall columns, scrambling over the tumbledown remains of walls and roofing, or sitting on the steps and gazing out over the sea.

It was breathtaking. Vivian could almost see King Menelaus and the Spartan ships, sails tall and proud, as they made their way to Troy, pausing to give homage to Poseidon as they passed beneath the shadow of his temple.

As the sun sank, and the sky was painted with swaths of orange, pink, and gold, Vivian laid her head on Thomas' shoulder and breathed in the beauty of it all.

Then, as the sky darkened, they both stood, glasses filled with the last of the wine, and raised them high in tribute.

"To the wine dark sea," Thomas said.

"To the wine dark sea."

~2019~

"We sailed home on the Queen Mary. She was a beautiful ship, and held so much inspiring history of her own. At any rate, there you go. I've taken a great deal of your time, Seth," Vivian said. "I do hope you didn't mind my taking so long."

"Not at all. It was fascinating," Seth responded with enthusiasm.

"Thank you. Now," Vivian turned to Tia. "Tell me about your interview. No need to go into detail about the other subject," she cast a glance at Seth. "I can read it in both your eyes."

"It went well," Tia said. "He said he'd meet with some others and set a date for an oral board, and if I pass, there'll be a psych review, then some head scratching, the usual. But he seemed pleased with our talk, and I sure was."

"That's wonderful news," Vivian said. "Now, before you go, let's make sure of which charms we covered." She fingered each one to the side and she named them. "English crown, the beer stein, the Burg Hornberg shield, and the Caryatid muses, from the Erechtheion Temple on the Acropolis. Yes, we've done well."

Vivian carefully dropped the bracelet back into the pouch, and handed it to Tia. "That'll do for today, and tomorrow there's going to be a luncheon for all the new arrivals, of which there is only one this week. Me. I shall be lavishly feted, I'm sure, although I do hope all those old people will be able to stand the strain of such a wild party. Perhaps you can drop by the day after? Let me know. I'll be here."

CHAPTER NINETEEN

"I WAS THINKING WE COULD TAKE A ROAD TRIP, GO SEE SOME sights," Seth said, a slice of pizza hovering near his mouth. "I've got another six days left on my administrative leave. Sound good?"

"Sounds great. Do they make wine around here?" Tia asked. "We could do a winery tour."

Seth took some time to finish his bite, but by the look on his face, she could tell her idea wasn't hitting a home run.

"No wine?"

He swallowed and shook his head. "Oh, there's wine. There's plenty of wine, but now I think of it, I've been wanting to do something more like a distillery tour. I've always wanted to visit Lynchburg."

Tia wrinkled her nose. "I'm a Scotch girl."

Seth looked stunned and dropped his slice of pizza on his plate. "Blasphemy! I don't think I can be seen with you anymore."

She laughed and flicked some of her beer at him. "We could compromise. Some wine, some whisky? You could try to persuade me to come over to the dark side."

"Done."

Tia's phone buzzed, and she turned it over to see who was calling.

She looked at Seth and frowned. "Work. My boss. I've gotta take this."

Seth nodded, then crooked his neck toward the bathrooms, and let her have her space.

"Hey, Steve. How are you? What's up?"

"Good, good, how're you? He asked, without waiting for an answer. "So, I was contacted for a character reference yesterday. A Lieutenant Hollings?"

"Oh, yea." Tia squirmed inwardly. *Damn!* This was not how she wanted them to find out.

"Care to elaborate? Are we losing you?"

"I...I honestly don't know. Right now I'm testing the waters, seeing what they have to offer, trying to figure out if this is a move I want to make," Tia replied. "I'm being straight with you. My great-grandmother asked me to consider it, and for her sake, I am. That's all—"

Seth slid back into his spot.

"That's all it is for now," she finished. But it only took a single heartbeat to realized she was blowing smoke, at her boss, and at her own feelings. That *wasn't* 'all it was right now.' Not by a long shot. She thought of the list she'd made, and she knew. She was certain.

"How long do you expect this leave to last?" Steve asked. "No pressure, but honestly, we need you back. We're short-handed, you know that."

"I know, and I appreciate it. I'll get my ducks lined up and give you a call tomorrow with something firm, okay?" Tia asked.

"Okay, talk to you then."

Tia put her phone in her pocket.

Seth leaned on his elbows and gave her a questioning

look. "Problem?"

"No," she answered honestly. "No problem, just terror. Sheer terror."

Seth had a look of concern on his face. "What's going on?"

"It seems I've been drifting while I've been here."

With furrowed brows, Seth took her hand. "Drifting? How do you mean? Drifting doesn't sound good. Drifting, as in, just passing time? Not being serious? What?"

"Drifting," Tia answered slowly, allowing her thoughts to coalesce. "Drifting, as in, I'm happy, everything is so right, so easy, I don't even have to try. I'm...happy, peaceful, like, in my heart peaceful."

Seth suppressed a smile, but he couldn't suppress the sparkle of delight in his eyes.

"Clarification?"

Tia took a deep breath, put both hands flat on the table, and looked him in the eye. "Clarification is: I'm in love. And I feel like I'm home. This is where I belong, where I need to spend my life. I know it."

"Damn, when the girl has something to say," Seth said. "So this love thing extends to...?"

She leaned in and smiled her best Cheshire smile. "It extends to the South, and Greenville in particular. It extends to GG, for sure. And..."

Seth leaned in, too, and wiggled his eyebrows at her. "And?"

"Naomi, Stephanie and Rob. Yep, love 'em all."

"You're not getting another slice of pizza until I hear—"

"You, Seth," Tia said, her voice husky. "I love you. I am crazy in love with you."

Seth leaned back with a happy smile, and lopped an arm over the chair next to him. "Then I guess you'd better pass your psych eval."

Tia started laughing. "Way to take the pressure off!"

Grinning, Seth went to the counter and paid the bill. When he came back, he offered Tia his hand, and she accepted.

When he pulled her next to him, he'd lost his smile. He was all business. "I love you, too, Tia."

Tia let her weight press against him. "Seth Lowe. As scared as this kind of honesty makes me, the truth will out. You've got my heart."

The pizza place was full of teenagers, and they were all gaping and making catcalls over the Seth/Tia spectacle. Time to go.

Outside, Seth leaned in and asked. "You want to come to my place, tonight? I'll pack, then we can stop by Altamont in the morning to get your things. Take off from there?"

"The big chez Seth reveal!" Tia said. "Are you in town, or out?"

"Out. Same general direction as Rob and Stephanie's place."

"Then let's go." She linked arms with Seth and they headed for his truck.

They drove in a companionable silence, Tia appreciating the evening lights, and rolling landscape. As they left town, there were fewer lights, and it was hard to make out much of anything beyond the car's headlights.

Seth gave a wide swath to a car waiting along the side of the road, which pulled out after they'd passed.

"This is my drive," Seth said, slowing and turning on his indicator. He made the turn onto a gravel drive. "It's a long one, but I have it bulldozed once a year, so potholes are minimal."

After they made the turn, Tia spotted car lights in her side view mirror. "Are you expecting someone?"

Seth checked his rearview. "I see him, and no. Nobody

has any business on my driveway but me. Did I correctly detect a weapon at the small of your back?"

"Yes."

"Good. Get it out, please." Seth pulled out his own weapon and set it in his lap, then handed his phone to Tia. "Here, call the dispatch number, and let them know what's going on. No need to think crazy. Just precautionary."

Tia dialed.

"Hey, Seth, thanks for calling back. We've been trying to get a hold of you."

"Hi, this is Tia, Seth's girlfriend." Despite the tension, the words made her smile. "He had me call as a precaution. We're on his private driveway, and there's an unknown vehicle following us."

"Put me on speaker," the dispatcher said, all business. "Okay? I'm sending a car your way. Please advise Seth he was doxxed this afternoon. His personal information is all over the web. Him, Rob, and the others involved in last week's shooting. The vehicle following you is not one of ours. Be careful. It could be nothing. It could be bad. Copy?"

"We copy," Seth said. "Thanks. There are two of us in my personal vehicle. No description of the other vehicle other than a dark, older model four door sedan. Nothing on the driver, or how many there are."

"Copy. Backup is on the way, Code three."

"I'm at the house right now. I'll leave the phone on so you can keep track. Tia, grab the flashlight out of the consol."

They slowed, and Seth made a sharp U-Turn, and came to a halt facing the other driver. He put the truck in park, but didn't turn it off.

Tia found two flashlights, and grabbed both, shoving them into her waistband.

The suspect car stopped about twenty yards short of the

house, but they couldn't see much, since the headlights from both vehicles were blinding.

"They're not making contact. This is officially not good," Seth warned, loud enough for the dispatcher to hear. "Tia, get into the foot well. I'm climbing into the back seat, then I'll open the rear passenger door. The interior will light up, so we both need to stay low. When I give the word, open your door. We'll both get out on your side. Once we're out, we'll run like hell. There's a gravel path through the lawn at your door, but don't use it. It'll make too much noise. Get onto the grass. There's a big Magnolia about tens yards out where we can take cover."

"Got it." Gun in hand, Tia waited for his go-ahead. The door opened and the cabin lit up.

"Go!"

Shots pelted the windshield, and they both slid out of the truck, staying low. She knelt behind the protection her door offered, until she felt Seth's tap on her shoulder. They both took off at a sprint.

Once behind the tree, Seth shouted, "Greenville Police. Put down your gun!"

"Piss off, asshole!" came the response. It was a woman. Another series of shots rang out, and they both hit the ground. Trees worked for visual cover. As cover from bullets, not so much.

"I'm good," Tia whispered.

"Me, too. Sounded like she hit my truck plenty, though," Seth said from behind clenched teeth. "I'm officially pissed off."

He stood, positioned behind the tree, then shook his head. "I can see a little movement, but not much. I think there's only one, and she's behind her car."

Tia kept checking their surroundings for any movement

closer in. "Is there a way to get behind her without being noticed?"

Seth turned and flashed her a grin. "Yes. Hold on." He crouched and swept the ground with his hand, then stood when he found a fist-sized rock. He threw it at the far side of the suspect car, which drew fire, then he grabbed Tia's hand and ran for the cover in the opposite direction.

They were soon in a wooded area, twigs whipping at their faces and bodies as they advanced. Once they were well inside, Seth stopped, and whispered in her ear.

"We're on a trail. It's narrow, so hold the back of my coat and follow my lead. It comes out at about the halfway point of the driveway. We'll be about thirty yards behind her."

Tia nodded, and they started along the path.

Two more shots, and the sound of breaking glass.

Seth increased his speed slightly, but he couldn't go too fast in the deep dark.

Finally, they came to a rise, their feet finding gravel, instead of dirt.

Three more shots hit metal, wood, glass. "Come out here, coward!" their attacker screamed.

"Sonofa..." Seth muttered angrily. "You have the flashlight?"

"Yes, two. There was a big Mag, and a tactical."

He took the tactical light, then looked at her. "How do you want to do this, Officer?"

Tia kept the big light under her waist band at the small of her back, and scanned the area, but could make out very little. Some distance down the drive, the glow of the car lights was easy to spot. The suspect could be seen moving on the near side of the drive.

"Go in dark. She'll be backlit as we approach," Tia whispered. "Easy prey. If she hears us, I don't think she'll be able to see much when she turns around. She'll be light blind.

Let's go up, one on each side of the driveway. If she sprints, we tackle."

"Copy."

They looked at each other with understanding. Seth used two fingers to point, side to side. They were a go.

Tia crossed to the far side of the driveway, and they made their way as quietly as they could. Even so, to Tia's ears, the crunch of each footstep sounded like they were announcing themselves with claxons.

As they neared the suspect vehicle, Tia could see a figure pacing behind the car. She was looking in the direction of Seth's truck, unaware of any movement behind her.

Suddenly, the figure raised her arms and fired three more shots. Seth's truck seemed to be the target of choice.

"Fuck you, Lowe!" she screamed. "I hate you! Die, motherfucker. Die!"

Tia hurried forward, counting as she went. At least a dozen shots fired. She had an idea, and signaled Seth. She pulled out the flashlight and showed it to him. He nodded his understanding. She tucked her gun in her waistband.

Fifteen feet. Ten feet. Seth raised his hand, and tossed another rock, which hit the front of the woman's car. Three more shots rang out.

Great. Psycho's got a freaking multiple mags, Tia realized, and got ready. She gave Seth a nod.

"Greenville Police," Seth shouted, keeping low and out of sight. "Drop your weapon, or I'll shoot!"

The woman spun toward the sound of Seth's voice, gun raised, and Tia swung with everything she had.

Five minutes later, the sound of sirens lit the night. Seconds after that, three patrol cars screamed in, to find Seth and Tia sitting on the trunk of the suspect's car. The suspect lay on the ground, wrists zip-tied at her back.

When the officers got out, Seth waved them over.

"Thanks, Jen," he said to the dispatcher, and shoved the phone in his pocket.

"EMTs have staged at the bottom of the drive," one of the officers said, then shook their hands. "Mike Almada."

Before Tia could respond, Seth made the introductions. "Tia Benson. Potential lateral recruit."

Mike nodded. "Cool. So, who've we got, here? I'm guessing Sissy Carter?"

"Yep. Marty's girlfriend," Seth replied. "Guess she wasn't too happy her guy decided to shoot at cops last week. Thought she could do a better job, or finish the job, maybe. Mostly she shot my truck, and my house. She was alone. Medics can come in."

"That's rough. She get hit?" Mike asked, then keyed his mic and called for the aid car to roll in.

Tia waved the flashlight. "Yes, with this. She has a nasty knot on her head, and I think she broke a couple of teeth when she hit the ground. But she was swearing fluently right before you got here, so I think she'll be fine."

"Better than getting shot," Mike huffed. "I need to take your official statements, then you can get out of here. Or, if your truck is out of service, we can get a car brought out here for you. Or, maybe you're planning on staying here tonight?"

He looked at Seth and tried to act nonchalant, but his gaze flickered to Tia.

"I'll check on my truck and let you know."

Tia smiled at Seth's non-answer. "You go check the truck. I'll give my statement."

The truck was functional, so after giving statements, patching the house, and gathering some clothes, they spent the night at Altamont. Neither wanted to chance another doxxing visit. They would drop the truck at a body shop the next morning, but both knew their whisky and wine trip was out the window.

Early the next morning, Seth and Tia went to see how Rob and Stephanie were doing. To avoid any uncertainties, they called ahead.

Rob met them at the door, his left arm in a sling, his right hand holding a gun. He stepped aside and let them in. "Welcome to Fort Knox. How's the truck?"

"Windshield's toast. Took out the driver's side mirror. Set a few in the grill, and one or two in the hood. House has some holes, too."

"Shit. Truck engine's okay?" Rob was surprised.

"She used a .22 semi-auto, if you can believe it. Enough punch to make for a hefty repair bill, not enough to do any significant damage, thankfully."

Rob looked at him with skepticism. "Sissy was the one who doxxed us? I find that hard to believe. She can barely remember her own name."

"They're trying to trace it. Somebody probably saw it online and gave her the info."

Stephanie came in and passed everyone a cup of coffee. "They're posting a patrol car outside at night, but the days are up to us to manage. Gives me the creeps."

"Come and stay at Altamont until this blows over," Tia offered. "There's plenty of room, as you know."

The two exchanged a look, but didn't respond right away. "Thank you," Stephanie said. "We'll talk and let you know, okay?"

They visited for a while longer, then Seth and Tia made to leave. "I have to go in to the station," Seth added. "Tia'll be with Vivian this morning. We'll see you when we see you. If you're coming, bring dinner."

Stephanie laughed and hugged her brother. "Thanks again. I'll let you know."

Tia dropped Seth at the station and went to see Vivian. He was going to get the use of an unmarked vehicle until his truck was fixed, so they planned to meet back at Altamont.

When she walked into Vivian's room, she was greeted by a smile that quickly faded.

"My dear, what's wrong? What's happened this time?" she asked.

It crossed Tia's mind to whitewash the truth a bit, but if there was anything she'd learned from Vivian's stories, it was that this woman had borne more than most, and kept on swinging.

"It's a long story, GG, but it ends well, so no worries," Tia stated.

"Then you tell me your story, today. Mine can wait."

Tia sat near the window, and Vivian joined her.

With a deep breath, Tia dove in. She told Vivian about the shooting the week before, giving her more details than either the nightly news, or Stephanie, had covered. She went on to explain doxxing, and the subsequent stalking and attempt on their lives.

"What will happen to the girl?" Vivian asked when Tia was done.

Tia shrugged. "She's not a girl. She's in her thirties, I'd guess. She has multiple warrants, she was high on meth at the time of her arrest, and almost everything she did, or was, or said last night, was a parole violation. She's a mess, and should get attempted murder twice over, plus a slew of other things. I doubt she'll see the sky again any time soon."

"Oh dear," Vivian said. "Well, she brought it on herself by choosing the lifestyle. We all have to live with the consequences of the choices we make. I'm glad you told me. There's one more thing, though."

Tia looked at her, expecting another story.

"Today is the newcomer's luncheon. I'll make sure they set an extra place for you."

CHAPTER TWENTY

THE WELCOMING CELEBRATION AT THE SENIOR HOME consisted of two introductions, Vivian's and Tia's, and some polite applause. No confetti. Not even a balloon bouquet. Tia was fairly certain most of the folks survived the excitement.

Back in the room, Vivian had tea, and Tia opted for ice water.

She pulled the velvet bag out of her pocket and handed it to Vivian.

Vivian drew it open, and spread the bracelet across her lap.

"How much time do you have, dear?"

"Plenty. Seth is going to meet me at Altamont. We'll both get there when we get there."

"Perfect," she said. "Then I shall tell you about the ship's wheel, the pineapple, and the next couple of years. It was a happy time, for the most part. Even though there weren't a lot of charms from that period, it was quite eventful, as you will see. At any rate..."

· · ·

~1953~

For their second anniversary, Thomas presented Vivian with a small box.

"Mind you," he warned. "If you say no, then you'll have to give it back."

Knowing full well the nature of the item within, Vivian was still full of curiosity. She couldn't think of anything in particular that might warrant a charm.

Vivian lifted the lid. Inside, nestled in cotton, was a ship's wheel charm. Confused, she asked, "You want to buy a yacht?"

Thomas laughed. "Viv, we have spent so much time studying Ancient Greece, the Romans, the ancient world in general, you and I, I thought we might try to gain even more understanding, draw closer to them, as it were, by learning to do what they did."

Vivian tilted her head and peered at him, but understanding wasn't forthcoming. "You want to take a cruise around Greece?"

"Yes, but what I'd truly like, is if we learned to sail, like the mariners of old, and charter boats ourselves." Thomas leaned forward eagerly. "What do you think? We could take sailing lessons, or boating, if you'd rather have a motor. There are classes out of Charleston harbor. I've already looked into it. We could start right away, and it might take us a year or so to become comfortably proficient enough to rent a boat in Greece, but it would be so exciting. What do you say?"

Vivian liked the adventure of it, but the practical side of her cautioned restraint.

"Remember the sunset at Cape Sounion, honey?" He hitched forward on his seat, and grasped her knees. "And the ships we saw, plying the waters of the wine dark sea? We could be them. We could sail upon the wine-dark sea. Viv, think about it!"

She remembered those ships, that moment, and suddenly the tiny spark of interest was a flame of aspiration. Vivian caught his excitement, and locked eyes with him.

"Yes, Thomas, yes, let's do it."

IN THE QUIET of the night, they would lie, side by side, and talk about the trip they would take, the ports they would visit, all in the pursuit of their shared passion – the ancient world. From then on, every weekend was spent on the water, at Foundation events, or with yet another hobby she'd taken up, photography.

Vivian also pursued a related branch of research while they learned to sail. She studied the known aspects of Greek and Roman sailing vessels, and the prevailing seasonal winds, currents, and tides of the region. With this knowledge in hand, they eagerly mapped out where they would go together, and which season would be the best.

They both tried to get Opal involved, but at eleven, her older cousins had her more interested in makeup, fashion, horses, and the Billboard Top 100. She preferred to pass her weekends with them in Abbeville, so Vivian and Thomas dropped her with Michael and Miriam when they left for their sailing lessons.

That fall, they took time off from sailing to pursue a sponsored dig site of an Etruscan village near Chiusi, Italy, then spent a week in Sorrento, before coming home. They made the round trip, New York to London, on a Pan Am Stratocruiser. It was thrilling, first class all the way, and very, very long.

"You've been quite secretive, my dear," Thomas noted at the outset of their return flight. He nudged her with his shoulder. "All these journals. Are you keeping a diary? I must say, it looks a bit more substantial than that, so I'm very curious. Do I get to know about it?"

Vivian put her pen on the service tray and took a deep breath. "Well, you're right, it's not a diary. It's, uh, I've had this idea about writing a paper for submission to the Antiquities Journal, or actually, well, as a precursor for a book. I didn't want to say anything until I felt confident about the ideas I was putting together."

She cast a glance at him. "What do you think? Am I crazy? I haven't the credentials, so perhaps I'm overstepping?"

Thomas half turned in his seat to look directly at her. "Credentials be damned. Did Plato have credentials? No! He had knowledge and wisdom. You are hugely intelligent, Vivian. And when you take something on, you do it with everything you possess. You never let uncertainty get in the way, and when you are passionate, nothing, bar nothing, stands in your way. I have every confidence you will succeed brilliantly."

Vivian glowed under his praise, and his heated scrutiny.

"Additionally, I have no doubt you shall be asked to head the AJ, before long, once they get a whiff of your expertise."

Vivian chuckled. "Thank you for your support, but you haven't seen a word I've written."

"I'll peruse it any time you ask, and make suggestions, if you'd like," he said. "But let me repeat, you know your stuff, so I have every confidence the content is top notch."

"Thank you, Thomas." She looked at him for a long moment, then smiled and rested her head against his shoulder. As she tucked her hands around his arm, her eyes drifted closed on a thought.

He is so good to me…

.   .   .

THEY GOT a chance to sail the wine-dark seas the following summer, and once again, Opal chose to remain home with her cousins and her grandfather.

On the surface, the relationship Vivian had with her daughter these days bordered on pleasant, even non-confrontational, but deep inside, it bothered Vivian that Opal never wanted to spend any personal time with her. Opal and Thomas were close, so Vivian couldn't help but feel there was some private, hidden, animosity her daughter bore toward her.

She'd even gone so far as to interview a child psychologist once, who suggested Opal's animosity was due to the death of her twin, and deep inside, the child was trying to make amends for the life taken, in order to justify her own. Vivian thought the woman a charlatan, and knew if she insisted Opal take sessions with her, the rift would widen and fester, never to be repaired.

Try as she might, Vivian couldn't bridge the gap. She shouldered the blame, yet refused to stop her life in order to make the girl happy.

If only Opal could come halfway...

IN THE SPRING OF 1954, Vivian published her first treatise on Ancient Greek Philosophy and the American Democratic Experiment. It was met with acclaim, and a publisher soon backed a book deal on the subject. She and Thomas celebrated by joining with Dr. Carl McCarthy and his wife, Esther, who kept a newly restored Dunkirk Little Ship, the *Nostos*, meaning 'The Homecoming,' at Piraeus. Together with a hired skipper/cook, the four friends were to spend six weeks cruising Greek waters, beginning with the west coast of the Peloponnese, then island-hopping east to Troy, before making a circuit of the Cyclades on their return.

. . .

VIVIAN SAT on the aft deck and tilted her face to the sun, a hand clamped firmly to the crown of her broad-brimmed sun hat. They were making their usual six knots cruising speed, and combined with the light starboard breeze and sea swell, she had to compete with several forces to keep the hat on her head. They'd left Aegina in the morning, and planned to drop anchor that night in a shallow cove at the western base of Cape Sounion.

On their honeymoon, they had picnicked in the shadow of Poseidon's Temple, which overlooked that rugged point of land, and dreamed of the eons of sailors who'd plied those waters – Homer's wine-dark sea. Tomorrow they would add their names to the list.

"You could be Elizabeth Taylor lounging on her yacht, with those big sunglasses, dark hair, and perfectly tiny body," Esther said in her very posh British accent, and proffered a glass of sparkling water. "I bloody hate you."

Vivian laughed and took the glass. "Thanks, twice, but you're the blond bombshell, which is all the rage right now."

"*Pfft*," Esther replied. She sat opposite Vivian, and picked up a magazine. "I've got two stone and ten years on you. I've left any bombshell qualities I may have had in my distant past."

"Every Greek man we've met so far would beg to differ."

"They eat squid, dear. Their standards are quite low."

Vivian grinned. She could not have imagined better companions for this trip. The McCarthy's were both avid and competent sailors, and both had a deep love for, and knowledge of Ancient Greek history. Best by far, though, was that the two couples got along so well. They were fast friends by the end of their first cocktail hour.

Whatever Esther claimed, she was a stunning thirty-something woman, with platinum blond hair. And she was slim. And she was irreverent. And the Greek men followed her around like adoring lapdogs.

"I've asked Tassos to fix a picnic dinner for us tonight," Vivian said. "I'll make sure he only packs dessert for the three of us. Can't do a thing about your advanced age, but at least you won't get any bigger. How much is a stone, anyway?"

Esther lowered her magazine and mock-glared at her. "Fourteen pounds."

"Ah, I see," Vivian put a finger to her lips and squinted, as though deep in thought. "You do have unusually large, flapping feet. Yes, the weight difference must be your feet—"

Two of Esther's ice cubes pelted her torso, and both women laughed.

That evening, Thomas and Vivian watched the sun set over the Peloponnese from Cape Sounion for a second time, and enjoyed sharing the moment with the McCarthys. The next morning, bathed in the glow of the warm, morning sun, they all saluted Poseidon as they rounded the cape and cruised past.

They each raised a glass of Ouzo to his temple, then poured the drink overboard. They'd done the same when they first left port in Piraeus – it was always a good idea to keep the god of the sea happy when venturing into his domain – but this moment took on special significance since they were at the foot of his most hallowed home.

Gazing at the scene, Thomas wrapped his arm around Vivian's waist, and put his mouth next to her ear. "I never imagined this for my life. We were both set on completely different courses, with completely different people, and happy, so happy. And yet, here we are, happier still."

Vivian leaned her head against his chin, and thought about Harold, and what their life together would have been, had he lived. Nothing like this one, certainly, and yet, happy, as Thomas said.

"We were meant to be together, Vivian. How else to explain this? And we shall make the best of it. We shall do things worthy of this gift of each other, and worthy of the sacrifices of those we loved."

She looked at him. "Yes, we shall. We are."

By the end of the week they arrived at Çanakkale, mere miles from the site of Homer's Troy. They spent several days climbing over the site, photographing, writing, and reading excerpts from the Iliad. It was breathtaking and humbling. They walked the outline of the ramparts, and thought of brave Hector, a prince of Troy. Slain by Achilles, his body was dragged before his people in a gluttony of hubris and bloodlust.

Vivian kicked at the dry, dusty, hard-packed earth, once soaked to mud with the blood of Greeks, Trojans, and demigods. She then looked toward the sea, and wondered where, exactly, Achilles had stood athwart the gap, gleaming in his armor, in order to strike fear in his enemies, and encourage his men.

They spent their last night together sitting on a beach, and ordered a bottle of champagne from a local merchant. It took nearly two hours for the poor man to drive his moped to the nearest town, in order to procure such an extravagant item.

The drink was warm, and yet, just right, when they opened the bottle.

Quiet reflection, contemplation.

Perfection.

Back onboard the *Nostos*, all were quiet, wrapped in their own thoughts.

Tassos had served them a wonderful dinner, and made the rounds with dessert, port, and brandy.

Vivian knew he would retire to his berth after this, but had a question she wanted a Greek, not a scholar, to answer.

"Tassos, tell me what you think of Homer, and of Achilles," she asked. "I'm familiar with the scholarly works, but what of Greek lore, Greek heart, the legends you pass on among yourselves, outside the universities?"

Tassos looked wary. He was friendly and gregarious, but kept anything personal at arm's length.

He shrugged. "Eh, men, gods, war."

"Have you ever read Homer?" Vivian persisted.

She saw the others shift uncomfortably, and realized she might be stepping on sensitivities.

"I don't mean literally," she looked at Tassos pleadingly. "We all have our noses in books, but you, you live your legends every day. You are the descendants, the living blood-line, of every single story we slave over. I thought you must carry on stories, parent to child, about your famed past. What are those stories? What are the stories you tell about yourselves?"

Grizzly Tassos, with his black cap, and lavish, salt-and-pepper moustache, was always full of laughter and grand gestures, tall tales, and humorous anecdotes. Yet now, he seemed to be struck dumb by her inquiry.

Vivian placed her hand on his. "I'm sorry if I've made you uncomfortable, but academicians live in lofty towers, and take little account of the everyman, and...and sailors in particular." She shot an apologetic glance at the others. "I was raised on a farm. I milked cows. We have stories of the South before, during, and after our war between the states. They are very different than what the textbooks give you. They are personal. I thought you might have your own stories, your own...recollections, of the Trojan War."

Tassos looked at each person, gauging his audience, then shrugged. "We have many stories," he said, spreading his hands wide. "If you like, I tell you, but," he held a finger in the air with a smile, "the price is Ouzo, much Ouzo, which may mean a very late start in the morning!"

Carl and Esther had no problem sleeping in late, but begged off on the Ouzo-fueled storytelling. Thomas only lasted a half hour. Vivian was enthralled.

She wrote furiously, asked questions, and poured liberally, since Tassos evidently felt it wasn't his place to pour his own drinks from their stores.

The following morning, Vivian could recall, with some effort, seeing the hands of the clock in the Nav. center hovering somewhere near 2:00am, as she stumbled toward her stateroom.

Feeling ill, she refused Thomas' offer of coffee. With heavy eyelids, she noticed several fresh notepads lying on a shelf, which sparked interest, but the interest was not nearly enough to battle her hangover, or thwart her succumbing to a prolonged morning nap.

The rest of the voyage passed with unending thrills of discovery, poignant vistas, and stunning, historical absolutes. Battlegrounds, past glories, volcanic cataclysms, and peoples beyond count, who lived, loved, suffered, and died, in the deep depths of time.

Several days later, with dusk falling, they neared the island of Serifos, exhausted from an hours-long struggle against the Meltemi winds. They entered the port and found it, and the few moorage buoys it offered, full. It was a port of choice for taking shelter.

Their only options were to continue on to the next island, hours away, or tie off on the seaward, or external side of the breakwater. It was the logical choice, since the Meltemies blew out of the north, and the seaward side was sheltered and calm. However, there were no mooring buoys to hook up to out there, only the boulders of the breakwater.

Tassos and the others looked at one another. Their options were unpleasant.

"We can head back to Sifnos, with the wind behind us, but the sea swells will be behind us as well, which is not good." Tassos inclined his head and lifted his shoulders. "Or we may go on to Kythnos, but it will be dark long before we arrive. I leave it to you."

The two couples looked at one another, unwilling to make the call.

Finally, Vivian put her hands on her hips. "I say we tie off to this side of the breakwater."

"How do you propose we accomplish it?" Carl asked. "There is nothing we can tie to."

"It's calm enough on this side," Vivian answered. "And there are plenty of boulders to tie off to." She looked at Tassos. "Do we have line long enough to reach?"

He shrugged. "Yes, of course."

Thomas looked at her. "What are you getting at?"

Vivian looked him square in the eyes. "I will dive in and swim onto the breakwater. You toss me a couple of lines, and I'll secure them around the boulders. Then you can drop an aft anchor to two, in case the winds shift in the night."

Tassos smiled.

"I'm not comfortable with the idea," Carl said.

"No!" Esther said vehemently. "No damned way. That's suicide."

Vivian looked at her, eyes wide. "How is it suicide? I've swum in every river, lake, and puddle I could find since I was a kid. We're holding at fifty feet from the breakwater. The water is nearly flat on this side. This is easy. I'll barely get wet." She looked to Thomas for support. "It won't be an issue, and it'll be easier on all of us, if I do. I definitely don't want to continue on to the next island in the dark with these winds. I don't think *that* would be wise."

Esther gaped at her.

Vivian understood. Esther obviously feared for her friend, and swimming wasn't in her wheelhouse. Because her knowledge was minimal, her fright was pronounced.

Regardless, Vivian stood firm. "Look, if you prefer, I'll wear a life vest, and you can attach a lifeline to haul me in if I get in trouble, but I'm going in."

"She's a strong swimmer," Thomas added. "I don't think she'll have any problem, at all, and I'd also prefer to tie up here, instead of going on."

The McCarthys reluctantly backed off their misgivings, but Vivian caught a wink and glimpse of approval from Tassos.

Vivian got ready, then grabbed her camera and handed it to Esther. "Don't worry, Es. It'll be fine. Just take a picture, will you? I want photographic evidence, so I can brag when we get home."

Unsure of the depth of the boulders, or how far out they were piled, she jumped from amidships, then easily made her way to a slippery, but solid, foothold.

Vivian raised her arms in victory and posed for pictures, then a line was tossed.

Once she caught the line and secured it around a boulder, she accepted, and tied off a second line, before swimming back to the boat. A pair of aft anchors were set, and they were good for the night.

The next morning, they were able to tie up inside the breakwater, and after a couple of days of rest, they took off for two nights on Hydra, and only one week left in their cruise.

On their last night before heading back to Piraeus, they moored at Epidaurus, and attended a play by the Greek playwright, Euripides, in the ancient, open air amphitheater.

With a full moon rising overhead, it was a magical end to a perfect holiday.

WHEN THOMAS and Vivian finally arrived at the farm in Abbeville, they were surprised to see Michael's car parked in the drive. Dread filled Vivian's heart. He wasn't supposed to drop Opal home until the following day.

They got their luggage out, and made their way to the front door. It swung open to reveal her father, sporting a dark expression.

"What's going on, Papa?" Vivian asked.

Michael came around the corner, his expression equally concerning.

Thomas left the luggage in the entry and guided Vivian into the living room.

"Something has happened," Thomas said. "Michael, Thierry, what is it? What has happened?"

Michael stepped forward and put a hand on his father's arm. "Papa, let me explain. It was my house, after all."

He squared off on his sister and brother-in-law. "We will not have Opal at our house anymore. Besides being rude and disruptive, which we're accustomed to, it turns out she snuck boys and booze onto the property all summer long, a fact we've only recently discovered. She flaunted our rules, which are not for her alone, as she likes to believe, but for anyone under our roof. Last night she talked my daughter, Sally, into sneaking out of the house. They took Miriam's car, without permission mind you, and went into town, where they met two local hoodlum boys. They all started drinking, and in a drunken stupor, they went for a joyride."

Vivian sat with a thud, stunned. Thomas stood beside her, and put a comforting hand on her shoulder.

"I found all this out when an Abbeville police officer

arrived at the house before dawn this morning, and informed us all four were in jail, and the car was being towed out of a ditch."

Horror washed over her, and Vivian put her head in her hands. "She can't drive. She won't turn twelve for three more days. How can she be drinking?" She looked at her brother. "Are you sure it wasn't Sally? I mean, she's fourteen…"

She instantly knew it was the wrong thing to say, and put her hand out to fend off a wrathful retort from her brother. She knew Sally was not the instigator. These antics had Opal written all over them.

"I'm sorry, I didn't mean it. Of course it was Opal. I'm trying to understand, make sense, oh my God, I'm so sorry."

"Were you able to bring Sally home?" Thomas asked.

"Yes, I bailed them both out. I took my daughter home before coming here. She confessed to quite a lot on the ride out from town. Told me about all the goings on this summer. She is contrite. Opal was furious with her for telling, and cursed, actually cursed at her, at both of us, several times. You must understand our position. We will not have Opal in our house ever again, and I refused to even let her go inside to gather her belongings. She is not welcome. Miriam is gathering her things, and I will bring them to you tomorrow."

"Understood," Thomas replied. "Please know we are fully on your side, and of course we will cover any costs incurred. We are shaken and appalled. Tell me about the boys. What do you know of them? Do you have their names? Ages?"

Michael handed over some paperwork. "It's all in there. The boys are both fifteen. I can't…" his voice faltered, and he ran a hand through his hair in frustration. "When I think…" He shook his head, obviously distraught. "Miriam is questioning Sally very closely, very personally. We have to make sure those boys didn't take advantage…"

Vivian was miserable, weeping, her spirit crushed. It dawned on her drastic measures were in order, and the thought was daunting.

Ashamed, she stood, took her brother's hand, and apologized to him for all the hurt Opal had caused.

"I will do everything I can, whatever I can, to set things right," she said. "I'm sorry we've abused the kindness you've shown to her over the years. Somehow, I thought she only behaved badly toward me, but I find, far too late it seems, that is not the case."

She looked at Thomas. "We've been sweeping this under the rug, hoping it will get better. We have to do something. She needs to go somewhere that will do her some good."

They all looked at one another. To send a child away was a drastic step, but each saw in the other, the knowledge, the certainty, that it was necessary.

Sunnyvale School for Girls was north of Columbus. It was a boarding school for troubled girls. They were strict disciplinarians, and kept the girls on a rigid schedule. There were no phone privileges, and any letters written or received were read by staff before they were passed along. The girls rose early, and went to bed early. They wore uniforms, went to every class, studied, and took physical exercise under stern supervision. There were no televisions or radios, and weekends were spent on premises. Their choices for passing any leisure time were reading approved books, studying, or more exercise. There were no exceptions, and absolutely no coddling.

Opal was enrolled the next day, and dropped off on her birthday, two days after that. Vivian wanted so desperately to hug her, to get a hug in return, as they stood in the principal's office and signed the papers, but it was not to be.

Opal glared at her, and as one of the staff led her out the door, Opal turned around and stuck out her middle finger. "I hate you."

Thomas supported Vivian as they walked out the door and got into the car. She cried all the way back to Abbeville.

OPAL WAS to remain at the school for an entire year, with no visitations. An evaluation would be made then, and she could be released to return home, or she might continue at the school. Some girls stayed until they graduated.

Vivian wrote to Opal once a week. It was the maximum correspondence allowed. She talked about the farm, and all the goings on in the family and around town. She tried to sound upbeat, but it was difficult, and her letters rang false, even to her ears.

She never got a letter in return.

The school sent detailed reports once a month, with pictures, and examples of classwork. Some of the photos were candid shots, and sometimes they could see Opal in the crowd. They never saw a smile. Her expressions, in the photos she was aware were being taken, were angry and fierce.

The school got high marks from officials, and was carefully monitored, and they had a policy of never using corporal punishment. Still, Vivian worried. She wanted her daughter home. She wanted her happy and well.

Over the course of the year, Vivian dropped twenty pounds from her already slim figure, and she knew Thomas worried about her, as much as she worried about Opal.

BY THE FOLLOWING SUMMER, with three months of Opal's schooling left to go, Thomas was desperate.

One Sunday morning their phone rang, and Thomas quickly grabbed the receiver, as though he'd been anticipating the call. With a mumbled word or two, he drew Vivian over and handed her the ear piece with a big grin.

"It's for you, dear."

She put the phone to her ear. "Hello?"

"Vivi?"

Vivian looked at Thomas with wide eyes. "Lucy? Is that you? Where are you?"

"I'm in London, silly," she giggled. "I miss my big sister. You must come visit. You've never met my husband, or my babies, and I haven't met Thomas. I simply can't go on without you. Please, please, please come. Say you will. Check Thomas's front pocket, and tell me you will."

Vivian looked at Thomas, then noticed papers sticking out of the front pocket of his sweater.

He pulled them out, unfolded them, and handed them over to her.

"Have you looked, Vivi?" Lucille asked. "Say yes! I can't stand the suspense!"

"These are..." Vivian was reading as fast as she could.

"They are tickets to London for next week, silly! Let me hear you say yes."

A smile swept across Vivian's face, and warmth seeped throughout her body. They were going to visit Lucille.

"Yes, yes, yes!" she exclaimed.

~2019~

Dinner chimes sounded in the corridor. Tia sat quietly and watched the memories, and the sentiments they brought, wash over Vivian's face. Finally, her eyes focused and she came back to the present.

"We spent a month with Lucille," she said, with a wistful

smile. "It was wonderful. No ruins, or history, or travel. Just us. I couldn't have asked for more. A week before we left, Papa rang to say the school had called, and Opal was doing so well, they anticipated releasing her to us at the end of her year. I was over the moon, and it proved to be true. She seemed much improved, and we were all delighted to have her home."

"I'm so happy to hear," Tia said. "I was worried I'd never hear about any good times between you. It must've been wonderful."

"It was," Vivian confirmed.

"And about your dive into the sea to tie off the boat. Incredible. I bet you'd do in again, even now, wouldn't you," Tia asked with a smile.

Vivian nodded. "In here," she tapped her head. "In here, I am still the exact same person. Unfortunately, my body has chosen to take account of the years, even though my brain doesn't pay attention to such things."

"Out of sorrow, joy," Tia said. "You've said it before, and that's what Thomas was referring to on the boat, wasn't it?"

"Yes. It's hard to reconcile the two. Survivor's guilt, I suppose." Vivian sighed. "But we must keep on living. We can't simply stop, just because others around us have had to."

"From what Naomi and Stephanie have told me, you did write the book."

"Yes, and several others, along with innumerable articles, treatises, etc., etc. Yes, my published work is rather well known, in certain circles, and I'm quite proud of it, actually."

"As you should be," Tia said. "Did you ever cruise Greece again?"

"Many times," Vivian replied. "We always hired Tassos. Twice more with the McCarthys, and three times sailing with others. There were also several sailing trips in the Caribbean. That's where the pineapple charm came from. St.

Vincent and the Grenadines. Lovely area. Absolutely beautiful, and the people so warm and welcoming."

"Well, GG," Tia said, and stood. "I'll walk you to dinner. I wouldn't want you to starve, or be left to beg door to door for a crust of bread."

Vivian put the bracelet in the pouch and handed it to Tia. "I have one last little story to tell you while we walk."

Tia grabbed her jacket and they went into the hall.

"My father passed away early in 1956. The farm went to Earl's widow. It was their child's inheritance, after all. She remarried and had other children, but the farm is still in the family, still run by Earl's descendants."

They stopped at the door to the dining room, where there seemed to be a sea of white hair. Vivian patted Tia's hand. "We bought Altamont after Papa passed. It was a shambles, but we moved in right away, and lived among the construction while we restored it. It was such fun. Even Opal liked it. There were a few years between the boarding school and college, when things were better, so much better. At any rate, the restoration fired her imagination, and she became a good painter, an even better plumber, and she could wield a hammer and saw like no other, if you can believe it, even at such a young age. Those were the very, very best days."

CHAPTER TWENTY-ONE

Tia sat beside Seth in the Greenville police chief's office and fidgeted with the cuffs on her too-new white button down. It was time to fish, or cut bait. She had been in Greenville for nearly a month, and she was taking advantage of her own department's patience with her extended leave. Vivian was well, and moved in to her new home. There were no more excuses for staying.

Yep. Fish or cut bait.

They'd given statements, and gone over the events of the encounter on Seth's driveway multiple times, but t's and i's needed to be taken care of at all levels, including Chief Pearson's.

How awkward to be in an officer-involved shooting, while applying for a job.

The chief leaned back in his chair.

"You both handled the situation well," Pearson said. "Tweaker out of her head and gunning for you. A shooting in self-defense could have been justified, but you handled it without firing a shot."

They both responded with a brief nod of acknowledgement.

"So," Pearson turned his gaze on Tia.

She could see the assessing in his gray-blue eyes, could practically hear the cogs of decision-making going on in his head. He was fifty-something, she guessed, had no hair left on the top of his head, yet hadn't succumbed to 'bicking it,' as in, doing the full head shave. His skin was weathered beyond his years, so, he looked older than he probably was. Regardless, he was obviously fit, and didn't look as though riding a desk was a natural part of his comfort zone. He still had it, she was sure, and having a chief who wasn't all about the politics was as good as it got.

Tia smiled. Was he trying to gauge her discomfort with this long pause?

"So, sir?" she reversed the enquiry.

"So, Lt. Hollins is very complimentary of you, and recommends we move forward in the hiring process," he said. "However, he did mention your department was surprised to hear of your plans to move here. It's a big step. Are you serious about pursuing this? Or would you rather take more time to think about it?"

"I am very serious, Sir," Tia replied with confidence. "I was planning on having a conversation with them, but the shooting stepped all over those plans. I need to have the same conversation with my parents, although they've already guessed as much."

"And if the position here isn't offered? What then?"

"I'll stay," she said simply. "This is home now. It's…it fits. It's right. If this department doesn't pan out, I'll look to a county hire, or maybe something in one of the smaller towns in the area. I'm a cop. It's what I want to continue doing, so here, or somewhere close by, but this is my home now."

The chief smiled, stood, and held out his hand. "Very well,

then. We'll be in touch."

They all shook hands, and Tia left with Seth.

"I'm going back to Altamont," Tia said, as they left the station. "Like I told the chief, I have a couple of calls to make, and I doubt they'll be short ones."

Seth gave her a kiss on the temple. "Take your time. I'm back on rotation this afternoon, so I want to get out to the house and fix a few things before I start."

"Okay. I'll be with GG this afternoon. Call me if you want to come over after shift."

"Will do," Seth said, and headed for his loaner car, then stopped and turned around. "Hey."

Tia looked at him.

"Couldn't be happier about your decision," he said with a smile.

She grinned. "Me too."

She got into her car, her smile lingering. She couldn't wait to see the look on GG's face when she told her the decision she'd made.

~1964~

Opal sat on the back porch at Altamont with several college friends. They were all smoking, and listening to a very slender young man Vivian didn't recognize, bang away on bongos.

Her daughter was popular, with her dark hair, worn in a flip, and her blue eyes with heavy, wingtip eyeliner. Throughout high school she'd had dozens of girlfriends streaming in and out of the house, though Vivian hadn't seen most of them more than once or twice. They didn't seem to stick, for whatever reason. The boys, by contrast, seemed to stick a little too well, until Opal tired of them, and gave them the boot.

College had been much the same, although Opal rarely brought any of those friends back home with her. And on the nights Opal didn't come home at all, didn't offer any explanation, Vivian could only pray she didn't wind up pregnant.

Vivian looked at bongo boy with dislike. Long, dirty-looking hair, a goatee he was only barely able to grow, and a cigarette hanging out of his mouth as he pounded away, his eyes squinting against the smoke. Vivian hated smoking, and wouldn't allow it in her home. She had no idea Opal had taken it up. It was so typical of her to challenge her mother in this way, knowing full well Vivian wouldn't say anything in front of her friends.

She sighed, plastered her best southern hostess smile on her face, and opened the porch door. "Welcome! Y'all hungry? Can I make some sandwiches or something?"

"Sure," the bongo player said, rubbing his stomach. "It's about time we had some chow. I'm starving."

"That'd be groovy, Mom," Opal said, then blew a long stream of smoke out of her mouth and smiled. "Beer would be nice, too."

The others heartily agreed, but Vivian shook her head. "So sorry, I don't have a single drop. I have plenty of sweet tea, though."

There were shrugs of disappointed acceptance, and Vivian closed the door, then went into the kitchen, grumbling along the way. "Worthless, self-serving, lazy, idiots. They think the whole damn world is there to serve them. Pre-Copernican indeed."

No wonder they like Opal so much. Vivian felt bad about having the thought. She also hated that it was true.

"Mom?" Opal slammed into the kitchen behind her. She sounded angry. "What's going on? I know we have beer, and we're all old enough, so what gives? Are you trying to be a bitch, or is it coming from years of experience?"

Fuming, Vivian spun around. "First, get that cigarette out of the house. Second, I had no idea any of these people were coming. You might have done me the courtesy of calling ahead. I have work to do, and your damned bongo player could wake the dead. Third, despite your lack of consideration, I offered them food and tea. Fourth, I am under no obligation to serve any of them anything, and certainly shouldn't be *expected* to do so, as bongo boy seemed to suggest. Last, have you, or any of them, ever learned please, thank you, or may I help?"

Her daughter rolled her eyes dramatically. "Well, right back at you, Lady Tightass. I happen to like the bongos, and I like bongo boy, and you're always busy. Books, digs, sailing, jerk-off people who lived thousands of years ago. Be sure not to busy yourself with your daughter, *Mom*. I've got one more year until I graduate, and then I'll be out of your hair forever. Promise." Opal flicked her cigarette into the sink, flipped off her mother, and stormed out.

Shaken by Opal's tirade, the first of its kind in years, Vivian stared at the floor, frozen in horror, as options raged through her mind. She wanted to leave, but no, she wouldn't give them full run of the house. She wanted to kick them out, but her southern manners protested such behavior. She also wanted to scream and scream and scream. Oh, what bliss it would be.

She hadn't ever ignored Opal, had she? She certainly hadn't indulged the brat in her. She'd tried, endlessly, to include her, to share, to join in her interests, to be her friend, but Opal would only accept rapprochement if gifts and favors were included. If Vivian didn't come bearing gifts, Opal wanted nothing to do with her. Vivian had tried that game early on, but no such begging on Vivian's part had ever done a bit of good.

I'd keep her gettin' up...

How Vivian missed her mother. Her mother would have known what to do. Her mother would have offered wisdom and a patient embrace until the storm blew over. Oh, how she missed her mother.

Talking and footsteps in the foyer brought Vivian out of her stupor. Were they coming to help? Vivian quickly turned away and wiped her face, astounded to realize she'd been crying. She tried to look busy, and got the bread and peanut butter out of the cupboard, but before she could open the jar, the front door banged shut.

She swiped at her face again and peeked out the kitchen door. The house was quiet. She tiptoed into the foyer, then looked out the front door in time to catch a glimpse of Opal's car spitting gravel as it sped away.

Vivian relented after that encounter. She tried everything she could think of over the coming months to find a way into her daughter's good graces, with gifts of every kind, but Opal would have none of it.

She would greet her father with affection, then pass by her mother, nose in the air, as though she didn't exist.

Opal continued to smoke, although she didn't bring it home anymore. Regardless, Vivian could smell it on her from feet away, since the stink of it followed her around like a cloud. Lately, her daughter had added a new, skunky, cloyingly-sweet odor to the cloud, and Vivian suspected she did not come by it legally.

By mid-winter, Opal's darling flip hairdo, held back from her face by a thin headband, was gone. Now she wore her hair long and parted in the middle, a leather shoe lace tied across her forehead, as though she were an Indian. And her skirts were as short as her temper.

When she talked, she spoke of San Francisco. Anyone who knew anything was going to San Francisco, she said with arrogance. That was where the *big scene* was, where the *action* was, where it was *happening*. They were going to change the world, she and her friends. They would fix everything earlier generations had so badly mismanaged. No more war, just peace, and love, and daisies for all.

OPAL GRADUATED THE NEXT SPRING, and planned to pursue a Master's in the fall. She spent as little time as possible at Altamont during the summer, but thankfully, talk of San Francisco seemed to have faded to a distant memory.

It was a hot Friday night in August, and, like so many others, Opal was gone with friends, who knew where, for the weekend.

Vivian sat beside Thomas in the parlor.

"I want to tell you something," Thomas lifted her chin and looked her in the eye. "I want you to hear what I'm going to say."

Vivian nodded, curious, yet sensing she wouldn't much like the subject. She was also fairly sure what that might be.

"Ever since I've known you I have seen you turn yourself inside out for our girl. You need to understand something. It's not your fault. You are not a bad mother."

She appreciated his kind words, but the proof was in the pudding. Opal hated her. She had to be the reason, because Opal didn't hate anyone else. Even her expulsion from her cousin's home, so many years ago, wasn't because she hated them, but because of her bad behavior.

Vivian shrugged, and chose to side-step the subject. "I worry she's not going to pursue her Master's. She doesn't talk about it anymore, and doesn't respond when I broach the subject."

"Vivian," Thomas said. "We must accept she may not, especially since it's what we want for her. It's her contrary temperament. It's something inside her. No matter what you

231

do, it will never be good enough, because to her, you are everything she will never be, and she knows it, and seeing you reminds her of it every single day."

Vivian tried to think of a time, a moment, where she'd consciously acted superior toward her daughter, or bragged about anything in her life vs. Opal's.

"Hopefully, she will start on her Master's next month," he said. "I've already talked to her, and she seemed agreeable. I offered to let her live in the apartment in town. We don't need it. Maybe with some distance, some time apart, we'll all be better off.

Relief flooded through her at this news, and Vivian felt ashamed of herself.

"Honey," Thomas interrupted her thoughts again, and looked grave. "I repeat; you didn't do anything to cause this. It's in her bones to hate you, or act like it, anyway. What I started to say earlier was, I think...I think something is not quite right with her. Mentally, I mean. And I mean in a very literal, medical sense."

"Oh my god." The thought struck Vivian hard, because it rang so true.

Then, shocked by the revelation, and a sixth sense, she raised her eyes with dread, and the breath was nearly knocked out of her body.

Opal stood in the doorway, fists clenched, face crimson, a look of stunned fury on her face.

Vivian leapt to her feet. "What are you doing here?" she asked. "I thought you were away."

"So this is what you do when I'm not here?" she said through clenched teeth. "Talk about what a shit I am? That I'm crazy?"

"No, of course not."

Thomas rose and took a step toward Opal, his hand out. "Honey, sit next to me. Let's talk rationally, please."

"Don't touch me," Opal spat, and took a step back.

"Opal, it's true, we were talking about you, about you and me," Vivian pleaded. "We were trying to figure out how to fix what's wrong between us, that's all. We simply, we..."

"You think I'm cracked!" Opal screamed at Thomas. "You were the one person, the one..." She spun out of the room and ran upstairs.

"Thomas, do something," Vivian pleaded. "She'll listen to you. You can calm her. Please."

Her husband followed Opal to the second floor, taking the stairs two at a time, but as soon as he approached her door, Vivian heard her scream again, and then slam it shut.

Crushed, Thomas came back to Vivian's side and wrapped her in his arms.

"I'm so sorry, honey," he said. "I should never have said what I did. What have I done? What have I done?"

"Neither of us knew she was home. Regardless, it was nothing short of the truth." Vivian put her hands on his cheeks, trying to reassure him. "You were right, and I should have figured it out long ago. We might've done something. Now, I don't know. We need to tread lightly, and hopefully we can—"

Opal opened her door, then descended the stairs with a suitcase in each hand.

When Vivian approached her, she glared in return.

"Don't. Touch. Me," she growled. "I'm an adult. I'm leaving. If I want to talk to either of you again, I'll let you know, but don't count on it."

Outside, a dingy VW Bug sat in the driveway. The driver pushed the passenger door open as soon as Opal reappeared.

Vivian followed her out, Thomas close on her heels.

"Opal, please, come back in," Vivian sobbed. "Let's talk. I love you, honey. I love you so much. Please don't leave."

Opal tossed her suitcases behind the seats and turned

around, not a hint of sorrow or regret on her face. Only defiance, and self-righteous anger.

With her eyes locked on her mother's, she got inside, rolled down the window, and flipped her the bird as they drove away.

VIVIAN PACED ENDLESSLY, forcing herself to let the situation cool for a couple of weeks, but by early September, she was frantic. She tried calling Opal's high school friends, but none of them had talked to Opal since graduation. She tried the university where Opal was enrolled for her post-graduate studies, but she was a no-show. She also hadn't been seen at the apartment, or at the job Thomas had arranged for her in town.

Vivian had a book deadline, but blew it off. They had society engagements, but ignored them.

She tried to locate Opal's college friends, the ones she'd seen on the porch, but no one knew anything about them. Not who they were, or where they might be.

There were dead ends everywhere she turned.

She felt like she'd lost a baby all over again, and the pain was unbearable.

Thomas called the San Francisco police, but got nowhere. He was told there were indigent young adults by the thousands in the streets, and unless their daughter broke the law in a major way, they had neither the means, the legal authority, nor the interest, in tracking her. They offered to take her personal information, and keep a photo on record, should a Jane Doe be found dead.

By Thanksgiving, they were desperate, and flew out to San Francisco. They spent a long weekend wandering the streets around Haight and Ashbury, then along the wharf and Union Square, but she was nowhere. When they showed her picture to the crowds, people didn't recognize her, or were too drugged out to care.

For Christmas, Vivian bought Opal a St. Christopher medal, in hopes he would protect her daughter, and laid it on her pillow. She lit homecoming candles in every window, and the tree was put in place, but they didn't turn on the lights. There could be no celebration until Opal was home.

But she would not come home. Vivian knew in her soul, Opal was gone.

Forever gone.

Thomas and Vivian never put lights on their Christmas tree again.

~2019~

Vivian stopped talking, and they sat quietly with their thoughts as they gazed out the window.

Tia was appalled and ashamed of the woman who had been her grandmother. Every single detail fit perfectly into all Tia had ever felt, heard, or recently learned about the woman, and she had a possible label for it from annual training seminars at work. NPD, or Narcissistic Personality Disorder. The hallmarks, as she recalled them, were an expectation to be fawned over, a continual need for admiration and praise, a sense of entitlement, a lack of empathy, arrogance, needing to be the center of attention, and lying to make reality fit her version of events.

Barely treatable with psychological help in this era. Not at all treatable back then.

In the end, Thomas had probably been right in his diagnosis. So, despite her personal feelings, Tia knew there was room for understanding, and maybe even forgiveness.

She needed to let GG know what she suspected, but now was not the time.

CHAPTER TWENTY-TWO

SETH DIDN'T COME TO ALTAMONT THAT NIGHT. THINGS WERE busy at work, and he wanted his own bed. She understood.

She'd put off the calls she needed to make, but knew she had no choice the following morning. She had to call her Lt., maybe even the chief, and she'd have to make the call to her parents. She also needed to book a flight home, ASAP.

She didn't want to leave, but she needed to give work their two weeks. She needed to pack and arrange for shipment of her stuff. Paperwork, change of address forms, so many things.

And before she left Greenville, she needed to find a place to come back to. Altamont would be turned over to the Historical Society the minute she got on her flight. There was no way she would move into Seth's right away, even if he offered. Too much, too soon, could ruin everything. An apartment in the short term, a condo, if she could find one before she left, for the long term.

Needless to say, she didn't sleep well.

· · ·

TIA BROUGHT SOME DANISH, coffee, and tea to Vivian early the next morning.

Vivian's eyes were puffy, and other than those early days in the hospital, Tia had never see her so un-put-together.

Vivian thanked her for the tea, then took a sip, and let her gaze wander. After a few minutes, she sighed and re-focused on Tia.

"As I mentioned before, Opal's finger was the last communication we ever had with her. You've filled in the gaps since then." Vivian fidgeted with a bit of wayward, wispy, hair, then patted Tia's hand. "As I've said, out of sorrow, joy. I am so very happy you have entered my life. The pain we all experienced has wrought a diamond, and I shall be forever grateful."

They hugged, then sat quietly for a moment.

"I did some research last night," Tia said, and handed Vivian a folder. "You don't have to read it now, but it might help. Nothing is for sure, of course. But, from my very non-medical background, and with some expert instruction through my work, the pieces seem to fit. As I said, it might help. It might not."

"Thank you, dear." Vivian looked at her with sad eyes. "This early visit is unusual. You have something else you want to talk about, don't you?"

"Yes. I didn't come for a story. I have calls to make, things to arrange, so I have to get back to Altamont."

A look of deep sorrow welled in Vivian's eyes. "You're leaving."

It wasn't a question.

Tia smiled. "Yes, GG, but only for a couple of weeks. I have to make moving arrangements, find an apartment in Greenville, book flights, tell my parents. I have a lot to do before I can move here permanently."

As understanding dawned, Tia watched Vivian's expression transform from one of sorrow, to one of joy.

WITH STEPHANIE'S tireless help the following day, Tia was able to find a furnished apartment downtown, and sign a rental agreement. Two days later, she had her psych eval, then spent the night with Seth. The following morning, she drove herself to Greenville/Spartanburg airport to catch her flight...home.

IT SEEMED STRANGE, a part of a different life, being back at work. There was a lot of paperwork, many meetings, and she couldn't take lead on any cases, because she wouldn't be present to see them through, should her testimony be needed in court.

Tia was treading water, checking the boxes, and it was frustrating. She wanted to go home, to her new home. She could hardly wait.

She talked with Seth and Vivian almost daily. Stephanie assured her all was well. Rob was doing well, too, and back in the office on light duty.

Shippers packed away her entire life, including her truck, and headed toward South Carolina. She closed her condo in Snohomish, and put it on the market. She lived with her parents in Kirkland, and used a rental car to get to work. She couldn't get gone fast enough.

Even so, before she left, she needed to make one more breakfast stop at her favorite diner. She left her parent's home extra early and headed out to say goodbye before her shift started. She would miss the whole gang, terribly.

As she expected, saying goodbye was hard, and she made

a lot of jokes to cover the strange, sentimental emotions percolating inside.

Then, in the blink of an eye, her two weeks were done, it was time to say goodbye to her dad, and her two siblings still living in the Seattle area, and board the flight...home.

This time, her mother would accompany her.

Finally.

"THIS IS LOVELY, TIA," her mom said, as she looked out the living room window at the Greenville cityscape laid out before her.

"Thanks. I signed a month-to-month, so it's expensive, but it'll give me time to find a place," Tia replied. "Tomorrow we meet with the real estate agent for lunch, then I'll give you the lay of the land, but first we'll meet GG for breakfast. You will love her."

"I'm nervous. Gosh, my own grandmother," Cherry shook her head. "Unbelievable."

The buzzer for the security gate sounded.

"Dinner, at last," Tia said, and pressed the video intercom. "Yes?"

"Delivery for Miss Benson," the crackly voice said. The image wasn't very clear, but the ball cap-wearing delivery guy held a bag of food toward the camera.

She quickly pushed the gate release. "Come on up."

Within seconds, there was a knock.

When she opened the door, Seth stood there holding the food, a broad smile on his face. He handed her the bag, then, before she could react, he took her face in his hands and kissed her, long and hard.

Tia had no thoughts beyond the delight of being in his arms once again.

After a few moments, the sound of a throat being cleared penetrated her Seth fog.

Mom!

She backed off with a grin. "Seth, I'd like you to meet my mother, Cherry Benson."

His eyes widened in surprise, and a flush washed across his face, right along with a stupid grin. He stuck out his hand. "Hi, nice to meet you, Cherry. I'm the food delivery guy. Your daughter is an excellent tipper."

"HE COULD HAVE STAYED the night, that's all I'm saying," her mom argued as they entered GG's building the next morning.

"Mom," Tia countered. "You and I share a lot, but I don't ever want us to be *that* close."

Tia tapped on Vivian's door, then entered.

Vivian sat by the window, backlit by the sunshine outside.

"GG, we're here," Tia said quietly.

Vivian turned, her expression inscrutable.

As they approached, she stood, smiled, and held out her hand. She looked radiant, and Tia noticed she was beautifully coiffed, and dressed to the nines. She took a mental note to thank Naomi.

"Cherry, I'm so very happy to meet you," Vivian said, her voice choked with sentiment.

"Grandma."

They spent an emotional hour getting acquainted, and looked through a photo album of Cherry's childhood that held pictures of her parents.

They had lunch at a lovely little bistro, and shared stories with each other. As they neared the end of the meal, Vivian asked Tia if she'd brought the bracelet.

"Yes, but I haven't breathed a word to Mom. It's your

story. I wanted it to be your surprise." Tia brought out the blue velvet pouch and handed it over.

Vivian opened the pouch and laid out the bracelet for Cherry to see.

Cherry looked stunned, and covered her mouth with her hand, before speaking. "Mom never talked about you, as you know, but, but she mentioned your charm bracelet, many times. She, uh, talked about it as though it had been a great source of pain. She would never let me have one. She would say – gosh, I'm sorry – but she said they were evil."

Fresh emotions, fresh pain, for all three of them.

"I won't go into it here," Vivian said, putting the bracelet away. "But I've been telling Tia about the charms, how and why they came to be. It wasn't so very long ago I realized it was a kind of biography of my life. We've recorded all my tales, and Tia doesn't know it, but Naomi has had most of it transcribed already, so you can read it, or listen. I still have a few more to add, if you'd care to listen in, but I think it would be best if we went back to my apartment for that."

Tia pushed off her meeting with the real estate agent until mid-afternoon, and they all left for Vivian's.

~1964-1979~

For the next fifteen years, in addition to the Historical Society, and the Antiquities Foundation, digs, speeches, and books, Thomas and Vivian were active in local conservative politics. Life was full, except for the heartache of a lost daughter, but they continued their search for her, while simultaneously continuing to live their lives.

Spring of 1979 brought early heat. Vivian sipped sweet tea in the parlor, and gazed out the window at the wakening day. Suddenly alert, she realized Thomas' voice, faint and coming from his office, had taken on a tone she couldn't quite place, other than to peg it as unusual.

She left her glass on a coaster, and walked quietly to his door. They hid nothing from one another, so she knew he wouldn't mind if she listened in. She also didn't want to disturb him on what was obviously an important call, so she remained in the foyer.

"Well, I'm honored, very honored," he said. "This is a big decision, and one I can't make without including my wife. May I call you back with an answer on Monday?"

When he signed off on the call, Vivian stepped inside.

"I heard the tone in your voice. Is anything the matter?"

He leaned back in his chair, with a slow smile and a shake of his head. "Nothing's the matter. But we do have something rather monumental to consider."

Their local congressman, a good friend, had suddenly become too ill to stay in his post, and the phone call was the state party head asking Thomas to fill the vacancy for the duration of the term – almost two full years – or until the elected congressman regained his health and could resume his duties, which seemed unlikely.

After a weekend of discussions, Thomas and Vivian decided to accept the post, but stated, in no uncertain terms, they were not interested in running for the spot at the end of the term. Somebody else could make a career out of it, not them.

Vivian stood at her husband's side and held the Bible, while Thomas took his oath. She couldn't have been more proud, and beamed at him. He looked so handsome in his dark suit and brilliant red tie. She wore an indigo blue skirt, matching crop jacket, and a white silk blouse, with pumps and purse to match.

His office had been cleared of his predecessor's personal belongings, and for the time being, Thomas kept the staff already in place. His orientation would begin immediately after taking the oath.

Once her brand new congressman left for his classes, some of the other congressional wives from South Carolina gave her a tour. They stopped first for a bite in a little cafeteria somewhere underground, then visited the gift shop, before moving on to more important points of interest.

Vivian wore her bracelet, and bought two new charms for it – a Republican elephant, and the US Capitol.

They'd quickly found and leased a furnished brownstone in the nine hundred block of NE Massachusetts Ave. It was within walking distance to the Capitol, and Thomas' offices in the Rayburn, and that evening they would host a cocktail reception for the South Carolina delegation, plus some others, in their new home.

The state party arranged for wait staff, cooks, security, valet parking, and they ran the show as though they knew the house, and knew the routine, which Vivian guessed, they probably did.

All she and Thomas had to do was smile, greet, shake hands, and remember names.

Thomas wore his tuxedo, and Vivian chose a sleeveless, emerald green sheath dress with a hot pink lining, and matching, cut-away stilettos. She had emeralds at her throat, ears, and right wrist, and once again, her charm bracelet on her left. It was too heavy, and too noisy, to wear on her greeting arm. A recommended jeweler had rushed to get the newest charms soldered into place, and delivered it to her an hour before the party was to start.

"You look absolutely stunning, my dear," Thomas said. "You will wow the establishment matrons."

"You look stunning, too, Mr. Congressman. Very James Bond."

He inclined his head to accept the compliment, then

shrugged. "Men always look the same in tuxes. Seems pretty boring, to me."

"Oh, no," Vivian countered. "For one thing, its attitude. Can the fellow carry it off? Not everyone can. On some, it's just a suit, on others it looks sloppy and awkward." She wrapped her arms about his middle, wiggled her eyebrows at him. "And then there are those who carry it like Bond, James Bond. In my opinion, Mr. Double-O Seven would be jealous of you."

Thomas barked out a laugh, then leaned in to kiss her.

"Just keep this in mind tonight," Vivian added, wickedly. "A nicely worn tux is, for women, and especially this woman, the equivalent of fancy lingerie to a man."

Thomas chuckled. "I want this party over," he mumbled against her lips. "Now."

Life in D.C. was a whirlwind, and full of pitfalls, but they managed to steer clear, and soon grew accustomed to the city, its pace, and their place in it.

By Christmas of 1981, with a new administration voted into office, Thomas was preparing to hand over the reins to his newly elected replacement. They were either hosting, or attending, a slew of holiday functions during the festive season every evening, while Vivian packed away their D.C. life during the day.

One month, and they'd be back in Greenville permanently. She could hardly wait. They'd made many friends during their sojourn, but this life wasn't for them.

There was yet another holiday party to attend, and, as Vivian put on a pair of diamond earrings, Thomas called up the stairs.

"Coming," Vivian called back. She finished and hurried out of their room, but found Thomas on his way to her, his expression one of concern.

"What is it?" she asked, her heart in her throat.

For fifteen years, she had felt equal measures of hope and fear when unexpected news came their way.

"Nothing to do with Opal," Thomas quickly said. "I got a call. They're sending a car. Reagan has requested we stop by before going to the party. He apologized on the short notice, can you imagine? He said it won't take long. Ten, twenty minutes, tops."

Vivian stared at him, slack-jawed.

By mid-January, instead of heading south to Greenville, they were headed east, as an adjunct to the US Ambassador to France.

~2019~

"By my count, there are only four left," Vivian said. She smiled at Cherry. "This last story explained the Reagan Presidential Seal, the White House, the elephant, and the Capitol." She took a long moment to gaze at her granddaughter, then reached out and took her hand.

Vivian looked her straight in the eye. "The bracelet is simply a thing. The charms themselves are very much beside the point - a way to tell stories that create a bridge to the past," she said. "Let me say, I believe you have suffered the most through all of this. "Your mother had nothing to give you, nothing from within. You had to make your own way, discover for yourself what love is, and what it is not. If Tia is any proof, I believe you have succeeded splendidly. She is a woman of strength and character, and that doesn't happen by chance. Somehow, through all of this mess, you were able to find your God-given inner strength to stand tall, and raise children who are a reflection of the morals and character you hold dear."

Cherry looked at Vivian with a wide-eyed, and very vulnerable expression.

"You're right. I, uh, neither of my parents were there, not emotionally," Cherry said, her voice choked. "I learned from pets, from friends, from my friend's parents. I thought living in an emotional void was normal, but I learned otherwise, and I was fortunate enough to have people around me willing to take up the slack, without judging. And then there was my husband, of course, who has always been my rock."

Vivian smiled, and gently shook the hands she held. "My heavens, the strength you've shown. *Ex tristitiae, laetitiae.* From sorrow, joy, I say, and you are the very epitome of that saying. You were given nothing, and yet you blossomed. Oh, the strength you embody. Bless you, bless you. I am so very proud to know you, and so extremely proud you are my granddaughter!"

Tia sat back and smiled as her mom and Vivian had their moment.

CHAPTER TWENTY-THREE

TIA HAD SOME SOLID LEADS ON THREE DIFFERENT CONDOS, AND put in an offer on her favorite one by the end of the day. Unable to sit still, she and Cherry met with Naomi and her husband, Everett, for a quick tour of the Historical Society, then went out for dinner before heading home.

The next morning, Cherry and Tia took Vivian out for breakfast, but before returning to her apartment, Vivian asked Tia to take them to Altamont.

"The Historical Society has taken possession, of course, but I still have a key," Vivian said, with a twinkle in her eye.

As Tia drove the gravel drive, she felt as though she were coming home. She would miss this place, and couldn't' imagine the pain it cost Vivian, who'd lived here for nearly seventy years.

She glanced at her mom, who's eyes were nearly popping out of her head.

"Tara, indeed," she mumbled. "Holy cow."

"They hold a benefactor's luncheon here every Friday," Vivian explained, as she unlocked the front door. "I am the guest of honor any time I wish to attend, which is lovely, although that's not why I come. I simply enjoy being here, and seeing the old place come alive again."

They stepped into the foyer, and Tia watched with amusement as her mom did a slow-mo, gap-mouth spin to take it all in.

After a brief tour of the main level, Cherry looked at the stairs, and the balcony on the second level. "You say my mother lived here. May I see her room, please?"

"Tia, my dear, will you show your mom?" Vivian asked. I haven't the strength for all those stairs, anymore."

Tia obliged, but suspected there were other reasons GG didn't want to go do it.

The room was bright and cheerful, and decorated as it had been in her grandmother's time, although any remaining personal items had gone before Tia ever visited the place.

Cherry walked slowly around the room, looked out the window, ran a finger over the doorknob, and peeked in on the adjacent bath. "It's beautiful." She approached the window again, and Tia could see sorrow vying with anger in the set of her jaw, in the rigidity of her shoulders.

"She had everything, and I don't mean monetarily, although she obviously had that, too. But she had a family who loved her. She had opportunities galore. And not only did she choose to abandon all this, throw it in the trash in the most selfish and cruel way, she also chose, years later, to deprive us of this, of our past, our heritage, our *family.* These people weren't just *her* family. She made a hateful choice for us, too, without so much as a by your leave."

After a moment, they stepped out of the room, and Cherry quietly closed the door. "I always knew my mom was distant, emotionless. I'm coming to realize she was heartless, and willingly, knowingly so. I think, I think I despise her."

"Mom." Tia reached out and enveloped her mother. "I agree with all of it, but, in the end, she didn't win, unless we allow ourselves to be bitter over this. We have to let it go. We need to forgive. Plus, I gave Vivian some research you might be interested to read. I don't know if she has read it yet, and I'm no psych professional, but I feel it puts a framework on your mom that makes sense, and might make forgiveness a little bit easier."

Cherry hugged her daughter, then stepped back with a smile. "You are so wise. You either get it from your father, or Vivian's wisdom skipped two generations before landing on your shoulders."

Tia's phone rang as they reached the foyer. It was Lt. Hollings from the Greenville police department. She left Cherry and Vivian chatting, and went into the parlor.

"Tia, Lt. Hollings. How are you?" he asked. "I hear you are back in town."

"Yes, since yesterday. I'm showing my mom the sights. How can I help you?"

"The GPD would like to formally offer you a position on the force as a lateral entry officer."

A smile swept across her face. "That's wonderful news, sir. Thank you."

"Is there a time today you can come in? We need to go over some specifics, paperwork, start date, etc."

Tia checked her watch. "I've got some people to drop off, but I can be there in an hour. Does 3:00pm work for you?"

"Perfect. I'll see you then, and welcome aboard."

She was about to tell the ladies her good news, when her phone rang again.

"Sir?" she said, without looking at the screen. She assumed it was Lt. Hollings calling back with some forgotten tidbit.

"Hello, Tia? Its Courtney."

The real estate agent. "Oh, hi, sorry, I thought it was…never mind. What's up? Anything interesting?"

"Your offer has been accepted, no counters, no nothing," she said.

Startled, Tia had thought they were low-balling the owner. "Oh, crap, did we offer too much?"

"Absolutely not, don't worry about it," she reassured. "Personally, I think it's a divorce situation, and they both wanted out fast. Actually, they also want a quick close."

"Well, it shouldn't be a problem, I guess," Tia said, feeling as though she ought to be excited, yet getting the uncommon sensation her life was spinning beyond her usually controlling fingers.

But in a good way, right? she wondered hopefully.

She ended the call and took a deep breath, not wanting any more phone calls for the moment. Exhaling slowly, she reminded herself all was well, and even better than expected. It was the pace of things, not the things themselves, that was unsettling.

Reassured, she went back to the foyer to tell them her good news.

CHERRY CHOSE to stay with Vivian, so Tia dropped them off at the residence, and headed for the station. She debated texting Seth, but wanted to tell him in person. She kept her fingers crossed the rumor mill wouldn't inform him first.

Tia approached the station's main entry at 2:55p.m., and the door swung open as she reached for it.

Seth stood there, grinning. She should never have bet against a rumor mill in the south.

"You want to go out for a celebratory dinner tonight?" he asked. "Actually, you can't decline, because Vivian has already made the reservation, and your mom, Stephanie, Rob, and yours truly, have already signed on."

"Sounds great," she said with a laugh.

He gave her a hug and a kiss in front of God and everyone. "Congratulations. I need to get back out there. I'll call you later."

A receptionist at the front desk buzzed her into the secured reception area, and she waited only moments before Lt. Hollings came in with a smile.

AT DINNER, Vivian insisted on treating. She also insisted on taking them to Hall's.

They were seated at a round table on the second floor, overlooking the restaurant, and the glittering lights of the city outside.

"When do you start?" Stephanie asked.

"The first of July, so, two weeks and change," Tia replied. "I'll have about three weeks with a training officer, then off to the academy in Columbia for two weeks to learn the local laws. Then I'll be back with a series of trainers for another twelve weeks or so, after that, before they cut me loose to patrol on my own. First order of business though, my offer on a condo was accepted, so I need to move in before I start. All in all, it's looking like a very busy summer."

All eyes drifted to Seth, and Tia felt bad. She was about to intervene, when he shook his head.

"Y'all back off. She knew she was welcome at my place, but that's not how we chose to move forward," he said, then winked at her. "Not yet, anyway."

Rob raised his glass. "Well, here's to July first for one more reason. Its's also my target date for getting back on full patrol. I've had enough of riding the desk."

They all toasted Rob's return, then Stephanie shook her head. "I don't know what it is about your line of work. I'm proud of y'all, but I wouldn't do what you do for anything in the world."

Seth, Tia, and Rob exchanged glances, and then quiet smiles.

"Best damn job in the world," Rob said.

"Here, here." The three of them raised their glasses once again.

At the end of a very pleasant dinner, and after a chorus of thank yous for Vivian, everyone got ready to leave.

Cherry grabbed Tia's keys off the table. "I will drive Vivian home, and then I will drive myself home," she said. "I know the way well enough, so you needn't worry. You go with your guy. No arguments."

Tia had not spent any alone time with Seth since her return, and she'd never seen more than the exterior of his home. Her only other visit had been interrupted by a meth head and gunfire. This time the driveway was quiet, and as they approached the house in the growing dusk, she took time to appreciate its beauty.

It was a modern log cabin, with a wraparound porch, and dark green metal roof. There was a big chimney on the right end, and a well-manicured garden surrounding the whole. Garden lights were coming on as night encroached, and security monitors shone brightly as they made their final approach.

"Seth, it's beautiful. Did you build it, or buy it like this?"

"I built it, with some help, but mostly, it was me."

Tia looked at him in surprise. "Really? When I said 'build', I meant 'did you have a builder do it', but you actually did it yourself?"

"Spent a lot of time in the trade through high school and college," he explained. "Dad has a construction company, so I knew how to do most of it. Borrowed some big machines from him, and had his guys do the electricity, gas, and the roof, but I did the rest."

He got out and opened the door for her. "I think you'll like the back. It's my favorite part."

They went inside, and Tia felt like she might expire from the shock of seeing what she beheld.

Seth gave her a tour. They started in the foyer, where the hardwood floor gleamed. They moved around a short wall opposite the entry, and came into the living room. The far wall was floor to ceiling windows and doors. The couch, loveseat, and chairs were a natural color leather, and the very large rug beneath was a Persian design in bronze and cream.

"Wow. Seth, this is stunning." She let her gaze wander, taking everything in.

He smiled and shrugged. "I like natural, and comfortable. Wood. Leather. Not big on sharp angles."

The vaulted ceiling had to be twenty feet high at the peak, with arched crossbeams. A river rock fireplace covered most of the right wall. On the left was an open dining room, with an oversized, natural wood table, and beyond, an enormous kitchen. Past the kitchen, he showed her three guest rooms, a laundry, and access to the garage.

They retraced their steps to the foyer, and Seth indicated a descending stairwell along the hallway. "I have a daylight basement. There's an electronic shooting range, a gym, a woodshop, and access to the backyard."

Seth stayed put, but gestured in the general direction of the end of the hall, beyond the stairs.

"My office is there, on the right, and the master is at the end, but I want to show you one more thing, first," he said with a grin. "Otherwise we might never see the one more thing."

Tia chuckled, and knew he was probably right.

They went through the living room, and Seth opened the far door, then stepped aside to let Tia pass.

Outside was a broad deck, overlooking an enormous slate patio on the ground level, with a large fire pit at its center.

Tia leaned against Seth, and he wrapped an arm around her shoulder.

"It is breathtaking," Tia whispered.

"That's Saluda Lake."

"Did you come out here to swim in high school? Is that how you found this garden spot?"

"Been swimming here my whole life. It's family land. Has been since before the war."

Tia knew he meant the civil one, not anything more recent.

"My dad parceled it out a few years back. He lives over there," Seth pointed to the left. "My brother and his wife live on the other side of Dad's place. The sons each have five acres, and Dad has the bulk, another ten. My grandfather had two hundred acres, once, but sold off most of it back in the sixties when he stopped farming."

"Wow, I'm speechless," Tia said, and meant it. "So beautiful."

Tia felt Seth's lips touch her skin below her ear, and leaned into their touch.

"I'm glad you like it," he said quietly.

~1986~

Thomas stayed at his post at the French Consulate through Reagan's first term, then, one year into his second, Thomas and Vivian decided five years was enough. They needed to be home. And, as always, deep in the back of her mind, Vivian knew she wanted to be where Opal could find her. It was January, 1986. Her daughter, if she still lived, would be forty-seven in September.

They'd made friends around the globe, she'd renewed ties

with family on her father's side, and they frequently crossed the channel to visit her little sister, Lucille, now a grandmother of six. But home was home, after all, and they both missed their Blue Ridge Mountains, cicadas, and sweet tea on the porch.

Their trip home took a lengthy, circuitous route, beginning with another visit to several sites in Greece, Turkey, and Italy. From Rome, they flew to Egypt, a trip they'd always promised themselves, before heading to London and a final, extended visit with Lucille.

They flew into New York on the twenty-fifth of June, and spent a week there, then took the train to Baltimore on the second of July.

Thomas had saved a surprise for Vivian, and on the fourth, they left their hotel at noon and toured Fort McHenry, on the central jut of land in Baltimore Harbor. It was a beautiful day, and everyone wore patriotic clothing and waved flags. There were fife and drum bands, guided tours, and costumed trinket sellers. Blankets, chairs, and picnic baskets were everywhere, as friends and family enjoyed the festivities.

After touring the famous fort, they went inside the gift shop. Vivian browsed, but Thomas headed straight for the jewelry display, and purchased a tiny cannon charm.

He turned to her proudly, and offered his purchase. "To commemorate our homecoming. Now, hurry, because we have a taxi to catch."

Vivian laughed at his enthusiasm, and dutifully followed him to the taxi terminal outside the park. The cab took them back toward the inner harbor, and Vivian felt certain she knew the surprise Thomas had hinted at all day.

Their hotel had a lovely dining room on the top floor, with windows looking out over the harbor, the fort, and the upcoming fireworks celebration. It would be breathtaking.

When the cab stopped along the docks, she looked at Thomas quizzically, but he only smiled and leapt out to open her door.

"We're not going back to the hotel for the fireworks?" she asked, trying to keep disappointment out of her voice.

Thomas simply held out his hand.

He tucked her hand into the crook of his arm, and they strolled along the wharf. "I thought you might like this, since we are sailors, not land lubbers."

"Yes, of course, it's beautiful," she replied, a bit confused.

Relax she scolded herself. They had hours before dusk, hours to get to wherever they were going.

Thomas stopped to chat with a fellow selling brochures in a booth, and Vivian allowed herself to enjoy the familiar sounds and smells of the wharf and the sea. Briny air, creosote and diesel fuel, the creaking of dock lines, and the clanking of halyards.

She took a long, deep breath. Ah, the wine dark sea, or at least the edges of it.

"Vivian?"

"Yes," she snapped to, and focused on her husband's bemused expression.

"We're here. It's time to go aboard."

She frowned and looked over his shoulder. They weren't standing at a brochure seller's booth, after all. It was a ticket booth, for the dinner cruise ship, *Lady Baltimore*.

"We shall cruise Baltimore Harbor, then go out toward the Chesapeake over hors d'oeuvres and cocktails. We will be served dinner at the mouth of the harbor as dusk falls, and return to a spot off the point of Fort McHenry, for dessert, champagne, the fireworks display, and of course, the Star Spangled Banner."

"Oh, Thomas." She squeezed his arm in delight. "You have outdone yourself. I never guessed."

The afternoon was glorious, the evening better still, and when Thomas and Vivian finally put heads to pillows, in the early hours of the fifth, they couldn't have asked for more.

As Vivian drifted off, she looked forward to the next few days. In the morning, they would go to DC for a quick, overnight stop, and the following morning they would board the train for home.

Altamont.

At last.

~2019~

Vivian touched the ten Franc coin on the bracelet, the largest charm, by far.

"They discontinued this coin a few years prior to switching to the Euro. I still can't understand why they decided the Euro was a good thing, which meant, essentially, handing over their sovereignty and their national identity to others."

She raised her shoulders with a bright smile. "Ah well, nobody asked me."

She took Cherry's hand. "This is your last day, and it fills me with sorrow to see you leave. However, now that I have Tia here, you will be obliged to come often. Very often, because I have not had nearly enough of you."

Cherry laughed. "And I feel the same. I will miss you both, and I promise to come as frequently as I can. Next time, I will even bring Don, Tia's daddy." She looked at Tia. "And I will make sure your siblings visit you."

Vivian spread the bracelet out on her lap. "We've gone through every charm," she said. "I'm so glad you were here, Cherry, to listen to a story or two. Naomi has arranged to have the stories transcribed onto paper, and put on the computer, as well, and they will be available in the Society archives, but you both shall have your own copies."

"I look forward to reading, and listening, to every word," Cherry replied.

As Cherry and GG chatted, Tia saw GG put the bracelet back in its blue velvet pouch, draw the strings tight, and then deposit it in the pocket of her cardigan, instead of giving to her, as she'd always done.

The stories are over, she told herself, sad to see it go. She'd come to think of it as an old friend.

She smiled warmly at GG, and reminded herself the bracelet was not the focus. The actual treasure was the gift of hearing the stories, of learning about her history, and of getting to know her great grandmother.

And all that from two little DNA tests.

CHAPTER TWENTY-FOUR

Tia hadn't seen much of GG since her mother left. She'd closed on, and taken possession of her condo, and her belongings had been delivered from the storage where they'd sat since she shipped them from Snohomish. Now that she was moved in, or at least living in the same square footage as all of her worldly belongings, she had time to relax, and wanted to give GG an entire afternoon of undivided attention. With only a long weekend left before she started her new job, time was growing short.

She arrived, and gave GG a kiss on the cheek. "It's a beautiful day. Would you like to drive somewhere, or go to Altamont and sip some sweet tea on the porch? I know someone who has a key."

GG smiled and shook her head. "Let's go out in the garden here. It's lovely, there's shade, and some of that misting stuff to keep us cool. There's sweet tea in the fridge, and a tray on the counter. Why don't you bring it out with us?"

Despite the heat and humidity – which gave Tia no end of worry, wondering how it would feel with a ballistics vest on

– they made their way to the garden, and sat in the shade of a fragrant Magnolia.

They chatted for a time about her job, her apartment, and the comings and goings of everyone in the retirement home, but something felt off, a bit awkward.

Suddenly, Tia realized their relationship, to date, had been about GG's storytelling. As wonderful as it had been, she realized now that the stories were done, there was a gap between where they were, currently, and true friendship. They were going to have to bridge the gap, based on the present, not the past.

"GG, tell me where you think you got the strength you have, to face what you've faced in your life."

Vivian looked at her quizzically. "You make it sound as though I might've gone shopping for it." She shrugged. "I suppose some are geared to fall apart, while others are geared to fight the fight. I'm a fighter, certainly, but I think my strength came out of every scar, every blow. You put your head down, you know? Put one foot in front of the other, and carry on until the storm passes. Hopefully, God will grant you a few moments to catch your breath before the next storm hits. The Roman philosopher Seneca once said, *"La vie, ce n'est pas d'attendre que l'orage passe, c'est d'apprendre à danser sous la pluie*. Of course, he said it in Latin, but everything sounds so much prettier in French.

Tia raised her brows. "Translation?"

"'Life is not about waiting for the storm to pass, but about learning to dance in the rain.' And that is so very true. I know the stories made my life sound rather harrowing, at times, and sad so much of the time, but truly, the Good Lord gave me far more time to dance, far more joy, than he did storms."

They sat in silence for a time, then Vivian smiled. "You and your mother are fighters, too, obviously. Your mother's whole life was a storm, but she kept fighting, until she could make her life a joy. And you, your whole profession is about the fight, the struggle against the storm, and it's the storm that brings you joy. Fighting it, helping others fight it. You are quite amazing."

Tia was about to respond with an 'aw, shucks' comment, but Vivian beat her to the mark.

"You know, now I think of it, Opal was a fighter, too. One hell of a fighter, except in her case, she fought to *be* the storm, and she fought hard, every day of her life, to make sure everyone around her had to struggle with it. She forced us to find a way to dance beneath her dark clouds."

Tia looked at her in amazement. Vivian didn't look sad, or angry, just matter-of-fact.

"Did you read the research I gave you?"

Vivian nodded. "I would say it describes her to a T. I guess there was nothing we could have done, but it doesn't take the pain away, or the wishing for what could have been."

"What are your doctors saying these days?" Tia asked, wanting to steer the conversation away from dark skies and gloom. "Are they going to allow you to resume some of your work schedule?"

"Oh, yes. They say I am cleared to do as much as I feel like doing."

Tia tilted her head, and regarded this woman she cared for so much. "But? I sense a 'but.'"

Vivian smiled at her perceptiveness. "*But* I find I rather like sitting in the garden, and listening in on the senior community gossip. I'll go in to work once in a while, or attend a function now and then at the Society, or at Altamont, but I find I like this new pace. It works for me."

Tia put an arm around her shoulders and gave her a kiss on the temple. "Then it works for me, too. Let me know when you want to go dirt-biking, though, and I'll be right over."

Vivian laughed delightedly for a moment, and then they sat in companionable silence.

"I have a house warming present for you," she suddenly said, and reached into her cardigan. "Or perhaps it's a 'welcome to South Carolina' present, or even still, a 'congratulations on your new job' gift. Better yet..." She opened her hand and held out the blue velvet pouch. "Better yet, let's say it's an 'I love you dearly' gift."

Tia sat, frozen with surprise. What she'd reached for so many times, she now did not want to touch. It was GG's, not hers. It made her feel as though GG was putting a final touch on her life, as though giving it away meant she considered her life story complete.

Vivian chuckled. "Go on, take it. It's not a bad omen, or an insinuation of anything dire. Not at all. It simply means I love you, and this bracelet, more than anything I can think of, links us as family.

She untied the strings, and upended the pouch.

"Take a look. Take a good look," Vivian urged, holding out the bracelet.

And right there in the middle, bright and shiny, were two new charms – a pair of handcuffs, and the state of South Carolina.

"I added them because you came into my life, as one of my brightest charms. Now, those charms have forever linked us, and have forged the transition from my bracelet, my story, to a bracelet about us, and now, a bracelet that is yours to carry forward.

Boy howdy, Tia thought, as Vivian laid the charm bracelet across her palm.

She looked at Vivian, her vision blurred by tears.

"Family," she whispered, and closed her hand.

EPILOGUE

Tɪᴀ sᴀᴛ ᴡɪᴛʜ ʜᴇʀ sᴡᴏʟʟᴇɴ ꜰᴇᴇᴛ ᴘʀᴏᴘᴘᴇᴅ ᴀɢᴀɪɴsᴛ ᴛʜᴇ balcony railing, and soaked in the view. All three of her siblings and their families, depending on ages, were either on the lawn playing Pétanques, or swimming in the lake, or chasing one another in circles.

Most of the historical society employees and patrons, including Naomi and Everett, were also milling around on the lawn, as were many from the Thomas Family Foundation.

Seth's extended family was mingling pleasantly with hers, while both sets of parents, and Rob and Stephanie, sat beside her on the balcony, overlooking all.

Tia thought the caterer had done a wonderful job arranging dining and buffet tables while they were away, and the air was filled with the smells of Southern cooking at its finest.

Everyone was here, and she couldn't be happier.

Correction, she thought. *Almost everyone, and she could be much happier.*

Seth pressed a cold glass against her arm, taking her out of her mixed emotions.

"Your sweet tea, darlin'."

"Thank you."

"They're tellin' me dinner will be served in twenty. That work?"

"Perfect," Tia said. "Come sit with me." She patted the open chair next to her.

Seth obliged, and settled in. He looked at his sister, then at Tia. "You two ladies wanna start waddling that direction now, or wait and be carried?"

Rob started laughing, and Tia punched Seth's shoulder.

Stephanie, sitting at the end, leaned forward and glared at him. "Step carefully, dear brother. Think fratricide."

Seth tried to look innocent. "I'm just sayin'. Y'all are both within what, two weeks of your due dates? I'm being chivalrous, here. No disrespect. Just askin' if it's to be waddle, or should I bring in a cherry picker and forklift y'all to dinner?"

Rob was howling with laughter. "You are so dead, man. So dead."

Tia's sister, Audrey, arrived with Rob and Stephanie's two-year-old girl in hand.

"Claire wants her daddy," she said with a smile.

The toddler crawled onto Rob's lap, and pointed at Stephanie's belly.

"Baby."

"That's right, Claire," Rob said. "Mommy has our new baby in her tummy. You're going to be such a great big sister."

Clair pointed at Tia's belly. "Baby."

"Yep," Rob agreed, again. "Auntie Tia has cousin Thomas in her tummy. You're gonna be a great cousin, too, aren't you?"

Claire nodded, then stuck her thumb in her mouth,

leaned against her daddy's warm chest, and watched the people on the lawn with sleepy eyes.

Tia put a hand on Rob's arm. "I've been meaning to tell you, congratulations on your promotion, Detective O'Connor."

Rob grinned. "Thanks. I'm looking forward to it, and I won't mind getting off patrol."

"Here, here," Stephanie said, raising her glass of sweet tea.

"I hadn't considered a change until Seth got the school resource officer gig," he said. "But it started me thinking, for sure, and I'm excited."

"Well, you earned it, and you'll be great," Tia added.

A bell rang – the sign dinner was about to be served.

"You know," Tia said, hitching her body toward the edge of her chair. "I'm thinking your cherry picker idea isn't bad. Not at all."

Audrey linked arms with her sister, and together they slowly descended the stairs to the lawn. "I can come back for the birth, if you'd like. I'm kinda loving the frequent flyer miles I'm racking up."

"Thanks," Tia said. They managed the rest of the steps in silence.

Once they reached the grass, though, Tia pulled Audrey to the side and waved everyone on, including Seth, who gave them a questioning look.

Tia glanced over her shoulder and smiled as her parents headed toward the tables.

She lowered her voice. "I know Mom wants to be here for the birth, she might even stay until then. It might be nice if you were here, too, if only to keep Mom from driving me crazy."

"I hear you," Audrey said with a smile. "Seriously, I'm game if you want me here. Just say the word."

"Thanks."

"So, tell me. Are you okay?" Audrey asked. "I mean, really? With today, and all?"

Tia heaved a sigh. "Yea, I'm fine. I miss her terribly, but I was able to have three good years with her, and it was a gift of time I can't overlook. I wasn't ready for it, but she was."

Audrey nodded toward the crowds gathering to eat. "Look at the lives GG touched, and this is a small fraction. She was wonderful. Mom is a different person, now she knows her past, and all those old wounds seem to have healed."

Tia nodded. "I'm glad GG knew about the baby, and that we named him Thomas," she said. She ran a hand over her stomach, and the charm bracelet jingled with the movement. She gazed at it and sighed. "Let's go. Seth was right. It still could take me ten minutes to get to the food, and you know I could go through everything like a freakin' badger if I get too hungry. It wouldn't be pretty."

As people quieted after the meal, and champagne was poured, Tia, Stephanie, and Naomi took their places at a small podium before the gathered crowd.

Stephanie and Naomi had very kind words to say about their time working with Vivian, and the contributions she made to the fields of Classical and American History, and the study of antiquities.

When they were done speaking, it was Tia's turn. She stepped forward, and smiled.

"Vivian Gardiner Henderson Weiss, or GG, as I called her, was my great grandmother, something neither of us knew until, separately, and in the very same timeframe, we both decided to submit DNA samples to the ancestral database. Those two decisions created a ripple, which became a wave, which turned into a tsunami. It made possible what was to become the most profound discoveries in our lives, and in the lives of those around us. Wounds were healed, love blossomed, families joined, or reunited, lives changed for the better, all because of those two little submissions, those two moments of bravery."

Tia paused and took off the bracelet, then held it in the palm of her hand for all to see. "My great-great grandmother, Effie Gardiner, presented this to GG on her eleventh birthday, eighty-seven years ago, and GG diligently added to it over her lifetime. It became the conduit by which she opened her life story to me, one that is available to everyone, through the auspices of the historical society. Now," she paused and motioned Naomi and Stephanie to rejoin her. "Now I would like to hand it over to the society, so people can see it, and understand how the storytelling came to be. It is, more than anything else, a portrait of the woman. Her highs, her lows, her loves, and especially her sorrows, which led to so much joy in her life."

Tia's throat felt like it was closing on her, so she took a deep breath, and swallowed hard. "She gave it to me, but it belongs with the stories." Tia pulled out the blue velvet pouch, dropped the bracelet inside, and drew the string tight.

She placed it in Naomi's hand, and everyone started clapping.

After some hugs, Tia lifted her champagne glass to offer a final toast, but paused when she saw Seth approach the little podium.

"Hey, y'all," he said into the microphone. "One more thing."

He looked at Tia and smiled. "We all thought my wife might do something like this, so we worked out a contingency plan."

Tia looked at him, confused, ready to protest, but she didn't want to make a scene. Then, she watched as Seth pulled a different blue velvet pouch out of his pocket, and gave it to her.

A replica? She wondered, and smiled. How sweet of him.

As she opened the pouch, Seth continued. "They say imitation is the truest form of flattery. We did not want to copy, but to imitate, and carry on the tradition Vivian, well, Effie, started. So, we" he paused while Tia pulled out a new charm bracelet, similar to GG's, but shiny and nearly empty.

"So," Seth continued, and turned to Tia. "I decided we needed to start a new charm bracelet for you. Someday you'll have grandbabies at your feet, and you'll be able to tell them the stories you heard, plus the stories of your own life, and all about your incredibly awesome husband."

Everyone laughed.

"Honey," he said, looking her in the eyes. "I love you so much. Why don't you tell everyone what's on your bracelet?"

Laughing through tears of joy, Tia named each one. "The first one is a double G, then a St. Christopher medal." Tia put her hand over her mouth, trying and failing to hold back her emotions. "There's a Washington State, and South Carolina, handcuffs, of course, Seth's astrological sign and mine, wedding bands on a disk with our wedding date inscribed, and baby booties."

Seth leaned forward, put an arm around Tia's waist, and said, "Haven't put a date on the booties, yet. Soon, though. Soon."

The crowd laughed again, and applauded.

Tia shook her head, then kissed her husband and thanked the crowd. Then, she raised her glass, and all followed her lead.

"*De tristitiae, laetitiae,*" she said. "Out of sorrow, joy. Here's to Vivian. I love you, GG!"

"Here's to GG!" the crowd cheered.

AUTHOR'S NOTE

Inspiration for this novel was born out of a comment at a Christmas party in 2018. A very funny lady I always enjoy seeing, asked about my charm bracelet. She knows I am a writer, and said, "So cool. You should write a book about it. A chapter for every charm!" Well, writers hear that sort of thing all the time, but she was right!

She was so right. I was in the middle of another book at the time, but no matter. It was instantly shelved, and I started on the manuscript that turned into *Out of Sorrow*.

My first order of business was to make a list of all 40 (and counting) charms – holy cow that would make for a lot of chapters! – and then figure out how I would present them. I never envisioned writing an autobiography. Nope. No way. Instead, I would use the charms as a guidepost to tell a purely fictional story. Eventually, however, it did become a sort of autobiography, an auto-ish biography, if you will. Only my mother will ever recognize the full extent of the personal tidbits I've inserted, and I had so much fun doing it. Archie, for instance, was our waiter on the Queen Mary for our transatlantic crossing in 1967. The Windy Deck was on the

SS United States, not the *Ile de France*, since the *United States* hadn't yet been built at the time I first had Vivian's fictional family travel to Europe.

So, things were stretched, manipulated, or mashed together, but except for the political job postings, the vast majority of the charm events are based on real-life events.

Some of the people and places do bear a marked resemblance to people in my life, such as Effie (my actual great great grandmother, and yes, 'I'd keep 'em getting' up' was something she said), or the people at the diner in Snohomish. However, this is in no way my story, but a story I thoroughly enjoyed writing, and one from which I hope you will derive an equal pleasure reading.

I invite you to visit Amazon, Barnes & Noble, Goodreads, or any other book outlet, and leave a review. Thank you very much, and see you at the next book!

Visit me at www.carymorgan.com or at www.morganoneill.com

ABOUT THE AUTHOR

Cary Morgan is a product of the Pacific Northwest, born, raised, and living there, still. She has a passion for history, both European, and that of her own family. She has logged thousands of hours and miles pursuing those histories, and much of her storytelling was born out of these twin passions.

She has co-authored several books with Deborah O'Neill Cordes – Roman and Elizabethan Trilogies, as well as a two-part series set in mediaeval Italy – and is looking forward to her career as a stand-alone author. Please visit her at www.-carymorgan.com.

Made in the USA
Middletown, DE
03 March 2021

34692500R00156